BODY LANGUAGE

Dan Gunn

Body Language

A novel

MAINSTREAM
PUBLISHING

EDINBURGH AND LONDON

To Nicholas Martin

First published in Great Britain in 2002 by
MAINSTREAM PUBLISHING COMPANY (EDINBURGH) LTD
7 Albany Street
Edinburgh EH1 3UG

ISBN 1 84018 572 4

A catalogue record for this book is available from the British Library

Typeset in Van Dijck and Opti Typewriter
Printed and bound in Great Britain by
Mackays of Chatham Ltd

ANATOMY

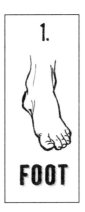

1.

FOOT

WHEN LAURA BROUGHT the foot home on Thursday, after taking time off work and going up to Phillips Auction House with her bid, she tried it out on her dressing-table, then on her bookshelf, then on her bedside table. Wasn't it one of the things she couldn't stand about living at home, the fact that she didn't have a decent place for anything. She couldn't just plonk it down wherever without subjecting herself to the inevitable comments of the rest of them. Consigning it to the bottom of the drawer with her undies was a temporary measure at best.

By Friday, however, it had migrated to the bed. She stared at it in amazement.

The sitting-room, when she stuck her head in, was staked out by her brother, Simon, and her father, both with their shoes off. They were ruining their backs in the bucket seats, newspapers in their hands, glued to the six o'clock news. One quick look was enough. So it had to have been her mother, who was most probably in the kitchen.

'You been in my room?' Laura asked her.

'No, dear, you know I don't go into your room uninvited.'

'So how come my foot's in the middle of the bed?'

'Is that what it is?' She raised a potato peel in acknowledgement.

'What did you think it was?' Laura caught a glimpse of her own reflection in the glass of the kitchen door. Despite her hair, what she saw did not please her. 'What in God's name were you doing in my lingerie?'

'Only putting away your clean things. Don't fret about it.'

'What, at the bottom of the drawer?'

Her mother concentrated on the potatoes' stubborn eyes. 'So what's it for then, this foot of yours?'

Laura's legs were aching from an afternoon of cutting and styling and sweeping. But the kitchen was her mother's orbit, so she pulled a chair to near the outside door. There was Candy, digging to Australia again. Wise dog.

'Well, dear?'

'What do you think it's for? It's a foot, isn't it?'

'Are you happy with it?' her mother surprised her by asking.

'Of course I'm happy with it,' she said, pulling a face. 'I bought it, didn't I?'

'Oh, you bought it?'

Would she never learn? Forever giving away more than she intended.

And there it was, dignifying the single bed she'd been sleeping in since the age of twelve, its shiny marble deep against the duvet-cover, whose pale green she'd agonised over in Habitat. Like it was at the bottom of a valley, waiting to be found. Her mother's busybody actions had only advanced the question of its ultimate home – though the idea that anywhere here could be ultimate, with the convent bed, the obnoxious mauve carpet, the Sanderson paper and curtains, the Pine World furniture, was too much even for a Friday-night-with-prospect-of-Saturday-off.

Candy, scratching at the door, would have to wait.

Laura mentally ran through the possible options. There were the shelves in the hall with plates marked 'Tyrol', inherited from her gran who had longed for Julie Andrews' Edelweiss. Two cuckoo clocks, both broken, one with its bird's beak permanently open, the other with its bird locked indoors. A sake set, which revealed naked women when filled. And last but not least her own ship-in-a-bottle, which she'd saved up for but which her brother claimed was fake with a false bottom.

Enough said.

Laura stretched out on her bed, arranged her long red hair on the pillow, and laid the foot on her stomach. It was cool, heavy, satisfying. Thousands of eyes must have admired it, when it was still attached to its body.

The only other possibility was the sitting-room cabinet, from which the Caithness Crystal never emerged. Threats had been made that its thistle-shape would match the new Scottish Parliament. The cabinet also contained her father's collection of pewter tankards and his flying swans from Venice. Enough said, yet again. Not to mention that her brother would then be free to comment.

For the moment she let it rest on her tummy. A size nine, by today's standard, men's measurements. Until she had the energy to put up a shelf, or convince her dad to do so, it would have to live among the knickers and bras, safe there, at least, from the marauding males of the house.

'And fancy free!' her brother yapped, incomprehensibly, in response to his father's question about how he would be spending his weekend. 'Now that the shoe's on the other – you know.'

Laura tried to translate her dish into Italian, Latin as yet being beyond her. The pasta was linguine, the Safeway sauce arrabiata. But the inevitable potatoes, on the side of the plate?

'You for the match, son?'

'What sort of match is that, Pa? Do you mean the rugby match, the cricket match, the lacrosse match, the tiddlywinks match?'

'You been drinking already?'

'If that were the case, then you'd really need to put your – hmm – down.' Simon stamped under the table for emphasis.

'What you blethering about?' his mother asked.

Laura shook her head in disgust. If only she could catch her brother's eye, she would halt him mid-flight. He was two years older, but ever since she'd shredded his Calvin Klein boxers and deliberately peed in his bed, he'd supposed she was cracked, therefore dangerous.

'And you, Pa?' Simon asked. 'You've really got your hmm in the door with that appointment at the Social. Treasurer no less. I trust you won't be letting in any of those who kick with the wrong – hmm – you know?'

His parents looked at one another, then at Laura, whose fork was constructing a pasta-and-mash dam. 'Something going on here, you two?'

'Something up?' Simon chirped. 'Something brewing? Something a . . .' He stamped again.

'Can I get down?' Laura asked, further enraged by her own request.

'You've got to eat, lass,' her mother sighed. 'You're wasting away.'

'Not putting your best one forward, Sis.'

Had her brother used his dictionaries or was he making it up on the spot? She'd always feared his tongue, though for the past few years that was the worst of him.

'So, Pa, you'll need to be careful not to waste any funds. Or to put it another way, squander or, eh . . . ?' Once more Simon stamped. 'Hmmer them, so to speak.'

'You're daft!' her mother decided.

'My hmm!'

'Could you tell us, Laura,' her father asked, 'what your brother is trying to communicate to us? Studying Divinity doesn't seem to be helping his vocabulary.'

'Tell us what you're doing tonight, love?' her mother hastened to ask.

Laura was headed for her room, despite the protests about pudding.

'And who'll be hmming the bill for the hmm?' her brother said, before she could slam the door.

It was only down at Bar Sirius, with the fourth or fifth Iguana cocktail inside her, that Laura considered forgiving her mother.

'You be able to do my hair Sunday, Laure?'

'Sure.'

'Can you do me like yours?'

'You'll need to let it grow some first.'

Laura's pals relied on her. Avoiding Enzo's Salon meant expenses only.

'Meet anyone interesting this week?' her friend asked.

'That woman who's the new MSP. What's her name?'

'And men?'

She knew there was no point telling them about Mr Glen, the balding lawyer from next door to Enzo's. They wouldn't understand.

She accepted a cigarette. 'There was that guy from STV, the one who presents that arty programme.'

'Not Okay Mackay?'

'Bit of dandruff but not a bad smile.'

'Fuckin' right!' It was the usual Begbie impersonation, even if its origins had been forgotten.

'Did you give him your number? You could have given him mine. How many interesting people do you think I get to meet, working in a bank?'

'What about Rory?' someone said.

'As in Rory-Consummation?'

The mirth round the table was general. The men at the bar looked like they'd do anything to join in.

'Who's for the club then?'

The drinks were nearly finished, the make-up was straight.

'I'm broke,' Laura declared, opening the clasp on her purse to prove it. 'I could manage the entrance but I couldn't pay the taxi home.'

'How's that?' came the Begbie voice again. 'A wee ride like you? I thoat you'd been savin.'

'Yeh, but now it's been spent.'

All eyes, and some fingers too, inspected the results: the top was the only thing new, and that was from Oasis so couldn't have set her back much. The handbag wasn't hiding a mobile or a mini-disc player, not even new lipstick. Explanations were expected.

'I bought myself this thing. Right?'

'This thing as in *thing*?'

Words were quickly replaced with actions and the men at the bar hooted as they spotted a hand held O-shape, vibrating in the air.

'You can lend it to me after.'

'It's antique,' Laura explained.

The pals looked dubious. 'As in a table or something?'

'A statue.'

'How did you know what to buy? They all look the same to me.'

'Fuckin' right.'

'I asked that Flora from the office above the salon. She's off with that Joe who works at Phillips Auction House. She said Joe doesn't actually know anything, despite him doing a degree, but that she'd ask Ian, her ex. He's the real expert.'

'What, him that's in Saughton?'

'Tit-Ian as he used to be called?'

'A right pretentious git.'

'Speaking from experience?' Sometimes Laura wished she could borrow her brother's brain, just for an hour, and download his retorts into hers.

'So what make is it?'

'You think they make designer statues? As in Versace Venus or Armani Aphrodite?'

This silenced her friends more than she'd intended. 'Anyway, so Tit-Ian, Titian, whatever he's called, says it's the genuine article, even if it's lost a couple of toes. Comes from the collection of the Duke of Montrose, being sold off because of some sex scandal. Tells me the maximum I should bid.'

'Which just happens to be the amount you'd saved?'

'I could always stay with one of youse?'

Normally, surely, one of her friends would have offered. Most of them lived closer than her to the centre, some of them even had flats of their own.

'And what's it of, then, this statue?'

Jackets were on, cigarettes extinguished.

'It's Roman, maybe Greek. Maybe a warrior or a god or something. Mythological.' She didn't mean to go into detail, but fortunately her friends weren't listening in any case.

'So, Laure, you sure you're no coming?'

Home was deathly after midnight. *Early Bed in Corstorphine*, the title of a horror film she'd direct: nothing gruesome, the camera would just move round the deserted suburban streets, peer at the bungalows, then penetrate inside to reveal the mindless decor, the floor-coverings, the furniture.

Her parents were snoring upstairs after their night at the Social. Candy was asleep in the kitchen, exhausted from the antipodes. Her pals would be getting tanked up in the loos by now, or out on the dance-floor, self-conscious only for the first few numbers before oblivion kicked in. She put on a video, plugging in the headphones to bring the whole thing closer.

'The Mycenae Gate,' said the voice, 'beloved of Agamemnon,' before a cut to Athens and the National Museum, where the statue of Poseidon was still throwing his trident. 'Follow the axis of the right arm,' the commentator continued, 'all the way to the left heel, as it concentrates its being into flight.'

She hit the pause button to give herself time. It was just as well, she thought, that hair didn't survive the way marble did. What would he look like with a mop of woolly black hair on top?

'Steve Backley!'

She tugged off the headphones, turned round. It was her brother's side-kick Stod; followed by Dan, aka 'Dan-Dare'. And her own darling brother, more slippery than ever with whatever the evening had coaxed down his throat. All that was missing was Ric, for the Famous Four – as she'd christened her brother's gang – to be complete.

'No techno-house-jungle-indie-garage tonight then, Sis? Here's us boys just back for a quiet smoke.'

It was one of the things she loathed about him, that he chose his friends among the half-wits who were bound to be impressed. He was standing there like some TV chat-show host: the Terry Wogan of Corstorphine.

'You're no leavin' us already?' said Dan-Dare over the mattress of papers he was gluing. 'You'll be wantin' a wee puff on this?'

She could hardly believe that only last summer she'd let him wheedle his way into her bedroom, and worse let him grope her and run his fingers through her hair, just because he'd said he was interested in her Venus de Milo poster.

And now he'd been thinking. 'Your brother,' he said, 'has been telling us about some statue you've bought.'

'Is it, like, an obelisk?' Stod had obviously been fed this question.

'Is that,' she sneered, 'is it like an obelisk? Or is it, like, an obelisk?'

'More like a phallus.' Her brother, of course, lighting up the overgrown spliff.

She knew she would regret it. 'Actually, it's a foot,' she retorted. 'Formerly part of a life-size statue. Ancient Greek or Roman.'

Dan-Dare lay back with his work-worn Nikes in the air. 'I could even take them off,' he offered.

'No! He's a one-a-week man,' Stod warned. 'You never thought of becomin' a chiropodist instead of a hairdresser?'

The question was so depressing, even by Stod's standards, that she failed to notice her brother had escaped. Instant hysterics when he appeared again at the door. Despite his suit, Stod had joined Dan-Dare on his back in order, presumably, to split his sides more comfortably.

Slowly, slowly, she turned to her brother in the doorway. The fact that he would pay for this was small consolation.

'And now for something completely different!' He spewed out the Monty Python theme tune, and only when he reached the raspberry at the end did he whip his hands out from behind his back and bring his sister's foot squelching down upon Stod's spare tyres.

'The Monty Python foot!' cried Dan-Dare superfluously. 'But what's it wearing? Is that a G-string I spy?'

'Seems to have got tangled up in Sister's smalls.'

Lovingly, Simon undressed the foot, tossing the feather-light garment into the lions' den. Dan-Dare made it first, and lofted it high as a trophy, before putting it to his nose and inhaling.

It was still early when she slid into her brother's bedroom. She knew where to find his *Shorter Oxford English Dictionary*, and she took both volumes before retiring to the bathroom. She'd felt it coming on since she awoke, though only now did she understand why she'd held it in.

She left a note on her brother's desk which read: 'FOOT: the lowest part of the leg beyond the ankle joint. FAECES: sediment, dregs, excrement.' Then she washed her hands, hid her statue in the ornamental cake tin, and headed for the bus.

She liked to pass Enzo's Salon when she wasn't working there, even if it meant a detour down to Howe Street. Here were her colleagues, looking wasted most of them, under thick cakes of make-up. One of them waved to her with the hand not holding the dryer. She waved back, though less to her colleagues, in fact, than to Mr Glen, the lawyer, who was staring out from his office next door. Back up on George Street, in the window of Morton's Vintners, there was a display of old rocks and pillars mixed up with bottles of Italian wine.

Instead of making her way along Princes Street, she urged herself between the columns of the National Gallery. The tartan-clad attendant was supposed to point her to the ticket office, but he told her it was for free. She didn't feel properly dressed, but she managed her way round the ground floor, spotting a painting on loan from the collection of her very own Duke of Montrose.

It was a shame about his short-back-and-sides, but on the way out she tried the attendant anyway. 'Where's all the antique stuff?' she asked. 'Greek and Roman, you know?'

She couldn't afford new clothes in any case, so she skipped Princes Street altogether. From the top of The Mound she gazed over the city through the hangover which caught up with her on the climb, and beyond that into the Kingdom of Fife.

There had to be so many people down there, she thought – so many that when a hairless man climbed past, she mentally thanked him.

The Chambers Street Museum had been tarted up since she used to push the buttons to make the steam-engines turn. She wondered if her brother would report her to their parents, and hoped he'd be too embarrassed, or scared of retaliation. On the second floor there were endless bits of pots, amulets, amphorae, and at the end of the aisle a few weedy-looking busts with broken noses. Not a single chariot-rider or colossus. Not even an emperor. Disappointment was relieved only by the thought that if this was all the Royal Museum had to show, then she'd surely got a bargain. She leaned over the bannister, full of words like 'heft', 'lustre', 'arcane', and 'Carrara'. It wouldn't be so easy now to look them up.

In the museum cafeteria she encouraged the time to pass by re-reading the bit about Messalina in *Claudius the God*. She'd read it four times already, and she presumed once more would do it: twenty-two men in twenty-four hours. The most she had ever managed was three, and that was in her prime, when she didn't even require them to take off their socks. During a recent truce her brother had passed her a copy of *Penthouse* where an American woman had notched up 300, doing four at a time. 300 pricks meant 600 feet, some things coming in twos, others in ones. Not to mention countless strands of hair. Unless, of course, there were any amputees, which was a fair chance if the blokes had been a cross-section of Joe-porn-Public. Chopped off at the ankle, as may be.

Five o'clock on Saturday for someone like Okay Mackay almost certainly meant that he couldn't find anything better for the evening, a last resort. But he did have quite a nice smile and he was presumably interested in things other than pints and Hibernian FC, and most important of all he was innocent as a babe about her recent purchase.

'Okay?' she asked, finding the name ridiculous for the first time.

'And this is Laura? Very punctual too.'

'You'll have to speak up.' From his number she knew he was on a mobile.

'I called your home to tell you it was on for tonight. Though of course you must meet loads of TV types, working in a fashionable place like Enzo's. With hair like you've got too.'

'Loads,' she said, not to flatter him yet. 'So what do you fancy doing?'

'I must've got your brother. He recognised my voice from the telly.'

'That little toady.'

'He was going on about how you're interested in fossilised feet.'

'So where shall we meet?'

'Is that right, you're into feet? Clean ones too, I hope?'

'How about Indigo Yard?'

'How about stilettos? Toe-sucking?' He was joking, of course, but that wasn't much of a consolation. 'See you there around seven?'

She shuddered as she replaced the receiver.

'Suck on this, Mr Dandruff.'

She put another coin in the slot. An evening with her auntie Gloria would be just the job, with her gin and tonics, and the stories of her clients. Anyone with fantasies based on the royal family deserved to be stood up. Gloria could be relied on to have her mind on some bit of anatomy other than the foot.

And the morning confirmed she'd been right, despite its being Sunday, despite the tape-recorded bells from the hideous bunker up the street, despite the vapours of stale gin and tonic. She could almost have regretted what she'd done to her brother's precious books. It wasn't even raining. She could spend the afternoon, until it was time for her friends' hair, up Corstorphine woods with Claudius.

Her father was silent in the kitchen, alone, brooding over the Social Club accounts. Only when she had nearly finished her cereal did he start. 'Everything fine with you, Laura?'

Her munch conveyed a 'Yes.'

''Cos we've been a bit concerned, your mother and I.'

So Simon had clyped on her.

'Maybe, we were thinking, maybe it's time you got your own place. Now you're twenty-two. We could help you get started.'

She'd wanted to hear it for years. Now she felt banished. 'Simon's two years older and he's still living here,' she petulantly retorted.

'Simon's a student, he's not earning a wage. Simon is Simon.'

She reminded herself how delighted she should feel. 'What's brought this on?'

Not bothering to get up, her father pointed to the ornamental cake tin. 'Not that we want to criticise, mind. You've always been grand about housekeeping. How you spend your savings is your own business.'

So he hadn't clyped on her after all.

'But, you know, what'll you be doing for your holidays? That friend whose hair you do was on the phone, tells us you're not going to Spain with them this summer.'

'I thought maybe Greece.'

'But with what, if all your money's been spent?'

Her father's fry-up was heavy in the air. She went over to the window. Candy was digging again. Wise dog.

'I mean, we could always lend you some, I'm sure. But is that what you'd want? Maybe you'd rather just sit in a dusty room surrounded by relics?'

She was about to cry until she saw her brother through the door. He came in on tiptoes.

'Not interrupting, am I?' he said, sweetly. 'Good.' He filled the kettle.

'If you see what we mean, Laura?' her father concluded.

'What the . . . ?'

She bit back her astonishment, deducing that to scream would be to admit defeat. Her father, blushing over his books, had failed to notice. She refused to be rumbled. It was her foot yet it was not her foot. Identical in size and shape, but a different texture, surely, a different colour too, like it was made out of plaster.

It was made out of plaster. And there was a hole in it, from the top of the arch to the sole, through which passed a piece of string that went up around Simon's neck.

'Did you know, Pa?' her brother said. 'Had you ever realised that stigmata is the plural of stigma?'

How had he done it, the wee fucking bastard? Had he really hunted it down in the ornamental cake tin, taken it to a shop like the one in Stockbridge where they made plaster casts of hands and faces? He wore it like a pendant or a chunky gold medallion.

'More like an albatross,' he said, reading her mind. 'Still,' he went on as the kettle began to whistle, 'I'll really need another, I think, if I want to use them as earrings.'

She almost knocked him over as she tore from her seat to the cake tin.

Finally her father looked up. 'What you doing, Laura, dear? Where are you going?'

Sure enough, her foot was covered in an icing of plaster.

She thrust it into her handbag, and without even putting on a coat, ignoring the laughter of her brother, the groans of her father, then the frantic knocking of her mother from her parents' bedroom window, she fled down the street, past the church, in the direction of the woods.

Her hair unfurled as she ran – it'd soon be for the chop – while the foot in her bag gave her ballast.

2.

LIVER

'I DON'T KNOW if I saved his immortal soul, but he seemed happy enough when he left the surgery.'

The man in whose arms Heather is curled, naked and conch-like, seems sceptical. 'Even now he's probably denouncing us to God. Or worse, to some Local Authority.'

'He looked me in the eyes before he went. Performed some sort of blessing with his rosary and cross.'

'I can't believe it. Why would he come to the infirmary with a crisis of faith? Why wouldn't he have gone to St Mary's, or to the Bishop's? Somewhere else? The French Consulate?'

'It was seven in the morning. You can't always time these things, you know. He needed someone to talk to. Accident and Emergency seems about right, now I think of it.'

The man, 'Roger Morton' according to an embossed leather ledger lying closed on the desk, must be twenty years older than the woman in his arms. Grey, thinning on top but not on the ears or shoulders: unworthy, one would think, of the bright and fulsome, if tired, young lass in his bed. He makes to turn out the bedside light, then changes his mind.

'Well,' he starts, 'my day was nothing like so uplifting. A surprisingly good Château Cantenac Brown, they must be getting their act together there at last. Ordered two dozen cases. Mr Barr, the packager, came by, looking awful, eyes bulging out of his head. I managed to sell him a bottle of Yquem for over a hundred pounds.'

He thinks for a while, then disentangles himself, climbs out of bed and goes over to the window. Below, the garden is prim and hushed. Though it is well past midnight, with the moon out it's still light enough to see.

'I wonder if the hedgehog will cross the lawn tonight,' he says, before turning back to face the woman. 'Tell me about it again. In detail this time. What really happened.'

Though she is obviously weary, she sits up in bed. It is one of those rare spring nights where no pyjamas are required, and he cannot resist walking over and cupping her breasts for an instant, weighing them like bunches of almost-ripe grapes.

'You'll have to let go of these if you want the whole story.'

He obeys but reluctantly as if imagining what it would be like never to be permitted to fondle them again.

'Are you sitting comfortably?'

He resumes his stance near the window.

'Then we'll begin.'

He nods.

'So I was coming off night-shift: two Coca-Cola bottles shattered deep inside orifices; one earlobe to stitch back on; three windscreen-jobs; and someone asks me if I can stand in for her for an hour, her wee one's running a fever.'

'Why you?' asks Roger, almost indignant.

''Cos I'm there. 'Cos I don't have a wee one. I don't know. Quit interrupting me if you want to hear.'

'I want to hear you tell me you didn't tell him.'

'So there's a couple of dossers with cuts and scrapes, nothing serious. I get them out in minutes. Then in walks this minister, priest more like, with collar and cassock, the full works. He's looking pretty awful, as no doubt I do too, like we've both been up all night. Just the sight of him's enough to set me off, I'm seeing the flags of St Giles, longing to hear some church choir singing, get away from the sound of trolleys and the sight of scalpel and suture.

'"Excuse me, Madame," he mutters, and it's already obvious he's foreign, French probably. "I do not know where to go."

20

'"So what seems to be the problem?" I ask him.

'"It's . . ."

'He seems pretty desperate, puts his head in his hands. He's a big bloke, sturdy, maybe your age. Probably attractive too if he weren't looking so awful. He's got a really lovely voice, like out of a Cointreau advert.

'"I not know how to say it. But here," he goes, "I have a crisis of faith."'

The other man, Roger Morton, the one listening by the window, clucks his tongue. 'Are you sure, Heather, that's really what he said? Those were his exact words?'

'Well, actually he said it in French, a *crise de foi*. I was about to get him to point, when I realised that wouldn't help much, pointing at heaven. All our trips to Burgundy must have done some good after all, as I figured it out for myself. Crise equals crisis, de equals of, foi equals faith.'

Roger peers to see if she is joking. When he confirms she is not, he scuttles out of the room and down the stairs to the kitchen where the remains of the dinner he had prepared for her are visible. He takes the empty jar of over-priced liver pâté, the foie-gras with its offending 'e', and stuffs it deep into the bin, before checking the doors are locked and climbing more slowly back up the stairs.

'Are you interested in hearing this?' Heather asks him.

'Of course. You know how neurotic I am, just had to check the doors.'

'So I'm thinking how I wish that ponce who ran the people-skills course last week could see me now, with all his nonsense about how I don't have an "empathic ear".'

Roger slips his hand between her pillow and her back, where he guesses the liver to be. One day, he may be thinking, hers too will give out, no amount of faith can cure that. They will leave no children behind. He dreads losing her so badly that for an instant he almost feels like throwing himself out of the window to avoid ever seeing the day – not that it would help much, the window being on the first floor, with his fall doubtless broken by the privet below.

'I'm wondering what in hell's name to say to him, aware there's probably a queue of patients needing patching and stitching, and here's this priest in crisis.'

'What colour was he?' Roger can't resist asking.

'What do you mean? I've told you, he's RC through and through. And I'm realising I haven't been to St Giles in years, not even for Midnight Mass, not since we found each other in fact. So I ask him: "Please tell me."

'At which point, right, he gets up and starts yanking off his dog-collar. Stuff this! I think. I'm not having him give up the cloth, not right here in my surgery. "Stop!" I order him. "Halt! Sit down!"'

'He obeys me, a bit surprised.'

'I can imagine.' Roger has been trying to remember exactly what the organ's function is, attempting to forget that of the calf which, accompanied by a bottle of Clos Vougeot '69, he polished off alone two nights before, soaked in Xerès vinegar, to console himself for her being on night-shift. To balance the hormones, was that it? Or something to do with the digestion, surely? Or the blood?

'"What's your name?" I ask him.

'"Call me Clovis, Brother Clovis."

'"So when did it start?"

'"Two years about," he says.'

Hepatitis, Roger thinks. A and B, was there a 'C'-version too? And they could burst in accidents. And jaundice, of course, like his mother had suffered as a child, which meant she felt guilty whenever she saw a blood transfusion unit, since they never wanted hers. She would have understood her son's current life and its predicament, he felt sure. Unlike his father, who would murder him if he knew. Unlike his sister, Deirdre, for whom he was 'The Monster'.

'"And what seems to have brought on the crisis? Sight of all our Protestants?"

'He didn't seem to get the joke. He's shrugging his shoulders like he doesn't have the foggiest.

'"So what are you here in Scotland for?" I try.

'"On a pele-grimage," he says, "to Iona. Maybe the . . ." He can't think of the word, so he draws it. Says something like "mules", but what he's drawn is like, you know . . . ?'

Heather draws it in air for her lover.

'Yachts?'

'Cunts, to be frank. And he's making as if he's getting stuck in to some heavy-duty cunnilingus.'

Roger shakes his head. Her language! She didn't learn that at Mary Erskine's. Yet is it not one of the very things he adores her for?

"'M . . . m . . . mussels," the priest finally remembers, with a big sigh of relief.

"'Right," I say. "Nice euphemism." I remember reading about how pilgrims hang strings of mussels round their necks as a sign they've risen above the temptations of that particular female trap.'

And she's not far off there, Roger thinks, admiring her distorted logic, *moule* being slang in French for *pudendum*.

"'With one of your congregation?" I ask. He doesn't get that, so I have to do some bleats, imitate some grazing. "Your flock?" I try. Finally I think he twigs.

"'No mouton," he says.

"'A spring lamb, I guess then, a young-un?"'

Roger, repressing a smile, thinks of how Heather taught herself Lego, then Meccano, building impossibly baroque edifices which she would go on constructing until they crashed to the ground. Her willingness to give it a go, contrasting with his own finickiness, his aesthete's need to apprehend his own sensations, his connoisseur's sense of the *juste distance* – it was what endeared her to him from the start. And when, later, she allied her gusto to her surgeon's dexterity and nerve, she became formidable.

In his last will and testament – for he certainly intends to 'predecease' her (as the lawyer inscribed it) – he has bequeathed her all his limbs and organs, reserving only the shell of his carcass for the flames. He wonders, briefly, if she will retain his *faith*. What will it look like pickled in a jar beside the bed?

She brings him back to the present by tweaking a hair from his chest. 'So what would you have done?'

Not a wince, he notes, her very persecutions instantly converted into pleasure. 'I wouldn't have known what to tell him,' he admits. 'If I exclude vintage Pommard and Montrachet, my only God is you.' He is aware it sounds melodramatic, especially coming from lips which are used to measuring, calibrating, sagacious judgement. Yet he also knows it is true. 'I'm not sure it counts as faith when it's mortal, fragile —'

'—And forbidden,' she interrupts him.

'The world's loss is our gain.'

'Gain, my arse,' she snaps.

Roger looks away, momentarily defeated.

'Anyway,' Heather says, 'I'm losing patience now with this priest and his pangs. "Why don't you love the lamb," I tell him, "if that's the problem. You don't honestly believe in all that chastity nonsense, do you?"

'I'm feeling utterly exhausted, and this big hunk of a man is moaning to me – to *me* – about a crisis of conscience.

'"You're not trying to tell me," I say, "that anyone still believes in abstinence, anyone other than John Paul II, who's thoroughly past it in any case? Gee's a break. It's downright perverse. I've been treating priests for years with every sort of STD – that's sexually transmitted disease, to you."

'This seems to make a hit. "You're not gay, are you?" I ask him.

'He shakes his head.

'"So just give it a bit of confession afterwards. You're damn lucky to have that going for you, all we Presbyterians have is permanent guilt."'

That very afternoon, Roger remembers, the retired civil servant beyond the privet hedge had interrupted his weeding to ask how his fiancée was keeping.

Oh, he knew it: Barnton would quake to its suburban core, if it realised. The waters of Cramond would cover the land in sin-sweeping flood!

'He still didn't look like he wanted to move, the priest, and I'm just getting more and more worked up there, thinking how fortunate he is to be free. So what if he's in love with the abbot's sister or screwing the archbishop's spaniel, he's got a god who will forgive him. And not only that.

'"Look," I yelp at him. "Look around you. You see these grey walls?

Bloodstained surgical gloves? Poor critters with Coke bottles up their arses, noses blown off with the other sort of coke? Pain and dying, and the rest of my time spent fighting with the bureaucrats to avoid their cut-price gauze and bandages."

'The priest jumps off his seat and starts pointing somewhere above his kidneys. "Oui!" he hollers. "Pain!"

'"You sit down there, Clovis!" I order him. I'd really had it by now. "Listen," I shout at him, "who are you to moan? You spend your days in the luxury of spirit. You're surrounded by beautiful music, skies, heaven, paintings. And don't tell me the Catholic Church is short of a bob or two when it comes to patching up the conscience." That puts him in his place.'

Roger goes to the window. The night is more silent than ever. He looks down upon the lawn. 'I thought it might be the hedgehog. But no such luck.'

There are tears in her voice when she starts up again. '"Look at me," I tell the priest, "if you want to know a thing or two about crises of faith. I'm thirty-two years old, it took me over ten years of hard training to get to where I am and I'm still working fourteen-hour shifts."

'I don't know if he can understand everything I'm saying, but at least he's listening now.

'"And all this cutting, grafting, sewing, all balanced on one great big lie. My parents haven't spoken to me in over seven years. If my grandfather found out, he'd drag himself from his wheelchair, he'd crawl all the way to Barnton from his nursing home in Newington, on his hands and bleeding knees, to execute his only son."'

'You didn't say that – tell me you didn't say that. Not about my own father!' Roger, in his dismay, is none the less aware that there is something vaguely ridiculous about his paunch, as he paces round the room, not to mention the incongruous semi-erection he is sporting.

'Why not, Roger? It's true!'

'What if it is true. Is that any reason to tell a stranger?'

'He's a priest! He puts his hands together like he's about to pray. "You suffer?" he says to me. Then he calls me "ma fille", which is of course all it takes for the dam to burst, and it's waterworks all over him. The big starched hankie he pulls out only makes it worse.

"'It's all right for you," I'm snivelling into his chest. "You can have all the children you want, so long as you do it on the quiet. Who's going to care, it happens all the time.'"

Roger waits for Heather's anger to pass. 'So you call him "brother",' he attempts a joke, 'and he calls you "my daughter"! Somewhat confusing, no?'

'Very funny,' she says, without laughing. "'Then say me all," goes Clovis. "You speak," he adds, with that deep voice he's got.

'I wait till my sobs have subsided a little. "There's not much to tell you," I finally get out. "I'm in love with my uncle. Always have been in love with him, since I was a little girl. Eight years ago something happened that meant I found out he was in love with me too."

'Then the priest opened his hands out wide, a beautiful gesture. I took it to mean that the world is big enough for every aberration.

'So I'm really gushing now. "My uncle keeps a diary," I explain, "his 'ledger' he calls it, and eight years ago I read it, not really by accident. It's mostly about wines – he's a wine-taster, a merchant – but he also keeps notes about the day, little stories he tries to write, diary entries. I suppose I was curious. For years, ever since I was a teenager and realised what love is, I'd been longing for him.'"

'Please!' Roger moans.

"'The brother of your papa?" the priest asks.

"'My mother's. When I secretly read his ledger I realised he felt the same way about me as I did about him. He'd made a vow never to let me or anyone else know. That night, eight years ago, I seduced him.'"

'Pleeease!'

"'It was the first time sex had really meant anything to me. When my parents found out they disowned me, threatened to tell the police. I haven't spoken to them since. We live in terror of being found out. He tells the neighbours I'm his fiancée, but we can't go out or socialise. He's offered to have a vasectomy, I keep thinking about having myself sterilised."

'The priest shakes his head, like he's finally understood.

"'We live in fear, Brother Clovis," I tell him. "In love and fear.'"

Roger, agonised and enthralled, sits on the bed beside his niece and touches her bold lips. It will be hard, he thinks, to get all this into his ledger, describing it all from his usual dilettante's distance.

'The priest passes his hand over my face and mutters a few Ave Marias. Then he gets up, goes over to the medicine cabinet for some reason, studies the pills for a while, grabs a few bottles and shoves them inside his cassock. Then he turns to me.

'"All must die, ma fille," he says. "Some soon, others later. Love will do you know you have lived."'

Roger stills his niece for a second in order to work that one out.

'And then he opens the surgery door, and he's gone.'

Hardly does Heather finish recounting this before she stretches out and falls asleep, exhausted by her night, her day, her tale.

Roger sits down at his desk and opens his ledger. 'Purified' might be too strong a word he reckons for what just happened; 'cleansed' perhaps closer; or 'racked', more precisely – racked oenologically.

> Let his God not forget his failing French liver.
> Let my hedgehog cross the lawn, and quickly find its slug.
> Let me end this entry here, climb under the sheet, do love to her.

3.

BOWEL(S)

HE COULD HAVE sworn her smile was just for him when she returned from the toilet – the 'restroom' as she was learning to call it. As if she wanted him to know she'd been successful. Though before the honeymoon, before touch-down in San Francisco, rarely a mention of such things between them. Of it, of them – of *it*.

Later, after rupture, after words he'd never thought he'd say to anyone, let alone a woman, let alone his wife, he claimed this had been the start of it, when she had emerged from the restroom at the Museum of Modern Art, looking so pleased with herself and wanting him to know it.

'He started it, weirdo!' she would recount. 'Stuck in some primeval infant stage.' She was referring to when they'd only just arrived. It was in the motel in San Francisco, and he was going on about how light he felt. 'Drained,' he said, 'like of old.'

By the time of the honeymoon they'd long since got over any embarrassment. After all, they'd been practically living together these past seven months, mostly in her Morningside flat, whose plywood doors and en suite didn't leave much to the imagination. He had even found it a relief, back then: Flavia, his ex, who'd been his teacher when he'd tried to learn Italian, said it was normal for her to be disgusted. *Il scoreggio* (masculine; pl. *scoreggi*): *the fart*. She could hardly bear to pronounce the word, so deep was her disdain, an act which was taboo in her own culture; nothing like this Scotch *schifezza*, this *filth*, where people thought no more of it than blowing their nose.

Whereas Una, now, she had nothing Italian about her bar her name. The second time they did it, standing up in the close behind Bannerman's, she merely laughed at his involuntary ale-filled phut. So relieved was he, in fact, he almost lost his erection.

'There's no need,' he said, a month or so after Bannerman's, staying over at her place, which was warmer than his. Six inches of snow outside, and the view was grand up to sledge-tracked Blackford Hill. 'There's no need,' he repeated, 'to run the cold tap every time you take a pee.'

He smiled to himself as the tap was turned off, snuggled deeper into her bed, admired the tog-value on her duvet, and for the first time wondered if he wasn't, in fact, in love with her. It'd be high time. He'd be thirty-six next week, and his wild oats risked running to seed. His place in Sparta Athletic wasn't in doubt, but Coach had suggested he think of moving back to midfield.

'Sparta Athletic? What sort of a name for a team is that?' Una had asked him at dinner the night before.

'Coach'd like to have been Greek. Eighty per cent gay, the team.'

'Like queer?'

He didn't know her well enough yet to tell if she was using queer in the way his father did when bitching about his prisoners, or in the way Bobby their goalie did, turning insult into accolade.

Anyway, he was still fit enough for fifth-division Edinburgh Amateur, if not so fit he could forget his age as ninety minutes approached. And she was no youngster either, though she hid it well when dressed. He liked the way she looked: all legs and elegance, her Paul Smith suits. She'd been with the Widows for nearly twelve years and was already head of some corporate investment branch – no mean achievement with no degree behind her. But the dimples showed when the suits came off, and when he leaned too heavily, her flesh was slow to spring back. Maybe she was ready for more too. She said she liked the fact he worked in banking, even if he was no match for her with figures, and she hadn't batted an eyelid when he told her his old man was a warden at Saughton. She thought it was 'quaint' that he didn't own a mobile phone.

'See, Una,' he expanded, when she finally came out of the bathroom, tiptoeing to avoid the freezing granite flagstones she'd recently had put down – 'see, Una, you're my one and you're my only.' It was the first time he'd sweet-talked her, and he was doubly pleased that the Italian was still there and that the lessons hadn't been a waste of time after all, despite Flavia's jibes about his 'haggis-accent'.

The wedding was what she called 'a simple one': registry office then a reception at Est Est Est on George Street. Rory was trying to keep his father in check. Una, taller than ever in high heels and hair up – 'bellissima' was her husband's verdict – went scampering back and forth trying fruitlessly to bridge the gap between her colleagues and her parents, who were themselves swithering between pride at the only one of their brood to have made it, and embarrassment at the sound of their West Lothian voices.

'Our Una's choice of course,' her mother was explaining to anyone who would listen. 'She's always been big on the New World. She'll be the one who's wearing the breeks in future. Rory would've been happy with Ullapool.'

Una pretended she hadn't overheard it. In truth, it would be the first time across the Atlantic for both of them, since her business trips to Atlanta hardly counted – two days at a time locked in a smoked-glass office. She'd thought: real estate, Bill Gates, over-fruity Chardonnay. Rory had said he'd always meant to read Jack Kerouac. They didn't want to fall into the trap of Disneyland or Hollywood, so they'd plumped for San Francisco over LA.

Where, regardless of who started it, whether it was him with his comment about feeling drained, 'like of old', or her with her self-satisfied smile, they'd only managed five days and already they both knew that something had changed.

Maybe that's what it means to be married, she mused, one of the things it means, to be able to talk about such things openly, even find them intriguing.

'But I still don't know why you put it in the plural. You're the proud possessor of precisely how many bowels?'

Rory was concentrating on his lobster bisque, and a cable-car was going by the Hyde Street Seafood and Rawbar, clanging its bell, which may be why he misheard her. 'One's enough, it's pretty creamy. I couldn't do another.'

'Another?'

'Bowl. Of bisque.'

She let it drop this time. Her Chilean sea bass in papillotte was getting cold, and she wanted to savour the precision of its name – Chilean sea bass – none of your 'cod', 'hake', or generic 'fish'. Everything here in California was so mathematically precise, with fibre quotients, protein supplements, percentage-rated iron boosters, fat content reducers. Eminently satisfying, even if for some reason she did still feel hungry most of the time.

Later, though, in bed, after she had failed to arouse her husband with a display of 'downward dog', from her yoga class, and had also failed to turn down the air-conditioner, she came back to it. 'You make it sound like it was some extra anatomy you have. Maybe one day it'll burst out of your body like the creature in *Alien*.'

'I thought everyone had more than one, like with intestines.' He was weary. Somehow the jet lag was getting worse not better as the days progressed. 'Don't we have two intestines? An upper and a lower, large and small, or something?' He badly needed to rest, yet he knew that as soon as he passed out he'd awake in a cold sweat and it would take him a further two hours before sleep came to him again. For a second, after one panic-stricken awakening, he even wished he was back in his own bed, until he remembered he'd sold it as it wouldn't fit into Una's cellar, at which point he scolded himself for failing to make the most of his honeymoon. 'Or are the bowels not maybe part of the intestines? Could that be why you say bowels?'

'I don't say bowels.'

'Right, but I do. People do.'

'So you say. Anyway, even with only one I went twice today. Number twos.' Una's eyebrows rose as her hands measured ten inches. 'Impressive, no?'

Rory wondered if he was eating too much or too little. All the choices, with the tofu terrines and the avocado wraps, were getting the better of him. 'That, *cara*, is rather more detail than I needed to hear. But since you mention it, you'll be pleased to hear that the log-jam may soon be broken.'

She almost yelped, and, undressing to the lingerie he'd bought for her on the eve of the wedding, jumped astride of him and fondled his tummy. 'We're married now, you know,' she said.

'I know,' he echoed, smiling. 'It's a miracle.'

'You feel it there?' She prodded. 'The miracle?'

'What, in my numerous bowels?'

Finally he felt his tiredness leaving him. He tried to ease her out of her lingerie. But he'd only got as far as the suspender belt when he realised she was asleep.

The following day was the first she hadn't planned their itinerary the night before. During the first few days they'd done the obvious SF sights: the Transamerica Pyramid, the Presidio, the City Lights bookstore, where she'd finally bought him the Kerouac. It was her first three-week break since she'd started working for Scottish Widows, and she knew that if anyone was going to make the most of the tour it was her. Rory would tag along, as he did in most else.

That was if, she rued, she could get him interested in anything beyond his many-channelled digestive track. Since he'd left Edinburgh Airport he hadn't so much as picked up an *FT* or a *Wall Street Journal*, or even watched the business news on CNN. It was all she could do to stop him zapping pointlessly, trying to find the Premier League results – as if anyone in San Francisco was interested in the antics of Glasgow Celtic or Heart of Midlothian. As she looked at the California guide-book she wondered if she hadn't been starved half her life, surrounded by grey harling Bathgate walls, with the local bingo the pinnacle in entertainment. And Edinburgh too, the big city to which she'd fled when she was seventeen and got her first job, it suddenly appeared like some ancient archaeological site, like the charred bones of someone formerly famous.

Unfair, probably, but maybe it was time to be unfair – it was her honeymoon, no? She'd spent the last twelve years in hard graft to get to where she was now, battling with the bigwigs of the establishment, for whom the only thing that mattered was the colour of your school tie. It wasn't too original, she supposed, but everything here, even the light, which made her feel as if she'd just removed a pair of dirty Ray-Bans, and the colours too, even if they were spelt *colors* – everything seemed to say: It's Possible, It's New, You Can Do It!

So it was at the wheel of a gleaming red-finned Cadillac that they cruised into Sebastopol the following afternoon, after a morning in which she'd traced a route into the Wine Country and convinced Rory that she didn't think less of him for his not knowing how to drive.

Rory's vote for Taco Bell was vetoed in favour of Food For Thought, and as he hesitated between swordfish creole and stuffed portobello mushrooms (each one bigger than his palm), she strolled along the aisles wondering how anyone knew their way among the thousands of vitamins and supplements.

'How you doing there?'

She'd got used enough to the question to realise that this was not a long-lost friend, though she still wasn't sure how to answer.

'Can I help you with something?'

'Oh no, I'm just looking!' came her automatic response, which instantly struck her as so typically Bathgate – as if the assistant were about to drag her into a back room, tie her to a chair, and pump her full of spyrolina. 'Maybe there is something,' she corrected herself.

The assistant pushed back his visor.

'Have you got anything that might help . . . ? I've been having some trouble . . . Maybe it's just the change of diet, or the jet lag . . .'

'Right.' The attendant was nodding sympathetically. 'And so?'

'There's so much choice in all the food, you know. The added fibre, extra protein boosts, double this, treble that, fat-free, gluten-rich, all that sort of thing. And the smoothies.' Here she was now, proving she wasn't Bathgate by giving him her life-story. 'Eh, for the intestines?' She pointed to the bank of efficient-looking bottles. 'For the bowel, more precisely.'

'Laxative? I sure know that when I travel . . .'

'It's not really that. I'm fine in fact, just curious.' She was backing away. 'I should get something to eat, my husband's waiting for me. I'll maybe come back.'

'You could try these.' He pointed.

'I'll see how it goes.'

Rory had ordered for both of them, and since he couldn't decide, three plates were sagging with unnameable salads and dips.

'Were you at the . . . ?' he asked, as she took her first bite, starting with the triple-chocolate mousse cake.

She didn't mean to nod. It was her first straight lie. She could see from his eyes that it made her more beautiful.

'Successful?'

She smiled enigmatically.

'Diameter?'

She went on eating, till the cake was almost finished.

'I went this morning before we left,' he said, 'hoping to get rid of the backlog. But only rabbit-droppings.'

She raised her eyebrows, to whose movements her husband was so attached. He watched them as if in their arch and incline he could read his future.

And what a future! When he would cease to care about his place in Sparta and be worrying about his son's place – or daughter's, he was open-minded on that score – and when his beloved would be deciding the futures (plural; neuter) of the biggest investment trust at the Widows.

'You don't think it's a bit odd,' he said, 'our conversation?'

'Triple-chocolate mousse,' she purred, as in some erotic ad, licking the last of it off her spoon.

'Those pellets do add up though. Not to be underestimated.'

'An inch and a half at least.'

His fork in the salad seemed to spear defeat and transmit it to his mouth.

Yet by the end of the meal, most of which he downed without thinking, he was hopeful again.

'You shouldn't stuff yourself,' she smiled. 'What goes in doesn't always correspond to what comes out.'

'Miss Economist speaking.'

'Mrs,' she corrected him, licking her bottom lip provocatively.

'Have you ever . . . ?' he got out, before suspicion of his own best instincts got the better of him.

She knew she was supposed to dig, and wondered if she could be bothered. 'Something about my life before I met you?'

'Right. I was wondering if you'd ever been into, you know . . . anal?' He pronounced it as if it were the singular of 'annals'.

'Aaanal,' she said, imitating him, 'as in the planet *Your*-anus?'

A family of four rose in unison from the bench next to theirs and noisily piled their tofu burgers into sad cardboard boxes. Rory cupped his hand over his mouth and stared fixedly at the floor until they had left.

'Oh, shit!' he moaned.

'Or in your case no shit.'

'Well?' he tried again. 'In some former life?'

'I don't see what that's got to do with anything,' she said, with a metallic ring to her voice he'd never heard before. 'I suppose you're going to tell me you've got two of *them* as well!'

The day dragged for both, and their first trip to a winery in Russian River Valley made it longer still since after five glasses of Chardonnay Una kept trying to push the gear stick in a way that defied its automatic nature, and Rory, feeling queasy on the curves, lay down in the back seat and decided that never again in his entire life would he sleep soundly. Dinner at the four-star Guerneville Rapids Hotel was a five-course affair, all inclusive with local brews, and even going for the lighter option of fresh sardines and sorbet, they both felt over-stuffed.

'But not for long,' Una chimed, retiring to their first-floor suite, leaving Rory to his brandy and his dread of the four-poster bed with which the room was swollen: pretentious thing, he told himself, though he knew this was not quite it – something about the sculpted wooden posts.

There was still a glow in the west and the clouds were raked over the vineyards in a way that made Rory wonder if a brisk walk might not trick his ever-more-weary brain out of its now inebriated jet lag.

'Hey there!' came a voice when he was only a few shaky steps out the back door, though when he looked round he couldn't see the head attached to it. 'Down here.' Rory lowered his gaze, and there was the head, right enough, buried up to its neck in the ground – like David Bowie in that Japanese film, whatever its name was. Identified now as that of the hotel manager, shrouded in steam and with a champagne bottle where his body should have been.

'Hot tub?' the head asked, and when Rory looked befuddled, 'Feel free, there's some shorts over there if you prefer.'

For a second Rory imagined his wife might be watching him undress from their window – from the bathroom window even, as she scored another triumph.

'Feels good, no?'

Rory felt his skin scald as he lowered himself into the water.

'Enjoy the dinner?'

The manager was talking to him, Rory realised, as if they were buddies. Fair enough, he supposed, since who was he to insist on any p's and q's when he had competitions with his wife about the most unmentionable things. But he didn't want to talk about the dinner, anything but, or sardines au sorbet would soon be forming a slick on the steaming surface.

'Redwood?' Rory asked, banging the tub rather too hard with his fist.

'Enjoying your trip?' the manager enquired.

'Pretty bad jet lag. Can't seem to get more than two minutes' sleep. It's our honeymoon, you know. I've probably been eating too much, certainly overindulging in your fine wines . . . You know what I mean?'

The manager pushed the champagne bottle his way, and Rory, figuring it was the custom, took a long swig from the bottle. 'Thing is,' he went on, 'it's, eh, a long way frae home.'

'I was just in Scotland,' the manager said. 'I got the accents down now. Buying antiques for the hotel. Braveheart, you know. Got myself a kilt.'

The fact that he should have felt flattered, being normally so nationalist, only made Rory more despondent. And hot. And drunk. 'I'll just take another swig, if you don't mind.'

'Be my guest,' said the manager, chuckling – a line he had evidently used before.

'You mind if I ask you,' Rory started, dimly aware that he didn't give a tinker's curse if he minded or not, 'but do you think it's normal, I mean, between a newly married husband and wife, to get competitive over things? Little things?' His voice seemed to boom in the dark over the bubbling round his feet. 'How about you and your wife, if you're married?'

'That'd depend, I suppose, on what sorts of things.'

'Like, say, personal things. Little things. Personal, eh, hygiene?'

'Sure, why not. You seen the bathroom products I'm stocking? I go all the way to Paris for them.'

'Or, say, like physical performance?'

'You got the keys to the hotel gym.'

'Or, say, I know this may sound ridiculous, but then I've never been drunk in a hot tub before . . . So how about intestines, guts, how about say . . .' He noticed he kept saying 'say' and guessed it was because he really was going to say it. 'How about bowels?'

'How many you got of them?'

Some ominously large bird, an owl or a nightjar, broke the silence which followed with a sweep of broad dark wings. Rory feared that when next he spoke he'd sound like a lobster screaming. 'I mean, between you and your wife, for instance?'

The manager's head was straining out of the water, suddenly looking indignant. 'This is a gay hotel, sir, if you hadn't noticed.'

Though he hoped it was hours, Rory knew it was only minutes later when he awoke, naked, with the four-poster threatening to crush him. His first thought was none too original: he'd been taken advantage of during his swoon, maybe that was even the manager's intention in luring him into the hot tub on a full stomach and plying him with champagne. His second thought was more cheering: that it might loosen things up down there, get them moving again after the pellet-hardness of the past few days. *Stitichezza*, the Italian word, he'd forgotten he'd ever learnt it, but it seemed to sum things up better than 'constipation'.

His eyes slowly came into focus in response to the cold towel Una was applying to his forehead. She might have a better head for figures, he thought, but he had it for languages and translation: mind into matter, investments into yield, matter into . . . more matter.

And sure enough, like a reward the next morning, after breakfast, despite the sleeplessness and hangover, despite the foolish flush at not having noticed how the waiters and guests were all patently gay. 'More goats this time than rabbits,' he informed his wife.

The fact that Una looked far from relieved when he reported it only made him the more chuffed. So much so that, though it was time to hit the road, he asked for another serving of hash-browns on rye instead.

'All that glitters is not gold,' he joked.

To underline his point, he opened a notebook which he'd named 'Translations' on the cover. He must have bought it since they'd arrived, Una deduced, since it had a picture of the Old Faithful Geyser on the cover, spurting a hundred yards into the air.

On the first page he inscribed:

```
BREAKFAST
one bowl (heaped) granola
two hash-browns on rye
melon and papaya side order
three double lattes
```

to which he added a big equals sign:

$$=$$

His wife's clothes were looking crumpled, he thought, though they had hung in the closet all night as she slept like a babe. He had spent the night pacing the room avoiding those four posts, yet he was looking fit and well-pressed this morning, he could tell it from the looks he was getting from the waiters. And the vigil hadn't been wasted, either, since at last he'd opened the guide-book and got to making some plans.

'I'd like to visit the Petrified Forest today,' he said, pointing to the relevant page.

'We haven't seen any real sequoias yet, and you want to see dead ones?'

'It says that Robert Louis Stevenson visited it in 1880 on his honeymoon there with Fanny what's-her-name. Seems appropriate.' He attempted a smile, but was defeated by the sudden thought that they hadn't made love since the first night in San Francisco.

'We've come all this way to end up where some daft Scotsman

stumbled over a hundred years ago?' She was failing to conceal her irritation. After all, what did he have to start reading the guide-book for? She was the one who'd be expected to do all the driving, in that ridiculous liner of a car. 'I thought we could go to a winery,' she improvised. 'This Korbel place down the road is famous for champagne.'

'On the way then.' His hackles rose as he tried to think of a Stevenson story other than *Jekyll and Hyde*. 'I've always been a fan of . . . eh . . . Long John Silver.'

'Pieces of eight!' she snapped back at him. 'Pieces of eight! Put that in your accounts book and chew on it!'

The champagne at Korbel was fizzy but tasteless, and Una had been further disgruntled by having to move out of the four-poster room into a more modest suite on the floor above, as well as by the complacent smile of the manager and deliverer of her husband, the knowing look in his close-set eyes. She'd said she wanted to change hotels in that case, move up to Calistoga and the spas, but Rory had insisted, claiming he was too tired to pack his things into the car again.

Though apparently not too tired to go chasing the shadow of what he now claimed was a great Scottish author – he who hadn't read a thing but the financial pages during the whole nine months she'd known him, and whose bookshelves in his dismal bachelor flat had been stacked with beer mats and football annuals. So she was pleasantly surprised when she stepped into the gift shop-cum-ticket office at the entrance to the Petrified Forest, where fossils of every colour were on sale, thin agate slices, ripe plums of nickel that felt soothing in the hand, and smooth stone baby squids, polished like arrow-heads. She abruptly felt a weight lifted from somewhere inside of her as she surveyed these relics, resurrected from under the lava and mud, and living again like a vow that nothing was ever truly wasted or lost.

Rory called to her from the counter, where he'd paid the storekeeper for tickets and was swotting up on his Stevenson, the volume on sale there clutched in his eager hand. For a moment she remembered why she'd married him, and stroked his sweating scalp, blessing his boyish enthusiasm.

'Listen to this,' he said. 'It's from *The Silverado Squatters*, which is all about this area apparently. Listen. Robert Louis says:

> 'Scotland is indefinable; it has no unity except upon the map. Two languages, many dialects, innumerable forms of piety, and countless local patriotisms and prejudices, part us among ourselves more widely than the extreme east and west of that great continent of America.'

At several points she wanted to stop him, to interject it wasn't true, that they didn't speak in dialect and were hardly pious; but the words seemed to form a tide against which she could not swim, like the time she'd been caught in the swell at Cramond as a teenager.

'"When I am at home,"' Rory persisted, '"I feel a man from Glasgow to be something like a rival, a man from Barra to be more than half a foreigner."'

What a load of nonsense! Just because they were Scottish. Maybe she'd decide to become American. Stuff all that and settle here in California. She'd find a job easy enough. By herself if need be!

'Let's do the trail,' she pleaded, alarmed by her own thoughts.

It was an easy stroll, too easy perhaps given the circumstances. Rory had hoped some serious exercise would clear the air between them, take their minds off the present. And the trees themselves, enormous redwood trunks which had fallen more than three million years before, were somehow disappointing too. For bark and wood had been so perfectly replaced by rock that they still indeed looked just like fallen trees. It was only when he tapped one, and felt the resistance of solid stone, that it came home to him. He was the more eager to get to what the leaflet said was the final great specimen, called 'The Robert Louis Stevenson Tree', in memory of the meeting between the Scotsman and the discoverer of these enormous tree-stones.

They stood, wondering, in front of its giant eight-foot diameter, and followed the mineral trunk to where it broke off in segments, then buried itself in the ground. The annual rings were still visible, though witness now to millennia as well as humble human years. An oak grew out of a crevice, its leafy effusions and even its sturdy trunk ephemeral above the epochal presence of this petrified survivor.

Rory smiled. 'To think,' he started. 'To think it's been here three million years. And that Robert Louis once stood right here gazing at it, just like us.'

'As one could say about most of Edinburgh, in fact.'

'You what?'

'You know,' she said, 'what it reminds me of?'

'Hmm?'

'It reminds me of one of my stools.' She was smiling too.

'Your what?' he grunted, disgusted now – offended.

'Right colour, shape.'

'Fucking dimension too, I suppose,' he growled at her. 'Here I am busy remembering a great bit of history, Robert and Fanny, my favourite author, and you're talking about turds! You're fixed, that's your problem – fixated I mean, that's what you are!'

She wanted to shout back at him that she was talking about history too, but if she didn't understand what she meant herself, then how could she expect him to. She'd never seen him furious before, it distorted his features in a way she might have found attractive, were she not so full of fury herself. 'I've been twice today already,' she sneered. 'So I know what I'm on about.'

'Well, I've been three times,' he bawled at her, then steamed off into the surrounding forest, swiping at the undergrowth. 'Must have been thanks to the servicing the fucking hotel manager gave me. He was a lot more interested in it than you!'

'You gonna sign him up?' she hurled back at him, along with the jar of laxatives which she found she was clutching. 'For Sparta Athletic?'

'Tollie!' he fumed. 'Shithead!' Then, remembering: 'Culo! Cacca!'

'Queer boy!' she cried at his disappearing back. 'Terminator!'

The tears were streaming down her face. So blinded was she, indeed, that for a moment the trees were just trees, divested of their epochs, the woodchips just woodchips, and she kicked a big one with the full force of her long right leg.

'I don't know which hospital,' the storekeeper said, when finally, having lost his way several times and been terrified by what he was sure was a grizzly, Rory found his way back to the gift shop. 'But the ambulance man said it was a clean break.'

Rory stared round wildly, but all he could see was trees, their tall trunks reaching on for miles.

'Here,' the storekeeper said. 'She left the car keys for you.'

.

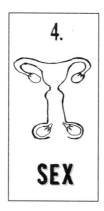

4.

SEX

IS THAT WHAT it amounts to: a big cock in one hand (Joe's) and a moist warm quim in the other (Flora's)? A few lines of Shakespeare?

It was more than enough for my warden and audience, who looked fit to dissolve last night, though not enough for my own tangled craving for perfection. Oh, the ambitions I had, nursed since incarceration. Looking forward to every minute away from the sewing-machines and compulsory recreation, to put my mind to it. Little suspecting I'd reduce it all to this.

Can it honestly be the best I'm capable of, when I've been aiming at a definitive dissertation, the ultimate essay on the topic, an epic, a lyric, a love-song?

Over my eighteen months inside Saughton Prison I'd managed to convince myself that there's nowhere better suited to such a project: that if I've been doing time, then time has also been helping me in return; not just freeing me from any responsibility for earning my bread, but letting the ideas ripen and mature like a bottle of good plonk. To survive inside, I've become a voyager down the *via negativa*, having convinced myself that, by doing without, I've also been turning up the dials marked 'Imagination', 'Intellect', 'Remembrance'.

I'm not much interested in my own sex, that's child's play. Added to which, my abilities as a mimic, combined with towering bulk and black belts, keep me from being pestered by even the most rampant of the pricks in the cells around me.

And my declaration too – words on paper (unworthy institutional paper: HMP) – of what the human sex means to me, this too would travel down the *via negativa*. For, not being the first to try and describe that delight, I'd have to start by saying what sex was not. The ground was littered (I switched metaphors, where switching cells or lives was denied to me), cluttered with hawkers and tents of exotic race and genre, and I couldn't just ignore them on the way to my own intimate strains. I tried to imagine little symbols to indicate the facilities in this campsite-of-the-mind: a Doric column for archaeological sites; a gilt frame for artistic masterpieces; a gothic spire to denote religious buildings; an open book for poems, novels, libraries; and then two little stick figures, one in a skirt, to indicate toilet facilities, suitable for both sexes.

And that was but the start of my inventory, listing traditional settlers in Sexville: the Venuses, the Kama Sutra temples, the Sapphos, the Symbolists. Deep down, I felt comfortable enough sharing space with them. But there were more recent migrants too, driven over the terrain by fickle winds of fashion, spoiling it with their chatter, staking out their claims on the sacred turf.

What I would emphatically not be talking about, I wanted it to be clear from the outset, was sexuality, gender, or any of the thousand-and-one gloomy tributaries of these sludge-filled modern rivers. I've had my fill of what it means to be a man, a woman, a daughter, a father, a third cousin twice removed, and, just in case I wanted more, I've had to put up with the monthly group therapy sessions in which these chestnuts get reheated. The very badges *masculine* and *feminine* make me want to vomit.

For the sex I intend is too real to care a damn about its gender, doesn't give a teenager's wank about all the frills and props of that stinking red herring, *sexuality*, infantile or adult. (And if this comes out paradoxical or mystic, then let me be placed in a dojo and used as a target for zen archers, or turned into a saint, like they did with that boring jailbird fart Jean Genet.) In short: hands off you feminists, gay-activists, tree-huggers! Macho-men, keep out! The sex I would write about, whether rising to salute me or snuggling along my fingers, has no obnoxious little *m.* or *f.* attached to it. The perfection that my time inside had permitted me to distil might indeed depend upon a man or woman for its existence (I'm not interested in hermaphrodites). But never should this define it. For as much as man may be man, woman woman – as much or as little – their sex is something else.

Which, to be honest, was partly what stymied me in the first place. For the apotheosis with Flora and Joe wouldn't have been thinkable without their pitiful worries about whether it made them more or less masculine or feminine; and the bullshit I spouted to allay their fears.

And then, if I tried to avoid that supreme example, I ended up abstract, in some Platonic cave before sex came into being, sounding off about willy-o'-the-wisp. I wanted palpable, palpitating. Instead, I got algebraic or ethereal.

Which left me where, precisely?

Going round in circles, wordless, devoid of discourse, like the dreichest days on the recreation ground, where I might as well have my ankles chained to my neighbour – at least it would give me something tangible to strain against. Or pointing, like the worst sort of culture-vulture I've always feared I could become, peering and pointing at the achievements of others.

'Oh look, there, at that primitive Yoni! Nothing but a vagina on legs . . .'

'My but that Pompeii Priapus has got a whopper, comes right down to his knees. Charming how he's weighing it. What's in the other basket of the scales, the whole mortal world . . . ?'

'That gargoyle, now, frightful and awesome, peeling back her labia upon the house of God . . .'

'The little tadger on that cheeky Caravaggio cherub, its very shrimp-like size a come-on . . .'

'Wow! *L'Origine du Monde*: the best painting yet of a woman's crotch, put it in the pantheon, far above more shiny types of halo . . .'

Till here I was, coming and going, talking of Michaelangelo's *David*'s dick; or worse, invoking Lawrentian bloodlust or singing the 'Body Electric'; worse still, given my proclivities and crime, actually trying to *imitate* the old masters. When what in truth I longed for was to put down my perfection, not theirs; the perfection I have known and held, entered and ingested.

There was no excuse. All this talk of campsites and colonies was just hedging my bets.

So I sit down in the prison library, finally, a few weeks ago, intending to get going. And what do I start with? Contemplation of climax – any sort of climax? Do I hell. I start remembering the new kid, three cells down.

'What you in for?' he asks me on the way to the chapel.

Shame it's nothing more spectacular: slashing a Rubens, or impaling myself on a stone phallus from Delos.

'Art fraud,' I tell him, seeking refuge in brevity. 'I worked at Phillips, the auction house.'

He can't believe he's ended up in Saughton for what he's done, insists it was just a lark. It'll mean missing a whole year of studies, not to mention the stigma of having been in the nick.

I can see he's not going to give me any peace until he's spilled the beans, so I utter a few long words to make him feel at home, somebody a uni-type can confide in. What he tells me sounds apocryphal, or like he's been reading too much *Trainspotting*, but that doesn't stop it rattling round my mind for days to come.

He's a medical student, he tells me, in his final year, one of whose perks is that he's been given his own corpse to dissect. He does this dutifully, confirming what he already knows, what pumps into where, the shin bone connected to the knee bone, the knee bone connected to the thigh bone, and so on. Then, at the end, rather than incinerate the whole thing . . .

'The stiff's just a young bloke,' he says. 'Not bad looking he's been, not that I'm that way inclined, despite necrophilia being the vogue these days. He's been a junkie. And so I think – maybe I've been spending too much time in the operating theatre, getting macabre, it's one of the risks of the trade, they say – I think, what if I kept a bit?'

(This, patently, would not do as the opening stanza in my *Ode to Sex*.)

'So before he gets reduced to ashes I cut off his prick and take it home. A few nights later I get stoned with some mates and for some reason I decide to sew it onto my jeans. Then we go out down the town. Causes quite a sensation, people screaming and hooting. Till finally a policeman comes up to me, the gentle sort.

'"Come on now, sir, put that away, you know that sort of thing is not allowed."

'So I whip out my scalpel and slice it clean off. Which is where my problems really begin, since the cop doesn't just faint, he falls so badly he breaks his arm. I'm had up for indecent assault and causing grievous bodily harm, which seems pretty far-fetched to me.'

I warned the medic he'd better keep his story to himself: there's folks in here who might get the wrong idea.

'Cheers,' he tells me. 'If you ever need some repair work when you get out.'

(He's going to specialise, he's decided, in plastic surgery.)

And who knows, maybe I'll take him up on his offer when I do get out of here. Though what I'd get him to improve I don't know. Most of the time my organ does its business – *organ* is fine for what I've got, no need to dignify it.

I could get him to remove a rib, I suppose. That's a thought. I read somewhere that someone had this operation done. I'd hoped greater flexibility might be one of the fringe benefits of all my karate exercise.

The sacred circle!

Babies have it right in this respect, learning the world through their mouths. The poet Leopardi could auto-fellatio naturally; maybe as divine compensation for having a hunchback. When I read that, I was never able to read his poem about 'The Infinite' in quite the same way again.

So books, paintings, sculptures, tales from those in the clink, contortionist fantasies . . . Most recently it's been Shakespeare ('Groping for trouts in a peculiar river'), and dictionaries.

Whiled away a whole afternoon last week with a slang dictionary and a Scots thesaurus. Everything from 'crown jewels' to 'one-eyed trouser snake', from 'pintle' to 'tirlie-whirlie' (obsolete), from 'bacon sandwich' to 'twat'.

Nor have I neglected research into that other essential function which the human sex performs, and I've digressed into golden shower memories of several provenances, the kind reputed to douse the aboriginal fires, and the kind, no less marvellous to this primitive's mind, which floods downwards.

And of course, even without the urging of my warden, I have, in deference to my Edinburgh Academy schooling, notwithstanding my claims about the sexlessness of sex, the incommensurability of male and female, gone in for a good bit of 'compare and contrast', transfusing life into the academic exercise with the blood of reminiscence.

Yet this is all fair play. The wellspring of transcendent memory remained unsullied; by keeping perfection to myself I was compressing it like a perfume squeezed from flowers.

Nothing remotely like what I did last night.

'You used to play in that team o' poofters, right, Ian?'

I'd wondered why this particular warden, 'Ol' Brockit' we call him on account of his incomparably ugly mug, always went out of his way to be kind to me (what he imagined was kind). He'd taken to paying me a wee visit in the cell of an evening, starting about nine months ago.

I give him my bored professor look. 'You're referring, my good man, to the noble culture of Sparta?'

''Cos ma son Rory plays fir them too.'

'Demon striker, your Rory. The Billy Dodds of Canonmills. I know him well.' I try to make it clear no intimacy is implied. Indeed, he's not a bad sort, if a bit underdeveloped above the shoulders.

'When you got put away, he asked me to keep an eye on you.'

'Much appreciated too.'

'He's taken up wi a bird, mibbe you know her? Called Una, a real corker, tall as anything.'

I nod appreciatively, hoping he'll spare me the details.

'It's quite a relief to me, I can tell you, son. I was starting to wonder, you know, wi' all his runnin' about wi' the jessies on that team. You ken what I mean?'

'I wouldn't have any worries on that score, sir,' I say obsequiously. 'He's a straight shooter, our Rory.'

That sends him away happy. I'm maybe in the clear.

And sure enough he keeps to himself for the next six months or so, during which time I'm left to my project; a privacy which, even if it doesn't see any real progress, does allow me to imagine that Flora No. 5 (pour femmes) and Eau de Joe (pour hommes) may soon be hitting our prison stores.

He keeps to himself, that is, until early this spring, when in he bursts, apoplectically happy. 'It's great news,' he tells me, sitting down uninvited.

I foolishly offer him a drink from my private supply.

'No bad!' he says, blissfully unaware that the whisky he's swigging has been kissed by sea airs for thirty-five years. 'So like I was saying, son, great news an a'. Our Rory's getting hitched. Splicing the knot. Doing the decent thing. For better or for worse.'

I'm starting to suspect Ol' Brockit's had his nose in my thesaurus. 'Great news indeed!' I agree.

'She works for the Widows, fair rakin' it in.'

'Long may they rake together!'

'San Francisco for the honeymoon.'

My fear that Ol' Brockit may somehow hear of San Fran's Castro district, world epicentre of gaydom, comes back to plague me, along with himself, two months later – months in which the final preparations have been underway for my grand summing-up.

'It's all off, Ian,' he moans. 'I canna believe it.'

My Islay Vintage is set to suffer.

'Rory won't tell me why. And he won't even get any alimony. All he'll say is something about "incompatible lifestyles".'

I barely suppress a guffaw: as if our Rory had a life in the first place, let alone a lifestyle.

'You don't think it could be . . . You know, like queer?'

'I honestly don't think it's that,' I tell him, for once using 'honestly' honestly.

I can hardly keep him out of my cell after this, overflowing with tedious trivia about the impending divorce – or annulment as it turns out she's asking for, claiming the marriage has never been consummated, which requires lots more reassurance about Brockit

Jnr's true-blue bollocks; which in turn, imperceptibly but none the less fatally, brings us round to yours truly and his own state of play.

'I'm the artistic type, sir,' I try, 'even if I haven't yet written anything much. Of course I do have a healthy interest in sex, but no, I wouldn't really be interested in a subscription to used copies of *Hustler*. I'm a great believer in what the poets call *sublimation*.'

I'm so desperate to get some peace that I almost tell him about the new kid on the block and his scalpelled penis. Then I almost break another cardinal rule and start up about the summation of sex I shall shortly be commencing.

'I see that, son. But I was askin' Rory, the laddie's round a lot these days, and he seemed to imply that, you know . . . ?'

I let him stew a while.

'Yer inclination, like?'

'Double-barrelled?' I help him. 'So to speak.'

'Aye, right.'

Embarrassment gets the better of him – this is a fortnight ago – and after another few tumblers he's off home for the night, leaving me to a last contemplation of the *via negativa*, which somehow turns into a dream full of Flora and Joe.

But he's back: like an incubus, he just can't keep away.

I'm thinking of asking the governor for solitary confinement, for protection from harassment by kindness. Could it be that Ol' Brockit, having developed the warden's bloodhound nose, has caught a whiff of the apocalypse, the anchovies and truffles with which Flo–Joe dreams are scented?

'Is one more, how should I put it, eh, satisfyin' than the other?' he's asking me. 'I've no experience in that domain, you ken, son.'

I pretend to consider it. 'Each has its own special beauty, sir.' I refrain from reading him some Bardic sonnets.

'But I mean, when it comes doon to it? You ken what I mean?'

I do know what he means, though I wish I didn't.

'Maybe you could gee us some examples, like.'

The silence hangs heavy, lulled by the snores on the block, the occasional moan of a prisoner who, willingly or not, alone or accompanied, is escaping from his cell.

'I'm no interested in they wankers and faggots,' he says, gesturing. 'They couldna describe it, let alone make a comparison, not if they had fanny and tool there starin' them in the face.'

Still I keep him hanging. I'm thinking how Joe used to sail round the showroom in his cut-off jeans, always ready with a smartass comment. I barely knew why at that point, but I didn't miss a chance to introduce him to Flora, taking care to explain to him how satisfied I was – in every sense – to be with her, the one great love of my life. I fostered her interest in the degree Joe was taking. His interest in her vegetarian cookery.

'At first,' I finally say, and Ol' Brockit shivers, 'at first, my plan wasn't so daring. I had the idea of just bringing my lover, Flora, together with Joe, the man I most fancy of all the men I've met. I only wanted to play the pimp, leave it at that, imagine the rest.'

'What?' he groans. 'Yer own bird?'

If he wanted comparisons, I'd give him comparisons. I'd force-feed him, served up as salacious-spread on toast.

'Try to imagine what it's like, sir. The sex you've loved since you were a teenager, finally meeting with the one you've been lusting after for months. Each so beautiful.' I think to stretch his lexicon: 'Paragons both: chefs d'œuvre.'

'Aye, well, when you put it like that, I suppose.'

'So I need say no more!'

Disappointment incarnate.

'Think about it a bit, sir, you'll have it figured out for yourself.'

I spend the next day, yesterday, when in my few spare moments I should have been memorising the Bard's greatest quatrains, with my nose stuck in *Richard* III, rather fancying myself in the lead role. I don't even get so far as taking my pen out.

He arrives like a punctual ghost, letting himself into my cell when the quiet reigns.

'You were sayin', son?'

'You've given it some thought?'

'Been thinking of nothin' else, I assure you.'

I can't believe I'm about to do this: rampage through my perfume plant in the company of Brockit!

'The female sex,' I start, 'is a marvel of nature, as of course you are aware, sir. But have you ever thought how wonderful it is that it's there, as it were in waiting, even when a woman is dressed and working, or doing the dishes, or putting her bairn to bed? In which it contrasts completely with a man's tadger, which, despite whatever he's doing, cannot be forgotten – by me at least – not even if he's dressed, not even if he's announcing a catastrophe on the nine o'clock news.'

'Hmm. It's an interestin' idea, son.'

'Then of course there's what I call' – extemporising – 'ehhh, the *manifest factor*.'

'I canna see that,' he says (proving my point).

'Think of it this way: a man's down to his kecks, right; it's pretty clear if he's genuinely interested or just going along for the ride, so to speak. That can be reassuring, but there's also not much mystery about it. Whereas a woman, now, well, barring very rare exceptions, it's not going to be clear until she's fully undressed, and maybe not even then. It means you've got to be bolder, but the uncertainty is also part of the thrill.'

'Ahh! Right enough.'

Suddenly I see who it is Ol' Brockit reminds me of: he's Clarence, the one Richard III calls 'G', stuck in his prison cell, waiting to be murdered, thinking about this dream he's had in which he's discovered an underwater world he never knew existed: more strange, more terrifying, more beautiful. Which, since I've had time to re-read today, let me snippet here – a little of Clarence remembering:

> What dreadful noise of waters in my ears;
> What sights of ugly death within my eyes!
> Methoughts I saw a thousand fearful wrecks;
> Ten thousand men that fishes gnaw'd upon;
> Wedges of gold, great anchors, heaps of pearl,
> Inestimable stones, unvalu'd jewels,
> All scatter'd in the bottom of the sea.

'And then, G,' I say to Brockit. 'You don't mind if I call you "G", sir, seeing as how you remind me of this guy I know called Clarence?'

'That'd be "C" wouldn't it, son? No that I want to quibble.'

He's got me there, right enough. (And even on the re-read I haven't figured out why 'C' becomes 'G'.) 'No flies on you, sir.'

'Feel free, son, so long as you dinna call me "Brockit".'

'So there's also this, G, not to be underestimated: that's the humidity quotient.'

Brockit is one huge ear.

'In the case of a woman, well . . . as you know yourself . . .'

But he won't be drawn into trading confidences.

'You're a canny soul, G,' I flatter him. 'Well, a man now, even if he has a tendency to produce a tad of fluid before the big spurt, is basically in search of the Triple M, as you know.'

'You mean, like thems that makes the scourers?'

'Not exactly. What I'm talking about is Mucous Membrane Moisture.' I surprise myself with this. I should start a seminar when I get out of here. 'We're taking it as given, aren't we, G, that dryness is the curse in this context. I mean, is there a word less sexy than "dust"?'

'Sandpaper.'

'Right enough.' I'll give him a free seat in the seminar for that. 'Yet lend your lugs,' I say, as if there were danger of him doing otherwise. 'Give that fatally dry male member a mouth, and that very dryness becomes a boon, if you catch my drift. Exploring every cavity, known and unknown, with no risk of super-saturation.'

'Aye but . . .' He spits as if he'd just chewed an unripe olive.

'Well, G, it's all a question of angles, you have to ensure the epiglottis doesn't take a battering. If you're interested, I could recommend some "How To" videos.'

G's head wobbles frantically from side to side.

Joe's was every bit as dry and tasty as expected. Something about his reluctance too, his very perturbation at the dreadful twist events had taken, which added a certain chilli to the salsa: he starts off the evening expecting to betray his old pal with his old pal's bird, and ends up suspecting he's a nancy.

It's not, let me assert this now, amid the ruins of my project, not, not, not a mere question of dimension – biggest, tightest, whatever;

nor, exactly, of mere aesthetic proportion, colour, hairiness, the sheen of helmet or the rubescence of lips, though none of the above are insignificant, or in the case of Flora and Joe anything less than ideal.

'As against the reward of a woman's moistness.'

G's nut has finally ceased shaking.

'Which somehow seems so personal compared to a man's erection, as if you and you alone could ever have provoked it. Though, with the inconvenience, as you know . . .'

I rub my jowls meaningfully, yet G will not bite.

'A certain, shall we say, swampiness? In extremis.'

'Ah!' G's nodding like a jobber's mate who's spotted a botched drain. 'And tell me, Ian, I mean, what about when it really gets down tae it?' He makes a fist and flexes his biceps.

I wonder if he knows that though I may have been a joke as Sparta Athletic's goalkeeper, I could, with a single well-timed kick, knock his prurient Brockit block off.

'Well, G, try and remember – I'm sorry to put it this way, but you did ask – try and remember the most satisfying shit you've ever had.'

It's all a bit much for him: what dreadful noise of waters in his ears! Water-closets!

'Try remembering, G, when Rory was a bairn, you must have noticed how perky he always was after his early-morning poo?'

That seems to work.

'Well, multiply that by a hundred times or more. And then think that the action, not to say motion, is in both directions, and can go on and on and on.'

I give him time to do so.

'Whereas with a woman, G, well you can . . .' I'm about to say 'remember that', when I glance across the cell and see that there's tears beaded on his hangdog cheeks. Then I remember Rory missing a match, three or four years back, saying it was because he had to attend his ma's funeral. A black armband for the next few weeks.

'Aye but,' he moans. 'Aye but . . .' There's snotter hanging from his nose. He'll be lucky to survive the night if he wheezes any worse.

I know I shouldn't, that it's a shortcut to perdition, that I'm pillaging the tomb whose relics have kept me sane here, that my ghosts will fly on the gust of my words, that I'll skitter away in anecdote the song I should have sung. I know I should tell my warden to fuck off out my cell, go home to his miserable Craiglockart digs, leaf through his dog-eared *Playboy*, run himself a nice warm bath, get into it, and then draw the electric heater in after him.

I know all this and more.

I say: 'Listen, G, I'll tell you. You remember about Flora, my bird, and Joe, the guy who works in the showroom?'

He's alive again.

'Two nights before I get put away, she finally decides to cut her losses and spend the night with him. They don't realise yet that I'm about to be sent down. They're under the impression that I don't know a thing about their liaison, when in fact I've been promoting it all along.'

Here's anchors, greater than ever; while I clutch the dead-weight of betrayal – mine.

'Up to now I've intended just to sit outside her house, imagining, at the most maybe trying to sneak a peek through her window. But knowing that in two days' time I'm going to be sentenced, it gives me new ideas.'

G breathes inaudibly, his cheeks aflame.

'They've finished their dinner, I can hear them from the porch. They're over their scruples, and finally getting down to it: my two favourite perfections, meeting each other at last. Can you see it, G? Can you see it?'

Great anchors. Unvalu'd jewels.

'I'll spare you the description of how I let myself in with the latchkey, how I watch them for a while, going at it like rabbits after months of denial, her moans, which sound different from that distance, his occasional obscenities with which he presumes to arouse her, then my gasp of amazement just before he's about to come – and of course the small-talk, all their desperate apologies, my expressions of astonishment and horror, Joe's terrorised wetting of the bed when he realises what I could do to him with a couple of kicks, Flora's touching attempt to cover her breasts with a sheet. Through my manufactured tears I break the news to them: that I'm soon to be locked away from the light of day, and that this may be my last night.

'Joe starts hunting for his clothes, until I invite him to stay. "Make that an order," I tell him.'

The bottom of the sea; G can go no deeper. I should disconnect his oxygen tube, but I just cannot do it.

'"Look," I tell them, "time is precious. Let's be adults. We all care for each other, in our different ways. Can we not make the most of it?"

'They're reluctant-going-on-horrified, but there's no getting out of it.

'You see these hands, G?'

From the pressure of the depths, my hands look alien to him, he hardly recognises an imperfect human form.

'I ease the left one under Flora's hips and raise her an inch or two. I put my right round Joe's prick, which, notwithstanding his momentary display of fear, is still standing at half-mast, and though I'm sure he's screaming blue murder inside, never having had a man's fist round him before, he knows there's no choice.'

A thousand fearful wrecks.

'"So where exactly had you got to?" I ask them, as I ease myself onto and into her, not letting go of him all the while. She holds me tighter than she ever has, and the look of apprehension slides from her face. Another look takes over.'

'Ahh!' Ol' Brockit sighs.

'Of hunger, if you will, G – though I might call it *love*.'

Inestimable stones. Wedges of gold.

'And then, borrowing from Flora's wetness, I place him behind me at the gate, twist my arm behind and begin to pull him . . . fill . . . be filled . . .'

G. Joe. Flora. Me.

Heaps and heaps of pearl.

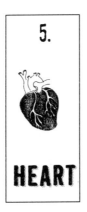

5.

HEART

Subject: Arrival

Wednesday 4 August

Dearest Deirdre,

Six in the Edinburgh morning; midnight here in Mexico. Dark as a coal-cellar. Yet the air is thick, active, pullulating, tropical. The last leg of the journey gruelling. After I called you from Cambridge Mass: Boston-NY-Mexico City was bad enough. But then I had to wait around for a coach, only to discover that the next three were fully booked. In the end I took a taxi over the mountains, Popocatepetl rearing its head above the smog, pictured Malcolm Lowrie brooding beneath it. Then on to uncharted terrain – for me I mean - into Tepoztlan.

Salgado from Harvard wasn't exaggerating: the house is unlived-in, 'virgin' as he put it, situated beyond the town, secluded, spectacular crags and hills all around, remains of an Aztec temple. Fire-crackers at dusk. The taxi-driver insisted I must know some film called *Clear and Present Danger* (Harrison Ford), which was shot among these mountains.

BODY LANGUAGE

Unpacked my clothes, more significantly set my laptop on the desk in front of a picture window with a huge view up to the ruined temple. I felt ready to begin, despite travel fatigue. Two weeks here should see me through the research, then home to write it up: 'The Case of the Tepoztlan Golf-Course', sixth and final chapter in what I've decided to call *20th-Century American Colonialism*. The bestseller the Edinburgh reading public has been waiting for! But seriously, maybe then my sabbatical won't have been a total waste, and I won't feel that all I'm fit for is Uni admin.

No need to tell me again: I'm a professor, a department chairman, too old for a mid-life crisis!

Very special atmosphere here. Only word for it: ENORMOUS. Awesome mix in landscape of life-force and harshness. The horticulturist in you would be overwhelmed, everything burgeoning.

Must go and shake out the bed: Salgado warned of scorpions' nests. There's you snug in your own, the milkman about to arrive - no innuendo intended!

All my love,
Peter

Subject: Testing testing

Thursday

Darling Darling,
I do hope this works. Despite your explanations and reassurances, the Luddite in me rises up. I'd prefer the old-fashioned method, even if I take your point about how you'd be home before yours reached me. You know I'm a slow typist, so don't expect reams.

Nothing much to report: nothing ENORMOUS about

Juniper Green! Unless you count Hearth-Rug finding a squirrel in the park and wearing out his puppy paws trying to catch it. (I do wish you'd chosen some other name for the puppy. I get the strangest looks from the widowers out on their constitutionals.)

Glad to hear the golf-course war will soon be under your belt. They're queueing at Waterstones already. Do be a bit careful with local politics and sensitivities, you know your tendency to barge in and polarise, not to say overdramatise. I shall see if I can't rent that film on video from Blockbuster. You know, don't you, that you didn't want me with you, getting under your feet.

Nasty premonition I was forgetting something today, then remembered it should have been Heather's birthday tomorrow.

Love,
Deirdre
p.s. Is this what's meant by 'cyber-love'?
p.p.s. Nothing virtual about the milkman!

Subject: Carfuffle!

Thursday

Dear Dee,
Yours loud and clear when logged on this morning. Do keep H-Rug on his leash. And yes, shall try not to play Boy Scouts. If the corporate interests win the day here, with their clubhouses, casinos, luxury hotels, leisure centres (read 'leeesure centers'), not to mention the massive great pipes they're going to have to lay to drain away most of the town's water-supply to keep the course from parching nine months of the year, then we can only hope the locals, most of whom will not benefit one iota from

the influx of tax-dodgers, White South Africans, and pot-bellied drug barons wearing Pringle sweaters, will take to the traditional guns and bombs. Can't believe that this is somehow connected to my childhood thrashes round Silverknowes with an iron and a putter (1s 6d a round).

Getting out of bed, remembered why Lawrence entitled his book about this country *Mornings in Mexico*: the whole world coming alive, limitless and abundant. Except yours truly, alas. Forget Harrison Ford and tune in to Hammer House of Horror!

Somewhere deep in the land of nod, dreaming of Jack Nicklaus as it happens, when there's the weirdest sound. Turn on the light, look at the time: 4.10 a.m. Pitch black outside. Salgado's house has three rooms downstairs and just this enormous open-plan bedroom upstairs in which a hundred creatures could live undetected. A rodent in pain? Or some sort of lizard? But it wasn't in the room, however vast. Somewhere outside, in the direction of the cottage where the housekeeper lives with her husband, the gardener.

How to describe it? The most unearthly sound ever. Like howler monkeys, mixed with a lion roaring, but with something irrepressibly human too, and female. Utterly unnerving. Five minutes it lasts, then recedes into the distance, going up the track away from the town.

Impossible to sleep after that. The dawn rose rapidly, cockatoos in the garden. Downstairs there was guava salad prepared, though not a sound from Faustina, the housekeeper. Too tired to start on golf-course investigations today, so a bit of tourism, then a nap in the afternoon.

Love,
P.

p.s. Milkman probably suffers from high cholesterol.

p.p.s. Your accusations of my being excessive are rich, given you're quite over the top with your future perfect tense about Heather's birthday. It IS her birthday today - her thirty-third - whether you like her present life or not. It pulls me apart not to simply call her up and wish her well, our only child. See, it even makes me split my infinitives.

Subject: Call that an explanation?

Tepoztlan, Thursday afternoon

Dear D.,

You probably haven't logged on yet.

Stroll round the town, wonderful market with unheralded fruits and flowers. Local church marvellous in its baroque way, built eighteenth century. Weary after the trek back down the long path on foot. Lunch set magically by Faustina. Salgado at Harvard told me a bit about her: twenty-four, an orphan, raised by local shaman, dominates her husband by her lore, spells, etc. Beautiful too in her squat Indian way.

She lets herself be enticed into the kitchen for coffee. After chitchat (translated for you since she hasn't a word of English, and even her Spanish is hard to follow), the tale of being woken in the night. If it had been Hammer Horror she would have pulled her shawl over her head and scuttled away; but she seemed unperturbed.

'That's the Llorona,' she explains, as if she were commenting on some species of bird. 'She walks at that time.'

'The Llorona': spirit of a woman murdered three months ago, a prostitute from Cuernavacca who was

carried here, dragged past the house up the hill
to the waterfall, raped repeatedly, then murdered.
As if that wasn't enough, she was then
dismembered, and the parts were scattered through
the woods and hillside.

(A gruesome tale to zap down the wires, but it
has quite disturbed me. The afternoon risks being
a washout. Only achievement is an appointment with
the manager of Golf Promotion Enterprises [GPE]
for tomorrow.)

The criminal was never caught. The police tried
to hush up the story so as to avoid upsetting the
golf investors.

'They pieced the body together,' Faustina says.
'They gave it a Christian burial.'

'And how do you know it's her, making that
dreadful noise?'

She looks over in a particularly blank way, as
if she were embarrassed - but not for herself.

'I mean, what's she doing out there?'

'She's looking for the part the police did not
find.'

My reminder that she was the one who said the
police had pieced her together only elicits
another blank stare.

'So what couldn't they find? Which of her parts
is she searching for?'

Faustina is halfway out the door by now. She
mutters something, but not a Spanish word.
Something like 'Duano'.

Hope, Dee, at least, this is a diversion from the
wrench of H's birthday.

Write soon. Love,
P.

BODY LANGUAGE

Subject: Not again!

Tepoztlan, Friday 4.30 a.m.

Dear D.,

Log in expecting to hear from you. That milkman IS keeping you busy!

As 'Subject' announces, it has happened again. Not so loud or bloodcurdling, more lamenting and mournful, more scary too after yesterday's conversation, however far-fetched. Doubtless there is some perfectly rational explanation. (As you see, my role must be that of rationalist sceptic.) A creature such as a . . . or a . . .

Trouble being, not even a gremlin in agony or a gryphon giving birth to the world would, in fact, sound like this. No need to worry about scorpions or snakes, no creepy-crawly in its right mind would put up with this every night.

Almost reassuring reminder of my own mortal body, sharp arthritic sensation in my left leg.

Love,
P. (Van Helsing)

Subject: Bleeding stakes

Friday lunch

Dear Van Helsing,

I can't say I've ever seen you as the rationalist-sceptic type. Far too much the enthusiast for that. As for Heather, future perfect birthday may sound harsh, yet appropriate to my mind. It's not even a 'wrench' as you put it. Anything that saves me from thinking about that creature, Roger Morton, formerly my brother.

Lots of work with Age Matters. The incorrigible Gloria. From the sound of you, with arthritis now, we'll soon have you on our books.

Hearth-Rug needing walkies. Less about the Ghoul, please, more about golf-course research. Call from Alex Haring at the Uni, moaning about admin, wondering when you're due back.

Love,
D.

Subject: handicaps

Tepoztlan, Friday late

Dear D.,

Lunch with Ruiz, GPE local manager: the predictable margaritas, toadying, pie-charts proving how beneficial two 18-hole courses will be for local economy. Balderdash the lot of it. Disney also interested!

After coffee Ruiz issues challenge to a match on the one sample hole they've already built. 'Coming from the home of golf, you must be champ, Professor Darling,' he says. 'Your handicap?'

Almost scare him with the truth, but too busy thinking that the real handicap is my right leg. I can't rid it of the oddest sensation, like it were swollen or bloated.

From the tee, a surreal sight on to one hundred yards of polished dichondra-green lawn in the midst of sub-tropical forest. Remember Fitzcaraldo?

'And the bet?' I ask him, far from sure I'll even be able to hit the ball, balancing on one leg.

'If I win,' he beams, 'then you will have to speak highly of me in your chapter.' How he knows about my chapter is beyond me, as I certainly haven't told him.

'And if I win,' I say, 'then you'll have to give me some information.' He looks dubious. 'Bugs

Bunny at the Royal and Ancient, that sort of thing.'

He tees up first, drives using a one-wood for 100 yards, just manages to keep it on the fairway, startling a pair of vultures. I'm balancing on my left leg, take an ungainly swing with a six iron. Amazingly, it lands on the green.

'That Jack Nicholson swing,' says Ruiz, creepily.

'As in *The Shining*?' I retort - but the joke's lost on him.

Then he tries to get me inside his electric buggie, but I'm stubborn enough to refuse, which means limping all the way. He chooses a four iron for his fairway swipe, overshoots wildly, landing in the back yard of a nearby shanty.

'Future bunker,' he informs me.

I get down in par three, leg notwithstanding (standingnotwith?). He's still hacking away ten minutes later.

'So I get to ask my question,' I tell him. He's heard of fair play; still, I can see he's riled. 'What do you know about the woman who was killed up by the waterfall?'

He's visibly relieved. 'Oh, she was just some peasant from a nearby village. She'd come to Tepoztlan church. She was captured when she visited the fountain, a sacred site for the Indians.'

'What happened to her body?'

'I heard cut up.'

'And put back together?'

'Dr Darling, you're surely not suggesting that GPE is involved in anything as crude as that?'

As I pogo home I have to admit I'm somewhat confusing my interests. Very melancholy evening, waiting for the night, wondering what's happening to my leg.

Hope, D., your own day was more fruitful.

Your

P.

Subject: Chilly willy

                    Tepoztlan, Sat afternoon
Dear Dee,
Nobody here to talk to, and can't keep the mind on research.

Woke feeling refreshed despite routine morning call. Pain gone from leg. Finally bumped into Faustina's henpecked husband, but in perfect Spanish he announces he speaks only Nahuatl. 'Tell me,' I say to him, not convinced for a second. 'What does "Duano" mean?' I try a few variants. Now HERE'S the truculent peasant of vampire films!

After breakfast, up the path towards the waterfall. Another world again as you rise into the foothills, all creepers, waxy plants, orchids, cackling birds, swarms of hornets. After half an hour, sounds of the waterfall, as it cascades out of the rock a hundred feet up. Time for a shower, with such a sweaty back. Magnificent view of Aztec temple on the mountain-top.

I'm drying off in the sun when I start to feel terribly cold, then a tingling in my hands and groin, like pins and needles. Oddest feeling. Wouldn't be a good place to pass out, miles from anywhere. My hands and penis have lost sensation, though when I bite a finger it hurts. Finally it passes and I make it back to the house. Exhausted.

You know all about the pact made with my body on my 50th birthday: I'll not abuse you. No cigarettes, limited alcohol, regular golf, once-a-week sex(!). In return for which, you are to act more or less predictably, let me get on with my work (my work! Haven't made a single note since I got here), announce any approaching problem with appropriate notice, and give me another twenty-five years, by which, even at the present rate, my book will finally be published.

Six years on, my side of the bargain has been kept (even if little luck with once-a-week). So what's happened to its side?

When I get back to Salgado's I have the strongest desire to call up our Heather, and to wish her a belated happy birthday. It occurs to me that Roger's company must have an email number. With a few of her plain blunt words she could cure my hypochondria, if that's what it is, a knack she had even before she did her training . . .

Oh well, another round of Faustina's burritos and failing to get her to expand upon the Ghoul. The account of the trip up to the waterfall had her repeating, 'Los aires, los aires' - bad spirits. She offered to pass an egg over my body, which she said would reduce the risk!

Good night/morning,
P.

Subject: Wobbling

Sun lunch

Dear Peter,
I am glad the leg has stopped giving you gyp, not least because you seemed undecided which it was. In one letter it was the left, in the next the right! These things are often the result, in my experience, of too much leisure. Idle hands, idle

legs, and all that. What about your research? I understood time was precious.

I enjoyed seeing your word 'balderdash', haven't seen it in years. How you do exaggerate!

The church at Currie was overflowing today as I passed on my way up the Pentlands. Hearth-Rug was frisky in the summer sun. I do envy you the flowers and vegetation though.

Speaking of wobbly, there's one thing I feel obliged to say. I categorically FORBID you to write to my brother, under ANY circumstances. What a suggestion! When all is said and done, Roger remains a monster. I do not use that word lightly. Let me remind you, since you seem temporarily to have forgotten: the betrayal was with his own niece, your daughter. I cannot forbid you from being in touch with Heather, but you know how pained I would be.

Let's hope your concentration picks up. As you know, many stuck their necks out when they recommended you for Chair.

Your Dee.
p.s. The milkman recommends I try organic!

Subject: Contact?

> Tepoztlan, Mexico
> Sunday 8 August

Roger,
Found your company email on the web. Wish to contact Heather, but don't have phone numbers, and in any case am reluctant to alarm with a call.

Will you pass on a message if I send one?

Peter Darling

BODY LANGUAGE

Subject: Odd request for Alex Haring

Tepoztlan, Sunday 8 August

Dear Alex,

Heard from my wife you called, so presume you're in circulation. Excuse this, but have caught some bug, health deteriorating at alarming rate, limiting movements. If you have a spare student, could you chase her/him up to the library to see if s/he could find a match for the word 'Duano'. Could be something approximate. Probable meaning, some body part. Try the languages of central Mexico: Nahuatl, etc. This elusive word somehow crucial to golf-club scam.

Home in a fortnight.

Cheers, Peter

Subject: Dictionaries

Tepoztlan, Monday

Dear D.,

Spare you the details of the nightly visitation and of my neck cramps. Vowed to quit malingering, with morning in local library, half an hour among the archives, searching vainly for minutes of town council meetings on GPE. Recognised Gandara from press reports (chief opponent to scheme, promoter of civil opposition), who invited himself tomorrow for chat.

Then, I must admit, the next two hours, as long as my neck held up, with dictionaries of local lingos and dialects, ropy old volumes. Finally awoken by a clerk who was closing up for lunch. Amazing to think that in the last Research Assessment the Anthropology Department was commended for its 'particularly assiduous research methodology'!

If you find 'Hearth-Rug' too much of a mouthful, then why not just 'Rug'? Or 'Hearth' for that matter? Or H?

Write soon.

Love,
P.

Subject: Answer

Roger Morton
Morton Vintners
George Street Edinburgh
Monday morning

Dear Brother/Father-in-Law,

I think it's rich of you after seven years of sepulchral silence. Yet how can I refuse? As you judge, so may you hope to be judged.

Kind of you, all the same, to ask how we're keeping.

Unrepentantly,
The Monster.

Subject: Out of the blue

Tepoztlan, Mexico, Tuesday

Dear Heather,

Roger has promised to pass this letter on to you. I know it must seem strange, my writing like this, and, what is more, on the email.

I won't write at length until I hear from you. And no: I haven't undergone a revolution in my view of your situation with Roger; still less your mother.

Sincerely,
Father

BODY LANGUAGE

Subject: Malingering

Wednesday

Poor P.,

Was I really so heartless as to accuse you of that? I haven't figured out how to do carbon copies on this machine, so I can't check if you're making it up. Anyway, I meant it for your own good.

Finally got round to *Clear and Present Danger*. Saw lots of menacing forest, mountains, explosions, but I'm not sure which were yours. Rug says it's high time you came home for walkies. Milkman disagrees.

Must run to Gloria's.

Love,

D.

p.s. You could always ring me, you know.

Subject: Problem

Tepoztlan, Wednesday morning

Dear Heather,

I haven't heard from you yet, but I'm writing in any case. If you are good enough to reply, I can rely on your characteristic frankness to tell me exactly what you think/feel about my unconventional way of breaking the ice. I've heard so little about your life these past seven years, I wouldn't know where to start with questions; they'd only reveal my ignorance.

Away from Edinburgh for over a month. Now in Mexico where I'm supposed to be doing research, but am falling behind through innumerable odd physical sensations - 'pains' wouldn't be quite right, more like bodily apprehensions so heightened as to be debilitating. And the sensations, or symptoms if that's what they are, move around. Damnedest thing, as if I were trying them out for size.

I hesitate to consult a doctor in the wilds here. And then, you know, don't you, that yours is THE ONLY medical opinion.

Hoping to hear from you soon.

Best wishes,
Father
p.s. I have not informed your mother I am writing to you.

Subject: Clarification

Tepoztlan, Thursday night

Dear Deirdre,

With the odd hours imposed by life here (life?), phoning seems impracticable. Idea at four this morning to call and let you share the Ghoul's report. But Mexican Telecom would not do justice, and you'd probably claim it was a cat in heat. And you certainly wouldn't appreciate my litany of discombobulations (guts now, despite being scrupulous about the drinking-water).

One week here already!

Homebound waiting for Gandara's visit, expecting skitters. Spent the morning pestering Faustina. The victim's spirit, she says, is in pain.

'Why does her spirit care so much about her body?'

'She was a Christian,' she says, as if that clarified everything.

'And the part she's missing? Do you know where it is?'

'Somebody knows,' she says, looking at me accusingly.

Dash to the loo.

Long afternoon in and out of toilet. Finally

Gandara arrives before sundown. He talks at length to Faustina outside her cottage, very deferential; she performs some fancy ritual with feathers. My colleague Alex Haring should see this, he loves all this sub-shaman hocus-pocus.

Gandara gives me an odd look when he comes in. He wants to walk. Chitchat until well into the forest. Then can't resist a question about what he knows of the murder. He believes she was a woman from the Taxco silver mines. He'd heard about the missing part; but must have found the questions pretty morbid since he suddenly turns round, claiming he doesn't want to tire me. Rather than the local opposition he's been mounting against GPE, he only wants to talk about the flora and fauna. Looks at me like I was a lost soul, then finally announces:

'I shall not exhaust you, Professor Darling, in your present state. We'll speak again when you are better.'

On his way out, another long visit to Faustina's cottage.

Curiouser and curiouser.

Must to loo again.

Your leaky P.

Subject: Info please

                    Tepoztlan, Saturday 14 August
Dear Dr Salgado,
Hoping to catch you with a couple of questions before you head off. You'll be busy with end of Summer School, so shall be brief.

What of Faustina and her powers? You hinted darkly at Harvard. Alas, I find myself somewhat incommoded.

What do you know about recent murder circa waterfall?

Thanks again for hospitality at Harvard. Your house here is everything you promised - and more.

Sincerely,
Peter Darling

Subject: Donkeys

Dept. of Anthropology,
Edinburgh University
Saturday 14 August

Dear Peter,
Diligent postgraduate (ex-Japes) collared and offered unmentionable favours for her participation in your attempt to thwart the extradition of St Andrews to Mexico. She even sacrificed the entire day of the eclipse for the search.

Sole vague correspondence, in Nahuatl, some word meaning 'dead donkey'!

Sorry not to be more helpful. Shall be glad to have you back, I can't get the hang of all this admin.

All best,
Alex Haring

Subject: Me again

Tepoztlan, Saturday

Dear Heather,
Has Roger passed on my messages? Forget the requests, this time it's an appeal.

I spent all of yesterday nailed to my bed by the most unaccountable headache: the sensation that my head was expanding, about to explode. I am starting to be genuinely concerned, not to say panicked. I believe that if we could put a finger on the symptoms, half the battle would be won.

I know I'm being insistent. But if I'm writing to you like this, you can imagine how desperate I must be feeling.

Your ailing
Dad

Subject: Lunacy

Tepoztlan, Saturday evening

Dear Deirdre,

Alas, all of yesterday lost, supposed to be the big day among the archives, as all movement impossible, even typing, flattened by a variety of migraine. Not pain exactly, but an awful overwhelming presence of head - hard to describe. Library closed today and tomorrow, which leaves only Mon, Tues, Wed, since the bus leaves Thurs to connect with plane home. Panic setting in.

And worse! In town today the indigenes were giving me the oddest looks and keeping their distance. Paranoia to add to my ills?

Faustina offered me a shot with the healing egg, passed it over my body a few times, but said that given my state her cure would hardly help.

Your lost soul in Mexican purgatory,
Peter

BODY LANGUAGE

Subject: Tepoztlan

Harvard, Mass.
Sunday 15 August

Dear Professor Darling,

So pleased you're finding my house comfortable,
though sorry you're not up to par. On your second
question: I do remember hearing stories of some
poor woman murdered at the waterfall. Macabre,
maybe ritualistic. A prostitute? A peasant?

As for Faustina, she worked at my previous
house, I've known her ten years. I can't say I'm
a believer; yet Tepoztlan would be unthinkable
without her. She has people come from miles
around for consultation. Her egg has done me
wonders. Explain it how you will. Tepoztlan is an
ancient site with powerful resources &
resonances. They say it tests people, newcomers.
In short, a small gratuity before you leave might
be an investment!

I'll be in touch again when you're back in the
solid granite of Edinburgh.

Yours sincerely,
Jorge Salgado

Subject: Ghostbuster

Tepoztlan, Sunday

Dear D.,

A few lines, between bouts: the most unnatural
sensation in my lungs, like asthma or worse.
Terrible foreboding. The contract is rescinded, my
body tells me, so now we'll see who's boss! Plague
victims sound the way I feel.

At 4 a.m. out on the path, shitting bricks, but
ready to confront, do whatever's feasible or
unfeasible, with no bunch of garlic or crucifix.

BODY LANGUAGE

The dread noise comes up the path as usual, then it skirts round and goes on. Not even a chance to cry 'Stop!'

Fitful sleep and dawn with seizure in the lungs. Would fear madness were thoughts not so lucid. Three days left, but shall be lucky to get out of here unscathed.

Know you'll deplore such sensationalism.

Wheezingly,
P.

Subject: Lunacy indeed

Monday morning

Peter,

As soon as I read your latest, this morning, I tried to call. It must have been one or two in the morning there, but no reply. I hung on for ten minutes at least.

Please call instantly. Then pack your bags. Then take the taxi. Then the first plane home. Spare no expense.

Whatever is ailing you, it's only getting worse, and you say you're lucid but in all the years I've never heard you like this - not even you!

I'll stay in, awaiting your call.

Deirdre

Subject: calls

Tepoztlan, Monday afternoon

Dear D.,

Thanks for uxorial concern, which seems to have gone from min to max overnight. Calling isn't possible now. Don't ask for explanations. Things must run their course here, whatever that involves.

Morning in library, despite alarming eructation of skin. Ruiz en route, who challenged me to another hole of golf, until he saw the skin condition. Couldn't face GPE and corporate take-overs, so hours through newspapers for accounts of the victim. Just as conflicting as verbal reports, and photos printed of two different women. No word of missing part.

Purchased a second-hand book on Aztecs on way home, the one you read by Glendenning.

Two days left. Something's got to break.
P.

Subject: Help

Tepoztlan, Monday night

Dear Roger,

No word from Heather, despite my appeal. Yes, you may feel bitter about my behaviour and Deirdre's. But I for one have never referred to you as 'Monster'. There are many things in heaven and earth beyond my philosophy. Your liaison with our daughter will remain one of them.

Another appeal to you to speak to Heather and ask her to write. Sore need of her words. The body's giving out on me. I'm dispossessed of a merest hold on the world, terrorised by what's in store. I'd call it 'despair', only this is too physical. Something will burst. This pressure literally intolerable. 'Possession' might be closer.

Tried to call the number I have for Heather, but a woman said she left six years ago and refused to give your number. Confess I tore it out of my book all those years back.

BODY LANGUAGE

This is the man who married your sister speaking, so you know how hard it is for me to say:

PLEASE HELP ME!
Peter

Subject: Trying

                                   Morton Vintners
                              George Street Edinburgh
Dear Peter (I almost put 'Dear Rogered'! The way I've often felt).
The nights are long, indeed, when the soul is troubled. I learned this some time ago. I shall refrain from preaching. I gather you do not believe your current problems would respond to conventional medicine?
I handed your notes to your daughter. She passed no comment and has refused to discuss them with me. You know how headstrong she is. All I can do is promise to pass on whatever you write. She would not receive your calls even if you had the number.
May one hope that these ills are some tropical malady, more alarming than perilous? I always find a bottle of Richebourg the best remedy, myself. Or let these symptoms, allied to your new volubility after all these years, be harbingers of some new state of self! But there, I said I wouldn't preach.
Sincerely,
Roger

Subject: Succour

                                   Tepoztlan, Tuesday
Heather, my child,
Come to my aid before it is too late! This is me speaking, your dad.

81

Subject: Signing off

Tepoztlan, Tuesday

Deirdre,

Body and face covered in sores. Stop trying to call me. Whatever's emerging, expect some changes: not that there's any way through quarantine in present state. And it's not over yet.

Jesus but these Aztecs were bloodthirsty. Victims flayed alive, bled to death, pulled apart, all in some imagined good cause. Trip into town forbidden due to leprous appearance. Walked up to waterfall. Hunted in the shrubs . . .

You don't want to hear this.

Demanded Faustina tell me all she knows about the victim. Threatened, shouting, to denounce her to Salgado. She just flicked through the Aztec book, studying the pictures.

The lawyer has the necessary instructions.

P.

Subject: Farewell

Tuesday night, 11 p.m.

Dearest Heather,

Roger assures me you'll receive this, my last. It seems decreed I shall not survive this night. Doesn't look convincing on paper - on screen - but this is how it is. A chill invests my body, making it no longer mine. I can hardly explain. Reading about the Aztecs, their unspeakable rituals. My whole self set to burst, contract, explode. I can hardly even type. I finally got round to calling the local doctor. His wife said he's out - playing floodlit golf. Doesn't know when he'll be back. I'm hours from the nearest hospital. This is Mexico. I don't blame you for not writing. I'd say

BODY LANGUAGE

I forgive you, only you'd say there was never anything to forgive. I still don't understand. I accept you, and ask you to accept me. My hands can barely move now. I must stretch out.

Subject: At last

Wed 2 a.m.

Heather,
Thrown over the Aztecs' killing stone the chest arched until the obsidian blade dives in to cut out the bright red pump still pulsing from the living body

Subject: Party's over

Wednesday morning, 18 August

Peter,
How dare you scare me like this? What in hell's name are you playing at? You're an unconscionable narcissist, a damnable drama queen, and I've had it with your amateur theatricals. You really think you can stage your own demise? What hubris!

You will find the house empty when you arrive on Friday. Hearth-Rug and I shall be in touch if and when you come off your Quetzalcoatl kick.

D.
p.s. Don't blame the milkman, blame yourself.

Subject: Epilogue

Tepoztlan, Wednesday midday

Dearest Heather,
As you can see, I'm still alive, if not yet kicking. You at least will believe this has not been play-acting.

I unplugged the phone, stretched out on the bed. Dark all around. My body went colder and colder. I seemed to be leaving it. The night got darker. My eyes blurred.

Sometime in the wee hours I'm aware of Faustina, the housekeeper and local shaman. She's standing over me. I have just enough mental activity to curse the fact I ever mocked your Castaneda books. She's carrying something in her hands, not the egg she's usually clutching. In my frozen delirium I'm convinced it is a human heart. She's muttering a word I've been obsessed with, 'Duano'. Finally I understand, rightly or wrongly, that it's her own private name for this organ. She passes it over my body, I don't know how many times. I hear the ghastly noise of the local ghoul outside.

I can tell you little of the rest of the night, but towards dawn I start to feel a tingle of warmth, which grows with the light. I slowly come awake. Even my skin doesn't look too bad. I could almost take the plane tomorrow.

Unless I decide to stay on here for a while, figure out how to stop a golf-course at the first tee.

Or just stay on.

I'm sorry if I scared you. It was nothing to how I scared myself.

All my love,
Me, Peter, your revivified dad
p.s. Time will tell what else has to change.

BODY LANGUAGE

Subject: Anew

The Royal Infirmary
Wednesday night

Dear Dad,

You did scare me, but that was the least of it. All that pompous language, your quibbles and your semi-colons, like you were talking to your lawyer! Fuck all that, Dad.

I hope you do understand why I didn't write before. I may be a doctor, a surgeon - I'm on night duty now. But what sort of responsibility would I be shouldering if I dispensed life-saving medical advice from this distance? What is more, to my own kin. To my estranged kin. Not to mention the rest, the seven years of silence.

But I did worry & cry a bit too.

I don't know what to say about your experience. It doesn't match the textbooks. The Greeks thought the womb could move around, a bit like the way your symptoms were doing. Hysteria, they called it. You'll have to tell me more when you come back - if you don't decide to go completely native, that is, and join some revivalist Aztec tribe.

I'm not a cardiologist, so all I can suggest is you've had what is commonly called 'a change of heart'.

You have my email number now. Maybe this is the start of something.

Love you, despite it all.

Heather

p.s. If appropriate, remember me to Mum.

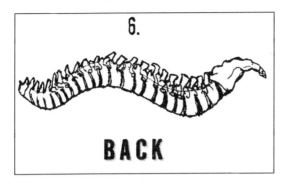

6.

BACK

ANYONE WHO'S BEEN there knows what I'm talking about.

There?

Angstville.

That's a bit glib. It's where you get to know that one part better than any other, every last vertebra, disc and floating rib, from the hours, the days, or in my case the months spent lying on it. Songless. Knowing that if you do get up, go out, what you'll see is fear and sickness, graffiti and broken glass, dog-shit and mobile phones, the limpers, shufflers, pretenders, failing to escape the chill from the gust that's about to carry them away.

When Janice left me, it wasn't definitive, she said. If I'd had the strength to call her up then maybe we could have worked something out. The monster from the deep must have been expecting me, mouth agape. I fell into its gullet, and it dived, spitting me out only when it reached bottom.

Its bottom, my back.

As no two routes down are identical, so I guess no two up. My own was slow; it involved forcing myself, physically forcing myself, to rise, sitting hours on end trying to hum to myself, further hours with the phone, trying to dial Janice's number. Then, having managed a tune or two, having failed to dial her number, it involved going to see a therapist – a 'psychoanalyst' Dr McAlpine calls herself – and sitting further hours in her armchair, twice a week, for nine months, talking about everything and nothing, in any case failing to say whatever it is I have to say to let me strain above the surface.

Convinced, all the while, that to rise I have first to descend, in order to reach vertical, *homo erectus*, I have to be supine again, this time on the analyst's couch, where I start unwinding, free-associating like in the textbooks I've read, and so begin my cure, become a singer again.

With the only problem, a major one, that she, the analyst, won't let me out of her armchair, won't give me the horizontal relief I'm craving.

'You're not ready, Mr Hutton,' she tells me. 'Not yet.'

It's like an itch I can't scratch, like sex with no penetration. That's what I've told her – though today it was something worse that I shouted at her before I stumbled and fell.

So, slowly, I started to feel slightly better about myself – less desperate at least, more simply furious. Joining a band was still beyond me, but a couple of mournful songs I squeezed out got taken up by some French pop group. Who knows how, but this led to my being asked to present a little-known French writer, Pierre-Loup Liberman, at the Edinburgh International Book Festival.

This might have been fine. But in the interim, between my being asked and now, August, Liberman's book *Pleasure Palace* became a runaway bestseller, embarrassing the organisers of the Book Festival for not having chosen someone famous to present the new celebrity.

It was daft to have accepted any appearance in public, in my present state. Certainly it was daft not to confess I've only smatterings of French; daft to have put off reading Liberman's book for so long; daft to have gone out alone and got pissed last night in the Kenilworth, rather than reading the last two-thirds of *Pleasure Palace*; daft not to have cancelled the session with the shrink for this morning, getting myself all worked up before I had to be a presentable presenter; and daft then to have filled the hour between arriving in Charlotte Square and the appointment with Monsieur Liberman with a visit to the Post Office Tent, where Andrew O'Hagan was set to spar on the subject of 'Architecture in Fiction' with Will *soi-disant* Self.

The weather was looking grim, rain clouds rolling in from the

Forth. Maybe, I convinced myself – great reasoning! – by hearing about 'Architecture in Fiction' I'd find something to say about the parts of *Pleasure Palace* I'd failed to read.

As I'll have to leave before the hour is up, I bag a seat near the door. I'm just thinking about how I haven't been on stage for nearly two years, since I quit performing my songs and became instead the depressed one, the one people look at in the corner of the pub, raise their eyebrows and whisper, 'There, but for the grace of God, go I' – when finally something that's been said drags me out of myself.

'What's new about the modern novel,' says Self, in his flatter-than-a-pancake accent, 'is that it takes us from the drawing-room *à la* Jane Austen and into the bathroom *à la* James Joyce.'

To which O'Hagan responds, in a voice whose seriousness is at odds with the cheery Glasgow accent, 'Right, but if you take the Scottish novel, it may have made it into the bathroom, but it's not yet made it to the bedroom. There's not a convincing sex scene in the whole of Scottish literature. Get a pair of Scots in the sack, and it's a recipe for literary disaster.'

Fuck me! I think (swearing like something out of the new novel O'Hagan has just been reading from). But fuck me if he isn't right. Maybe that was one of the reasons, it occurs to me, why I was having such a job getting through *Pleasure Palace*, giving up when the sex scenes got going. From the reviews, I knew these sex scenes filled the remainder of the book, and to judge from the one I started, they'd be amazingly vivid and convincing yet completely contrived at the same time, realistic but fairy-story – how did he get away with it?

Monsieur Liberman got away with it, I figure now, because he wasn't writing in the wake of *Waverley* or *The Monstrous Regiment of Women*, but of *Liaisons Dangereuses* and *The 120 Days of Sodom*. Who could fail to be sexy with Libertines as ancestors instead of men in pulpits with ponderous grey beards?

And one thing's for sure, I muse, as Self drones on, even if I were a writer it certainly wouldn't be me about to rectify that situation, not with my problems, the sex ones, not to mention the rest. None of which are likely to improve so long as she, the mistress of denial in the therapist's seat, maintains eye contact and refuses to allow me onto my back.

I'm hovering, as I always do these days, between Dr McAlpine's armchair and couch, waiting for her to invite me, permit me, let me take my due. Only, as always, to be ushered into the armchair, there to resume my tired-bored-disgusted look. She doesn't remark upon my smart suit, with which I'm going to charm the Edinburgh reading public later in the day.

Fifteen minutes at least of disgruntled silence. I'm so pissed off today at the way she's denying me the couch that I figure – none too logically, I admit – that maybe she's seen the Book Festival brochure with my name in it, and has decided to be specially nasty to me. I'm so pissed off, in fact, that for once I'm not even counting the money I'm wasting, sitting here saying nothing.

'Not that I couldn't call her if I wanted to,' I say. 'I could call Janice today if I was really desperate.'

She only smiles at me across the pastel colours of the consulting-room. I invent some story about how I've written a song about the hideous style of her clothes, to try and wipe the smile off her self-satisfied face, get her to show some emotion. Pity her name's McAlpine, if there was the remotest chance she was Jewish I'd have thrown in some anti-Semitism as well, anything for a reaction.

'Janice and yourself,' I try, 'like day and night, like Highlands and Industrial Lowlands, like then and like now, vaginal and clitoral, passionate and resigned, life and death.'

She uncrosses her legs at last. 'Are you talking about two women here, Mr Hutton, of whom you say I am one, or are you talking about yourself?'

'My Divided Self?' I parry, to remind her I'm not a complete ignoramus.

'Dividing, more than divided.'

Fuck you, I think, but resist saying, since the one time I tried it, figuring what I was paying for this service dispensed me from politeness, she asked if I was expressing anger, a wish, or both.

'Would you care to know what it's like to be thinking of Janice while sitting here with you?'

She refuses to respond, as she always does whenever I ask her a direct question. I must have been staring at the couch without realising it. She nods that nod of hers. 'You wouldn't by any chance be wishing to remind me of what it's like to be sitting in the armchair, having to face me, while wishing to be on your back on the couch, staring at the great white space of the ceiling?'

Bastard! Bitch! 'Sitting in the high-chair while dreaming of the cot? Is that what you're implying?'

She smiles to herself, unperturbed.

It's only when, ten futile minutes later, I'm halfway out her door, into the Stockbridge sunlight, that I wonder if I haven't somehow informed her, after all, about this afternoon.

O'Hagan v Self is coming to a close, and I'm so lost in my turgid ruminations that I've forgotten my author, whom I eventually find huffing in what's quaintly called the Writer's Oasis (a Portakabin with a couple of plastic chairs and a ferocious East-Coast draught).

He's tall, for a Gaul, lean, in his late forties, reminding me of photos of Jean Cocteau, wearing a crumpled linen suit that's seen better days, and that, given the fortune he's made on his book, I presume to be some sort of statement. He's drawing on a roll-up which has been extinguished by the rain. I suppose some women would find him handsome.

'Monsieur Liberman?' I say, needlessly.

'Vous parlez français?' he asks. 'J'espère.'

'Not really. A few Edith Piaf songs and an occasional Jacques Brel.' I demonstrate an inch-sized measurement between finger and thumb. 'I'm afraid I was chosen before you became famous.' In compensation, I lead him toward the One World Café. When we're seated, I ask him, 'So what would you like me to say about your book?'

'Say what you think,' he gets out, in an accent that's less strong than I'd feared. 'I only write it, you must speak about it.' Then he goes silent again, as he unsuccessfully tries yet again to light his dampened cigarette.

I offer him a dry one but he declines, and begins to roll himself another. I can't make up my mind if he's modest or wildly arrogant.

Either way, I'm going to have to say something about him. He's the only sell-out event today other than Harry Potter, and though nobody is coming to listen to me, I'm listed on the programme and they'll soon notice if I make some huge gaffe, and that'll be the end of literary festivals for me.

'Coffee?' I eventually ask, determined to make him grateful to me for something.

He nods, but when I bring it to him, in a paper cup admittedly, he merely stares at it. You'd never guess he was a bestselling author, the way he's hunched up in his seat.

'I'll just say a word or two of introduction,' I try, 'if that's OK, then I'll let you get on with the readings. How many passages?'

He indicates two with his fingers, and I understand he'll be reading the French original, leaving me to read the English translation. Then he marks the pages. Then he stares out of the tent at the rain that's heaving it down upon the Festival.

A few minutes' more silence, and it looks like our exchange is over, so much for the French art of diplomacy, I'm thinking, so much for the Auld Alliance, when suddenly he says to me:

'My publicist, he says the Scottish love my book. But . . .' He stares at me with sudden interest, representative as I now am of 'the Scottish'. 'But I worry. You think they do see it is one joke?'

'Is there a joke?' I ask, and almost give the game away by saying, 'I can't have read that far yet.'

His head is in his hands.

'I believe,' I say, 'I know they find it very sexy.' This much is true, I read it in the *Evening News* just last night. 'I've heard it described as "the most erotic thrill since *The Story of O*".'

He sinks further into himself. Stretching a leg outside the tent, he seems to find it consoling to watch his foot get soaked. 'But don't they see, don't you see it is entirely one joke?'

'A joke?'

'It is all parody. Blanche Neige and Casse-Noisette.'

The first one I work out for myself: 'Ah, Snow White.' But the second requires him to perform a charade involving a tree-impersonation, a squeeze of his testicles, and an attempt to stand on point.

'Nutcracker!' I finally exclaim.

'Snow White and Nutcracker meet the Marquis de Sade. Could it be other than a humorist work?' He looks genuinely upset.

'*Cosmopolitan*,' I tell him, making up whatever comes into my head, 'voted it the sexiest book of the year.' I almost start to tell him about Scottish literary bedrooms. 'I guess we must be hungry for it, up here in the windswept North.'

He's so upset, he's forgotten he's not supposed to speak English. 'I thought Scottish people are supposed to have a big sense of the humour?'

'Being Presbyterian means we're responsible and dour 24 hours a day, 365 days a year, with no respite. We need escape where we can find it.' I'm thinking of telling him about Janice, how songless I've been without her, when fortunately he opens his street-map of the city and asks me to indicate the most interesting graveyards.

For some reason I ask myself, all of a sudden, if Pierre-Loup is his real name. Peter-Wolf, maybe that's part of the joke? And Liberman for that matter: man being man, while Liber suggests book, no? Implies free?

So as to avoid putting both feet in it, or to sound smarter than I really am, or maybe just because I'm still caught up in the frustrations of my session with the shrink, I come out with:

'Sex and death, two activities best undertaken lying on one's back.'

He's put away his map and is looking anxiously at the clock. 'You think to them as activities?' he says. 'More like passivities, to my taste.'

When finally I make my entry, preceded by Pierre-Loup, the Beck's Spiegeltent is standing-room only, and not much of that, packed with people of both genders and every age from fifteen to four score. Tables have been removed to make room for extra seats. My old drinking partner from the Uni, Alex Haring, catches my eye; I haven't spoken to him since he mocked me for going to see a therapist. There's Morton, the George Street wine man. Typical Edinburgh, I know half the folk here, by sight at least, including that tall woman from the yoga class I used to attend (recall her amazing downward dog).

We sit, the famous Frenchman on one side, the former Scottish singer on the other. Thinking of yoga, a few deep-breathing exercises wouldn't be a bad idea, as the assistant attaches us to our microphones. Nerves don't even come into it, this is blind panic fuelled by disgust at myself for failing to be properly prepared.

'It is our pleasure today,' I start. Then stop, distracted by the door opening at the rear of the tent to let in a further glut of enthusiasts. 'It's my great pleasure today to welcome Pierre-Loup Liberman to the Edinburgh International Book Festival, in the context of the series called "The Wider Picture". Pierre-Loup is the author, I need hardly remind you, of a work which since its publication in English at the start of the year has taken the country by storm.'

Now I'm finding my voice, I'm even more sick at myself for not having read the damn thing. I stare pointlessly at my notes, which are nothing more than doodles.

'French literature,' I pronounce, 'has not, despite the Chunnel, had much success in recent years in our country, and I suspect there's many of us here . . .'

I pause long enough for the crowd to wonder if I really mean 'many of you'.

'Many of us would have difficulty naming more than a couple of French novelists alive and writing today.'

Further pause to give them time to confirm the truth of this. At the back, I notice a newcomer, I can't see her properly but she's surely someone I recognise.

'Across this Channel of Indifference Pierre-Loup Liberman's work has cut its way: proud, individual, oblivious to the swings and roundabouts of literary trends.'

In other words, don't ask me to place it! I'm starting to feel pretty pleased with myself, actually, and I'm even enjoying the sound of my own voice, remembering what it used to be like in front of a crowd, getting an echo of what it was like before post-Janice despair got its hands around my throat. (That's glib too, but I don't have time to improve it.)

'I hardly need to rehearse the plot of *Pleasure Palace* to you avid readers. Rather, with no further delay, let me hand over to Pierre-Loup himself, who will read in French, after which I shall read the English translation.'

Phew! With my mike switched off, I'm free to bask in the applause for a while, tell myself I was right all along not to script the introduction, that my impromptu intro came out more natural and spontaneous, the voice working well.

Pierre-Loup has begun to read from *Pleasure Palace*, where its protagonist, the improbably named René Perrier, has fallen into a decline, then a catastrophic slump. (I know I'd better tune in since we might have to chat about it later.) Aged forty, he's spent the past twenty years making an incalculable fortune and leading a crazy, varied, excessive, extravagantly active life. Yet nineteenth-century *ennui* has nothing on the po-mo end-of-millennium blues now afflicting him. Unlike me, he has retinues of butlers, valets, maids, courtesans, stunt-cocks and fluffers, yet none of them can stir him out of his lethargy and impotence.

Pierre-Loup pauses for a drink from a hip-flask. I can't help remembering, as I look round the crowd again and at that person in the back of the tent who seems to be concealing herself, what it was like to be in front of a crowd, singing, in my own right.

Meanwhile, crushed by inactivity (though by my standards he's still pretty hyper) René Perrier has decided that with the last stirrings of his flagging spirit he'll mount a competition. He'll advertise worldwide, in every bakery and post office, as well as in the national press of every civilised country, on the Internet, by carrier pigeon, smoke signal and native drum, for couples who believe that, by some demonstration of unheralded exotic charms, they can arouse him. The reward will consist of a prolonged stay in the fabulously luxurious Château Perrier on the banks of Lac Léman, with every conceivable expense paid, plus one million euros for every inch that the Perrier penis extends during the couple's performance.

Five couples will be selected, on an arcane basis which has something to do with principles of numerical combination and chance theory. (I faze out at this point, since maths was never my strong point, and in any case I'm getting an itching feeling that I do know who that is at the back.) For every continent there will be a couple (it occurs to me this is the Nutcracker connection) and these couples will visit the Château one a month, where, after being fêted and banqueted, they will be invited to exert their allure.

Trying to take my mind off the anger that's welling up in me, I look over the audience again. Here, in the fourth row, is that student I used to bump into in Greyfriars Churchyard, Helen I think her name is; she'd be searching for inspiration about the Covenanters. Amazing weight she's put on in the last few months. Sad, so sad, the way the desperate attract the even-more-desperate.

I realise I'd better tune back in to Pierre-Loup, who's deep in a detailed description of what René Perrier calls his 'Renaissance Chamber' (some pun intended?), where the couples will perform. Said chamber sports a vaulted gothic ceiling, bacchanalian frescoes, numerous alcoves (adorned each with some different precious stone) where the contestants are invited to refresh themselves before another orgiastic endeavour, banks of digital-sound and image-recording equipment by which the couples can reproduce their climaxes, acres of marble floor leading to a gigantic ornamental bed. Next to the bed, the centrepiece, a throne, elevated on a dais, from which the fizz-less Perrier will watch.

A ripple of applause passes through the crowd when I finish reading the English-language version of this passage. Even as I've been rediscovering my voice, adapting it to the formal sensualities of Pierre-Loup's prose, I've noticed the author peering ever more intently into his audience.

Now he turns to me. 'Not one laughter!' he groans beneath his breath.

And he's right, we might as well be in church.

'No more,' he sighs to me, covering his mike. 'If you cannot make them laugh, I refuse to read another word.'

I glance at my watch: if reading's out, then we'll have to drag through the next twenty-four minutes chatting about the two hundred pages of his novel that I haven't even glanced at. And with her – I'm practically sure it's her back there! the shrink! – watching me make an idiot of myself.

Laugh, you bastards, laugh!

Figuring I'd better get a question in before he kicks off on some detail of the conclusion, I try:

'So, Pierre-Loup, if I may ask you: Why . . . ehhh . . .' I'm searching, searching, got to make it quick. 'Why, ehmm, so many formal constraints? All the maths and number theory? Am I right in thinking that . . . hmm . . . we're not meant to take them all too seriously?'

He smiles for the very first time. He stretches out his legs. 'But of course not! It is a game. A serious game, if you prefer.'

Now he's relaxing, his English starts to flow.

'Serious uniquely in the sense that so many constraints, as you call them, may permit an escape, a release. A liberation which may sometimes occur not by adding to action but by . . .' He is searching. 'Do you say, letting go?'

I'm nodding as if I were an expert on the subject. 'Something involuntary? Is that the idea?'

'You cannot oblige yourself to laugh. It must arrive to you. So you cannot, or at least I cannot, oblige myself to – euhh?' He points at his groin again. 'Bander,' he adds, expecting me to translate.

I stare in panicked ignorance.

'Bander,' he repeats. 'Bander!'

'Nutcracker?' I exclaim, at a loss.

He shakes his head furiously.

'Get a hard on!' comes a shout from the audience.

'Thus,' says the author. 'Get a hard-on. The veritable affirmation of life has to pass through you. As I was saying to him–' He points at me. 'We need to learn to be passive.'

I don't remember that, exactly, but I'm not about to argue, it's filling up the minutes. And then it suddenly occurs to me that it's not such a bad thing after all, if the shrink is here as witness. Say I did somehow tell her – maybe I was right to do so.

'Now,' I whisper to him, passing him the Faber edition. 'You read to them in English, you can easily do it. And just you see, you'll have them rolling in the aisles.'

And it is her – shit! I knew it. I can see her clearer now, cowering in the back so as not to be conspicuous, I'm probably not the only one of her nutters here. Oh, it's her all right, no doubt about it.

Pierre-Loup, from somewhere near the end, is reading:

'René Perrier, dispirited on his throne, contemplated the collapse of his meticulously elaborated scheme: four years of planning, hundreds of millions of francs, four of the couples inspected, in all their beauty, exoticism, perversity, and longing, without the merest stirring in the groin.'

The faces staring up at us, famished. Then eyelids going down – hers too, no doubt. These four attempts may have failed to rebirth René, but for the audience they're the sexiest things they've slavered over in decades – 'Blasting apart the tired old categories of eroticism and pornography', as the blurb says on the garish dust-jacket. Oh, they've got *Pleasure Palace* audio-books, and they go all moist and mushy as Ralph Fiennes reads to them in their bath, or driving to pick up the wains, or thanking God they've just seen the back of another crazy patient.

'He had met the final couple, representing the European continent, at the banquet held in their honour the previous evening.

'How had they appeared? Like something out of Bruegel's painting of the blind leading the blind, like some ironic replay from Perrier's most distant past. Not only were they French, not only Breton, but from the very town of Saint-Lô where he had himself been born and raised.

'And dressed? They were dressed in their peasant clothes, as if they had just stepped in from the fields: two ancients, older than his own parents would have been had they still been alive, gnarled by the years, their wrinkled skin like bark, their backs bent like the scythes which once they must have wielded.

'His disappointment was as measureless as his wealth.'

Pierre-Loup has them eating out of his hands, yet not a sign of mirth. Couldn't she laugh at least, help me out here? After all I've paid her?

'And now, the following day, here they are walking in their clogs across the marble of the Renaissance Chamber, assisted by canes and crutches, where their predecessors cut capers and undressed as they moved in complex choreographed coils, where they bit, squeezed, pinched, pumped, tore, cupped, and lapped, on one occasion (Australasia) not ever reaching the giant ornamental bed, collapsing on the way there, from exhaustion and loss of fluids.'

What's Pierre-Loup twitching about when he pauses? Is it giggle and guffaw he's waiting for?

'Michelange,' he whispers to me, gnomically. 'And Marcel Proust. They both did it thus.'

Then he stares round at his audience, able to detect not a single twitter. They're on tenter-hooks all right, their hooks couldn't be tenterer were they watching a judge don his hanging-cap.

And how in God's name am I supposed to be setting the appropriately humorous tone, with her sitting over there, probably the only one splitting her sides in fact, but secretly, at the sight of yours truly about to make an even bigger fool of himself, with not a clue of how the damn novel ends.

Fourteen minutes to go.

'When the pair of crones finally reach the ornamental bed, what do they do? They do not remove a single item of their worn tweeds or aprons. They peer at Perrier through the cataracts of their wizened beads. They lay down their crutches and canes.

'Perrier asks himself again: How can it all have come to this? All my plans, my numbers, my euros.

'It is the she-crone who speaks first, if indeed she is a woman, the ravages of time having rendered the couple almost genderless. In the Breton tones of Perrier's childhood, she says:

'"Are you comfortably seated, Monsieur Perrier?"

'Perrier, filled with horror at what he is watching enacted before him, the final futile throes of all his ingenuity and expense, has barely the strength left to nod.

'Perched on the edge of the gigantic bed, the two look more than ever like arthritic elves. Slowly, with creaking joints, they stretch out to supine, not bothering even to remove their clogs. They do not move an inch now: so immobile they might almost have expired.'

Pierre-Loup is booming into the roof of the Spiegeltent, threatening to carry us all away with his words. In response, the wind catches the canvas ceiling and billows it into a sail.

'When suddenly the man's voice asks:

"'Listen now, Monsieur René! Are you really listening?'"

Stuff Perrier! I don't know how long it's been coming over me, but now it's me who's hanging on every word. The minutes to be filled cease to matter, and all that matters is what this ancient creature is about to say next.

I'm staring at Pierre-Loup, as he continues:

"'Listen, while we tell you," says the he-crone, with a lilt in his voice that has never been heard in this chamber before.

"'Please," pleads Perrier, leaning forward in his throne. "Please start."

'And so they do begin.

'The tale they tell, first he, then she, finally in unison, sneaks across the marble floor, climbs up the dais, and enters the curlicues of the Perrier ears. It is their tale at first, but as it enters and sedates him, it now becomes his. Until it reaches his core, where it begins its revivifying work.

'Does it tell of their youthful romance in the fields? Of the clearings amongst the poppies of their homeland? Of long summer days and long winter nights? Does it speak the language of hips and tongues and teats? Or does it use the chaste gasps of children?'

Pierre-Loup takes a long deep breath, looks round.

'When Perrier awakes many hours later, he does not know, nor can he imagine.

'He knows only what he can see: the crones have departed; the bed is empty and pristine as if it has never been used; his penis has strained so hard, it has burst through his flies and is menacing his chin.

'What more does he know? He knows that chance has nothing to do with the fact that he is alive again and renewed.'

Pierre-Loup closes his book and lays it on the floor between us. Though he must have read it a hundred times before, he tries none the less to start a fashion by forcing out a chuckle.

And maybe it would have been infectious, drawing the crowd from where they're trying to catch a final echo of that invisible, inaudible language . . . Maybe it would have worked . . .

Had it not been for me.

I just cannot stop myself, though I certainly know I should. I've been down on the seabed too long, and now I'm rising so fast I've got the bends. 'You hear that?' I mutter, forgetting my microphone is still switched on. 'Did you hear that?' I repeat, amazed at my own nerve.

The faces in the Spiegeltent turn towards me, no doubt wondering what I'm on about. I can see her smiling in the back, that supercilious smile of hers.

'You hear that?' I persist. 'And people wonder why there's never been a successful Scottish sex scene? I'll tell you why.' My hand rises like it's got a will of its own, and points at her. 'Because of killjoys like you!'

Not being completely demented – yet – somewhere inside of me I realise I'm haivering, making a disastrous fool of myself. But at least, I think, for once I'm not being glib!

And, curiously enough, Pierre-Loup doesn't seem to mind my unscripted intervention. On the contrary, he seems to find it amusing, and lets out a chuckle, a genuine one this time, his first. 'Enfin,' he sighs, 'un happening!'

'You hear that, Doctor Ball-Clipper!' I shout, getting to my feet, as she tries to make a dash for the door. 'Stop! Listen!'

I'm livid now, demented. I'm out of my bleeding box.

'Listen!' I cry, with whatever is left alive in me of despair and ambition, so it comes out almost tuneful. 'Did you hear that, you tyrannical prick-tease? Moving mountains, making fizz, singing their songs, telling truths! And from where? From their backs. Their backs!'

If it hadn't been for the microphone cable which had slyly wrapped itself around my ankle, then surely I'd have caught up with Dr McAlpine, rather than plunging headlong from the podium, Pierre-Loup's laughter joined to that of the crowd now, ringing in my ears.

And so I wouldn't have woken up in the Writer's Oasis ten minutes later with a pain in the very part of my anatomy about which I was screaming.

But nor would I have realised, with a start, that maybe I'm really ready to call Janice again, find out if she's willing to see me.

Right: straight after the next session with the shrink. Where I get to confirm to her what a cunt she is.

In a song, as I must.

From my back, of course, on her couch.

7.

THYROID

THE JULY TRADES HOLIDAY was about to start, but that was no reason for slackness. Two whole weeks the plant would be inert. Business was booming, but it could always boom better. If everybody would only pull their weight, right down to the lowliest soul on boxing. If they'd only realise that though Barr Packaging Inc. had virtually cornered the market since his invention of the New-Condensed Crate, it remained a family business, in ethic and ideal if no longer in size. There were, he believed, values beyond the purely mercantile; even if he wasn't as fundamentalist in his views as his foreman, Hugh, who only liked to recruit from the flock of St Mary's, or failing that from the loyal supporters of Hibernian FC.

It was Friday afternoon, and Hamish Barr was overheating in his office. He took his temperature with the thermometer he always kept handy, but it read frustratingly normal. There was no getting out of it: he'd definitely be leaving for France in the morning.

So maybe it was time for a spot-check, he thought, calculated to keep them on their toes, send them off on holiday with a sense of purpose.

Up in Research & Development his best brains were hard at work on improving his own design for the award-winning New-Condensed Crate; not that he imagined real improvements were possible there; and in Customer Services his webmaster was inputting the most recent company figures, which, if read by his competitors, were bound to spoil their holidays.

As he took a self-satisfied stroll towards boxing, he was joined by Hugh, who announced the news about the millionth bottle packed since the start of the year. He strode through the open door and stepped into the warehouse wearing a smile which, when he looked around, turned into a fleshless gape.

'Anything wrong, boss?' Hugh asked.

'Who,' Hamish asked icily, 'is that ham-fisted fellow over there?'

'That's Simon, Stod as he's known to us. Been with us these past three months.'

'And what does he imagine he's doing?'

Hugh was used to his boss's jitters, especially before holidays. 'He's no genius, I grant you, Mr Barr. But he comes from a good background, and at least he's no smart alec.' As Hugh listened, his boss was becoming a ventriloquist's dummy, with every rising intonation in his voice.

'His father may be the John the Baptist, for all I care. How often do I need to remind you, Hugh? A Scotus education doesn't blind me to the Protestant virtues of hard work, intelligence and responsibility.'

The ventriloquist's dummy moved closer to the offender. 'You!' it shouted over the shop-floor.

Stod looked up and smiled, despite dropping on his foot the crate he had been wielding. A silence descended, as his work-mates sidled out of range.

'Boris Yeltsin on a bad day,' whispered a boxer to the conveyor-belt operator.

'I've never seen him look this grim,' muttered a work-mate. 'More like ET, with those bulging eyes.'

'What can I do for you, Mr Barr?' chirped Stod.

The boss surged up to him. 'What, precisely, do you think you're doing there?'

Stod was undaunted. 'Just loadin' these boxes, boss.'

Hamish turned to Hugh, as if to say: And you hired him? Then, to Stod: 'So to you it seems normal to force litre bottles of the squat Cardhu into crates designed for slim 75-fluid-ounce bottles of Talisker?'

Stod stared, as if the bottle of Cardhu had voluntarily flung itself into his right hand, and stuck.

His boss fumed for everyone to hear: 'It's just what I was saying to your foreman: the firm depends on the performance of all.' He turned, frothing, back to Stod. 'Now, what are you? Tell me that. What are you, man?'

Stod was confused. 'You mean, like, am I Catholic?' He spotted the vigorous shaking of his foreman's head. 'So, you mean a bit of an eejit? As you could say.'

'What are you?'

'A scatterbrain, sir, I suppose.'

Hamish turned to the crowd of Stod's fellow-workers, cowering in the corner. 'Come on,' he barked, 'the lot of you. You know I'm always encouraging you to be articulate. Study dictionaries! What is he?'

The suggestions came in embarrassed undertones:

'Eh, a simpleton?'

'A spam-heid?'

'A dimwit?'

'Come on!' he roared. 'You can do better than that.'

'A fool?'

'A moron?'

'No!' Hamish held up his arm as he used to enjoy watching the priest do. He turned again to Stod. 'I'll give you one more chance. If you get it right, then you can keep your job.'

'Eh, Mr Barr,' Hugh warned his boss. 'You can't really do that. There's codes of practice.'

'I'm a dunder-heid?' Stod stabbed. 'Is that it?'

'No! Wrong again. For you are a cretin. C-R-E-T-I-N.' He spelt it out. 'Cretin! Do you hear me?' He turned to his foreman. 'I never want to see him on the premises again.'

What came as such a shock to Hugh (if not especially to Stod) had, however, been predicted. And this prophecy had occurred in no more lofty a place than Clarks Bar on Dundas Street, three months before. It was 1 May, the pub doors were wide open, tempting the elements, and the Famous Four (as Simon's sister called them) were for the moment only three.

'You hear Stod's landed himself a job?' Ric's peeved tone matched his thick coat and boots, as if he believed the sun were trying personally to trick him. 'Down at Barr's.'

'That's Irn-Bru on tap then,' chirped his pal, Dan-Dare. 'Handy for the hangovers.'

'Alas,' said Simon, who despite his world-weary appearance was always first with the facts. 'It's Barr Packaging Inc., model industry of Donald Dewar's enterprise-friendly Scotland. Stod's gran used to attend mass at St Mary's with the foreman, a certain Hugh. The RC mafia.'

'Fair makes you sick,' commented Ric, who had been out of a job for over a year. 'My old man's a Mason, but does that win me favours?'

'Never fear, Ric,' Simon consoled his friend. 'Do you want to bet how long he's going to last?'

The other members of the Famous Four had long since given up gambling against him.

'You don't have to be strictly Antinomian, boys, to realise that Stod's fate is sealed. He'll last two months at Barr's, four months at most. Shall we drink to that?'

Their pint glasses were raised as the toast was solemnly made: 'To our mate Stod, predestined from before Creation . . . to failure.'

Four months on from the incident on the shop-floor, Hamish was feeling so bad he'd had to leave the office and come home. Forever encouraging his men to be articulate, he switched on his PC, since he had time before leaving for the doctor's, and called up the dictionary.

'Cretinism,' he read, not for the first time. 'The state of one with deformity and mental retardation caused by thyroid deficiency. Coll. A stupid person.'

Not bothering with the etymology, he impatiently switched off, swore at the cat, then left his house in Belford Park, slamming the door as he went. Though there was no rush, he sped along Ravelston Dykes in the Merc doing well over eighty successfully terrifying some young mothers collecting their children from playgroup.

'Anxiety, Hamish, I'm sure of it.'

What was it with doctors? Five years ago not one of them had heard about the mind; now even his ancient GP was a frustrated psychoanalyst.

'Been feeling like this for long?'

'Since just before the Trades, and worse by the day.'

His doctor smiled knowingly.

'What?' Hamish objected. 'Anxiety, with my whole body become foreign to me, running a permanent temperature, breathless, down two stone in weight, my reactions so fast that I can return my wife's best serves, a hundred ideas a minute, heartbeat over ninety, and the whole world running late except for me?'

Even the birds, with their ceaseless infuriating warble, were on the doctor's side. 'Has anything been stressing you unduly? Work? Home life?'

That was easy. 'It's been the firm's most successful year to date. If people would just stop confusing us with the makers of Irn-Bru we'd be sailing.' He paused for long enough to wish his voice sounded less like a dentist's drill. 'Zoë, the wife, she enjoyed France, even if I found it more torture than ever to be on holiday. I'm liking the theatre class I enrolled in at the University, though it's a struggle to get up the six flights of the David Hume Tower when the lift's out of order. We both love the new house in Belford Park, or I loved it until I started to feel so bad.'

Nothing he said seemed to make an impression. 'You still attend mass?' his doctor asked.

'What the hell's that got to do with anything?' Hamish snapped. 'It's a doctor I'm needing, not a priest! The back of my head feels like it's falling off, no amount of aspirin gives relief.'

'You've got to slow down, give yourself time to enjoy your successes.'

'Time's the one thing I've far too much of.' He glanced at his watch. 'Given I hardly sleep any more, and given that everyone else is moving round like the living dead.'

His doctor was ushering him out of the surgery, so he dug in his heels for a final attempt. 'So you don't think it could be my thyroid for example?'

'What? Aged forty-five?' His doctor laughed. 'Anxiety, Hamish, anxiety. You need to find new ways of relaxing.'

Relaxing by reporting him for malpractice, for example, his patient thought, five minutes later, as he slammed his foot down on the throttle.

'Look!' Simon ordered, blithely unaware of being stuck back in early July. He was pointing to a cluster of unapproachable well-groomed blondes, who were coming down Dundas Street, clad in short skirts and lycra tops.

'Friends of your sister, I wouldn't doubt,' remarked Dan-Dare.

Simon shook his head in pity, self-pity, pity for the whole predictable world perhaps. 'Though what I wanted you to note, rather, was the manner of Stod's dismissal.'

Ric gazed wistfully into his half-empty glass, the foam the more precious now that free rounds were over. 'Thus does he join the ranks of the lumpen unemployed. Those of us who have to beg for our Beck's.'

'I know you good Divinity pupils remember all about the great Scottish creed of Antinomianism, by which it is explained how all is ordained since the beginning of time: for who are we puny mortals to alter the unfathomable decrees of the Almighty by our prayers or good deeds.'

Even if they didn't remember, neither Ric nor Dan-Dare was about to spoil the fun.

'But not everyone can read the Divine Intention, and that's where I, the Elect, come in. To me, clearly, it's obvious who's been chosen and who's damned. For a moment, I grant you, it seemed like Stod, despite his Papist past, might be saved. But catch a hold of this, and forgive me if I temporarily promote Mr Barr beyond his true station, for dramatic effect.'

Even a second wave of blondes wasn't enough to distract them now.

'For the great God Barr trusteth not to Archangel Hugh, he for whom packaging is but a path through catechism to communion, but he cometh down in person from on high to smite the uncircumcised Stod, he who cannot tell a squat litre bottle from a slim 75-fluid-ounce. And verily he sayeth unto the idler: "Be gone from my lands, hither never to return. And a curse upon thy head".'

'What?' puzzled Ric. 'Cast out into the wilderness?'

'But Simon,' joked Dan-Dare, 'aren't RCs like Jews, don't they get circumcised at birth?'

Simon gave it thought. 'Well, my brethren, if Stod's got a foreskin, we can be sure he'll be the last one to realise it.'

'We can all drink to that,' said Ric.

And drink they did.

Fast forward to Hamish, speeding into the BUPA hospital in Murrayfield, six weeks after he'd almost strangled his GP; to find, to his chagrin, that it was built upon the grounds of Scotus Academy; the noble old building where once he'd been instructed, filled now with malingerers in pyjamas. He cursed himself for not having given to the appeal from his *alma mater*, until he was interrupted by the nurse attempting to show him in.

'And anxiety?' he asked the specialist.

'Who wouldn't be anxious, Mr Barr, with a time-bomb ticking away inside of them. The thyroid gland controls your entire metabolism, which means every last cell in your body is sick. Your gland is very enlarged, and the blood tests indicate you've got way too much T-4, that's thyroxin hormone, racing round your body.'

'You mean . . . like . . . I'm about to become a cretin?'

The specialist chuckled companionably. 'On the contrary, your hyperthyroid is the other end of the scale from thyroxin deficiency.' Since his patient still didn't look convinced, he went on, 'In layman's terms, you and a cretin would make the perfect couple.'

'No!'

'Yes, really. You would balance each other out.' Figuring his patient must be humourless by nature, the consultant took a more orthodox tack. 'Though of course, both afflictions can produce goitres, protruding eyes, panic attacks, diarrhoea. And have you been irritable at all?'

'Irritable?!' Hamish fumed.

'Hmm. Well, were you to have been, it would explain that too. What we shall do is blast the gland with the drug called carbimazole. Presuming your liver tolerates it, you'll start to feel better almost immediately.'

His patient looked far from reassured.

'And if that were to fail, there remains the more radical measure of radioactive iodine. Or, all else failing, surgical removal of the gland. The only inconvenience being, with one so young as yourself, that you'd be on hormones for the rest of your life.'

Given the fortune he'd be paying, now he'd resigned himself to going private, Hamish presumed questions were permitted. 'What concerns me, doctor,' he said, trying to recover his old voice, from the time before the swelling squeezed his vocal cords. 'What I'm really concerned with is the cause.'

'Question not the cause!' intoned the consultant, with a theatrical gesture.

'The need,' Hamish corrected. '"Reason not the need." *King Lear*. Been studying it in my theatre class, the one activity I do manage to enjoy. Yet I'd still like to know.'

'The death of a loved one? An accident, or trauma?'

Hamish stared into space, trying to match the words with what had happened in the warehouse. Was it, he wondered, just an awful coincidence?

'To be honest with you, Mr Barr,' the consultant concluded, 'it's beyond the ken of science. Your guess is likely to be as good as mine.'

Two months previously, on the second Thursday in September, phone calls and faxes had been required to summon Dan-Dare and Ric. 'As you can imagine,' Simon started, before drinks were even ordered, 'I wouldn't have assembled this august congregation without some heavy-duty news. So you really haven't heard?'

His friends were shrugging.

'Yesterday, only yesterday, there comes to earth a miracle. You know all about predestination and the Elect. But I regret to say there are apparently exceptions. Our own brother, Stod the Devout, while he lieth blootered in his crib, is visited by the Archangel Hugh, who inviteth him to lunch at Valvona and Crolla's.'

'What?' asked Dan-Dare. 'To fire him again?'

'I'll trip lightly over how Stod mistakes the balsamic vinegar for HP sauce and the disastrous consequences thereof to our Angel's wingèd jacket. Not to mention the waiter's reaction when he orders pasta and chips . . . So they're noshing away, Stod not daring to ask what the lunch is all about, when Hugh says to him: "It's Mr Barr who's charged me personally to take you out, see if you might be interested in rejoining the team." "What, me?" says our Stod, modesty incarnate. "Mr Barr admits he was slow to recognise your talents, but in retrospect, he says, he feels the firm could benefit from your enthusiasm and expertise." So Stod's waiting to hear the punchline, thinking it's some kind of practical joke. But no, it's for real, he's back with the firm.'

'But . . .' Ric objected, as disbelief turned to amazement. 'But you didn't foretell this.'

'And wait, brethren,' Simon added. 'He's no longer on boxing, he's been moved up to the orders office, where women work and folk have computers.'

This was too much for credence. 'He gets *this*,' said Dan-Dare, 'the bloke for whom a mouse means Rentokil, and a Mac is a garment for flashing in?'

'Take it from me, boys,' Simon reassured them. 'It'll soon end in tears. The Holy Roman Empire, with its good deeds, its charities, and its Hibernian–Hugh axis, may moveth mountains, but it cannot save our Stod.'

Though racing in advance of the world by compulsion of his hyperactive hormones, Hamish had to admit that Christmas was still consensual, in date if not in spirit. By four in the morning of that sacred day he was awake, his heart pounding as if he'd just sprinted the 400 metres: like when he was a child waiting for his presents, he thought ironically.

He counted his pulse at 150 per minute. He didn't even need to touch his wrist, all he had to do was listen to the pump and whoosh. That'd be sleep over for the night, he realised; though Zoë was still dreaming blissfully.

Straining for small mercies, he thought of the snow outside, which ensured that, with the heating off and only one sheet, at least he wasn't burning up. Saving on electrical bills.

Downstairs, he switched on one of the 40-watt bulbs he'd installed in all the sockets to save himself from having to wear dark glasses indoors as well as out. He reached for *Endocrinology*, the tome at the centre of his new library, but its weight defeated him even more than its incomprehensible diagrams, equations and graphs. His attention span was less than a pubescent house-fly's. His muscles hurt so badly he couldn't resist downing an extra two carbimazole, despite the yellow blotches behind the pallid sheen of his skin, and the warnings that any more medication and his liver might give out.

He read: 'I Just Want To Feel Normal Again', infuriated by the tone, at once whining and chummy, one of the chapter titles in *Thyroid Problems*, the paperback he'd picked up at Thin's the night before. Almost as infuriating as the way he kept repeating it to himself a thousand times an hour; or as the presents beneath the needle-shedding tree.

His whole life would be so much simpler if Zoë kept the house clean. If she got up at a reasonable hour instead of lying in till eight every morning – ten o'clock on Sundays! And if she weren't so damned attached to her bed, they could have opened their presents by now, incinerated the paper and ribbons. There was a time when he'd regretted having to sleep six hours a night. Now, he'd read all the plays they were studying on the Uni course, until he practically knew them by heart.

Though he realised his bladder was empty, he went to the toilet for the fourth time that night. Why, if he realised it, did his bladder not realise it too?

First light in the east sent a silver lustre across the snow-covered lawn. But surely he'd been right yesterday, he told himself, to offer a serious Yuletide present.

'That's magic, Mr Barr,' (he heard the voice again). 'I'll be able to get the drinks lined up at Clarks with this.' His employee looked particularly awkward in his suit. 'Or call Simon up when I'm at Easter Road and give him a running commentary.'

Was he schizoid as well as simple? 'Why would you want to call yourself up, Simon?'

'Not me, sir, my mate Simon. Have I no mentioned him? He's a right smart guy, studying Divinity, and he's got this real corker of a sister, Laura, who works in Enzo's Salon up on Howe Street, maybe you've seen her. Anyway, that's why they call me Stod, to avoid confusion.'

The boom and whoosh were as loud as ever. His skin prickled.

'And here, Mr Barr, I've bought this for you, as a wee token of thanks for all the support you've been showing.' He dragged it in from the door of the office: a 24-bottle crate of Irn-Bru, 'MADE FRAE GIRDERS' thoughtfully scribbled on top. 'As a bit of a joke, like, seeing hows you have everything.'

For a second all went quiet, outside and in. Whoosh-boom no more.

Could this fresh affront have sufficed? Was this what it meant to be well again? But then Hamish heard it, felt it, rising from the basement of his being, to where it almost extinguished thought.

Who was he kidding? Measure for measure, like in the current play he was studying. Who was he trying to kid. He'd hardly even begun to give.

Dawn was threatening the city. Even Zoë would be up before long, with some noxious scheme he'd have to spike, some plan for injecting joy into the dire hiatus of the holiday.

What had started ad hoc, with occasional readings from Calvin and the Auchterarder Creed, had hardened, way back mid-November, into a Friday-afternoon Assembly: two hours of information-sharing and indoctrination before the topic arrived in person. 'Sherlock-Simon', as the Moderator was christened, had seen his dog-collar ruffled and his deerstalker dented.

'Blackmail,' Simon announced, trying once more to dig his nails into the future, through the thickened air brooding over them. 'It would be one hypothesis, if we didn't know that Stod is constitutionally incapable of keeping a secret, still less holding a plan in his head for more than three minutes.'

'I saw him at Easter Road on Wednesday,' Ric reported. '"How's it going up in research?" I ask him. "To be honest with you, Ric," he tells me, "it's no really my cup o' Tetleys."'

The regulars at Clarks, proud to be party to such intensity of talk, left space around the table for the Assembly. The rumour had spread that Simon wasn't just a Divinity student, but an undercover agent working for Richard Holloway, the controversial Bishop of Edinburgh.

Ric held the floor. '"Back to the storeroom, then, Stod," I say to him. "Nah," he tells me. "The way Girder sees it – that's ma own wee nickname for Mr Barr – the way Girder sees it, firing me was like givin' me a clean slate, a boot up the bum, teachin' me a lesson, a kick-start, tabula rasa"–'

'He did not say "tablula rasa"!' Simon, upstaged, was indignant.

'"Tabula rasa", sic Stod, cf. Girder.' It was easy to forget that Ric had completed half a degree in Biology at Heriot Watt before his money ran out. '"So now," says Stod, "I don't see a way back, so much as up and on. I've been moved to Corporate Planning. Success breeds success, like."'

'Hence the suit.' Simon had kept the crushing news for last 'From Aitken & Niven, admittedly, where Barr Inc. has an account. But a suit none the less.'

Save for expressions of astonishment, Dan-Dare had virtually been silent. Now something twigged. 'I've been trying to remember the film. That one with Peter Sellers. No, not *The Pink Panther*, the one where he gets to watch Shirley MacLaine wanking. Where he starts out a gardener and ends up President of the United States.'

Before the final member of the Famous Four arrived, they agreed to convene two hours earlier the following week, to watch *Being There*, for tips.

One numb night in March, Hamish was trying to avoid being hurtled yet further into the future, by imagining it. This, he thought, is what it will feel like to be old, with limbs adrift and exhausted; combined with a thousand-and-one notions all clamouring for attention. 'Life In The Fast Lane' was how it was described in another chapter in the insufferably clubby *Thyroid* book: in the fast lane driving a Robin Reliant. One measly organ, shaped like a bow tie, now tightening round his throat until it throttled him. What did it imagine? That once his heart had given out, it would lord it over his carcass, waving its bow tie banner aloft?

Dimly aware that attention to time wasn't helping, he tried to project himself in space. Fortunately, the garden for which he had harboured so many hopes was coming alive with the light.

But then, as he'd soon be under the turf, what did he care about space?

This, he concluded, is not what it will feel like to be old. This *is* what it feels like. Worse, this is it, forget the 'likes'. With the heart beating in a permanent sprint, then old age and coronary were just round the bend, thirty years in three months, little wonder he was ahead of everyone else, ahead of them in his grave before long.

The early birds were chirping. With the telescopic mikes that had once been his ears, he could make out a starling, two blackbirds, a dove of some description. What would be the simplest way to eliminate them? Shotgun would be noisy. Netting would be silent but clumsy. A crossbow might serve.

He tried again to remember how it had felt not to be ill, not to have ninety per cent of his energy required just to hold himself at the window and resist screaming at the dawn chorus. Then he tried to remember what it was like to remember how it felt not to be ill. And he was almost there, he was sure of it, when the cat came in from snuggling with Zoë. He grabbed it by the tail. To think, he recalled, that once he used to feed seed to these rats on wings.

'Here,' he swore, as he swung the cat round his head, 'instead of lying about with my slut of a wife, go out and kill some birds!'

By mid-January, pre-empted by events, the Assembly had adopted the more modest name of Seminar. Still trying to catch up, Simon scheduled additional Wednesday meetings at The Abbotsford on Rose Street Christmas had come and gone, with gifts from Stod of HMV tokens and Hogmanay had seen self-defeatingly numerous free rounds.

'Maybe Stod's shagging Barr's wife?' Dan-Dare tried, in one of his less extravagant speculations.

'And he gets promoted for that?'

'If old man Barr's a voyeur, aye.'

'I skipped Medieval Theology class,' Simon explained, 'to get on the Web. www.barr.inc.co.uk; www.promoteyourcareer.com; www.black mail-for-beginners.' His disgusted tone spoke volumes. 'And there's worse. He called me from his mobile yesterday, and what does he say? "I'm no sure, Simon, that it'll be possible to be callin' me Stod much longer."'

'Never!'

'"But Stod," I remind him, "The Famous Four has already got a Simon." That gives him something to chew on. "Were you thinking, Stod, of rechristening yourself Giovanni Paolo the Third, or Richard

Branson Jnr, or, eh, Ewan McGregor, or maybe Irvine Fucking Welsh?" Excuse the language, boys. But that he should defy the destiny laid down for him is one thing. That he should try and steal my name goes beyond the pale!'

'The wee bastard!'

'"It's gist," he has the nerve to say, "it's gist that Girder insists on me being called Simon, like." So I just maintain this menacing silence on the other end of the line. Then: "So maybe we could call me Simy?" he suggests. "Or Simy-on?" I don't need a second chance. "That's perfect, Stod," I say, "we'll call you Simian from now on".'

'Like the Neanderthal?' cheered Ric.

'Tarzan and Cheetah!' Dan-Dare expanded. 'Planet of the Apes!'

Though aware of its being meagre compensation for the demise of a doctrine, when they left The Abbotsford two hours later they did so swinging through trees.

Forward in April, at the last class of term, while his fellow students went through their presentations, Hamish was furtively studying the brochures he intended to use in his bid to divert his wife from the sun. If she insisted on a holiday, then it would be a chalet in Reykjavik, or a fortnight at the Skeabost Hotel in Skye, where the ludicrous prices would help her forget the midges and rain.

'And you, Mr Barr?' the teacher asked. 'Who will you be presenting as your favourite character from the plays we've studied this year?'

He'd been meaning to prepare it, but his mind had refused to focus. He was shamefaced when he rose to his feet. 'I . . . I . . . My health, you understand . . . ?'

The stares were steely from the retired civil servants; the eyebrows raised on the nurses from the Infirmary.

'Antony!' he blurted out. 'Antony's my man.'

'Tell us more.'

Pacing up and down the classroom, for ten whole minutes he delivered an impromptu harangue which surprised himself as much as the Bruntsfield spinsters: how he admired the excess of the man, the exaggeration, the extreme irritability, even the fact that he was such a hopeless judge of character.

'And you know,' he ranted, alarming one elderly soul whose own choice had been Viola from *Twelfth Night*, 'you know what I love so much about this bloated basket of a play? The way it just goes on and on, cutting endlessly from Egypt to Rome, the way Antony goes on and on too, taking everything to the limit, his willingness to run the world to ruin, stuff the collateral damage.'

As he caught his breath, a broker in pinstripe raised his hand. 'Are we talking Kosovo here, with "collateral damage"?'

But Hamish wasn't listening. 'Here's a man who overestimates everything and everyone, including himself. Who's out of synch with his times.'

'Yeh, behind them,' came a voice from his right.

'He's so far in the future that we're still trying to catch up with him!'

The outburst was so unexpected that the class balanced perilously between enthusiasm and embarrassment.

'You make a convincing case, Mr Barr,' the teacher put in. 'Though Ventidius, Antony's own faithful general, might think otherwise – not to mention Caesar.'

'Stuff Caesar!' Hamish fumed. 'A man of maps and graphs. If he was alive today he'd probably be . . . a packager!' To his overwrought body this extra flagellation felt like relief. 'Caesar's a bureaucratic wimp.'

'Hear, hear!' cheered the Bruntsfield contingent.

When he got home, he vowed, he would send a cheque for £1,000 to the RSC in Stratford. But he wasn't home yet, and there was more to get off his chest.

'And when Antony's deserted by his old servant Enobarbus, what does he do? Does he swear revenge, the way Caesar would have done? Does he hell!' He knew the speech by heart, but he wanted them to hear it in his own words. 'Not Antony. He blesses Enobarbus and sends his treasure after him.' As he chanted, more than spoke, he reached his arms out in front of him. There were tears in his bloodshot eyes, his shirt-collar soaked.

Fortunately, perhaps, there was so much commotion, between the students recoiling from the violence of the outburst, and the others egging him on, that they failed to catch his closing line:

'Thus dies Enobarbus, slain by the generosity of his master's over-active thyroid.'

Rewind to February, from which premature perspective the future was looking ever less certain: Ric, po-faced, refusing to answer questions about his father's cancer; Dan-Dare shivering whenever the door opened on Clarks Bar, at a loss for even halfway plausible suggestions; Simon, defrocked, his deerstalker in tatters.

'It's disappointing, boys, I know,' he started, in a voice that sounded in search of itself. 'I got Stod to go through it again, thinking there might be a clue in the way he was fired. I figured he'd be lucid as we were watching the Hibees being wasted. "It was just before the Trades," he says. "In comes Girder. Looking right raj he is, people say he's got some big-time health problem, like something out of Hieronymus Bosch."'

Simon let his friends recover from the reference.

'"But what exactly did he say?" I ask Stod. "Look," he tells me, "he was right. Firing me was like giving me a clean slate, a boot up the bum, teaching me a lesson, a kick-start, tabula rasa, you know?" "Cut the impersonation," I bark. "The detail, man, the devil's in the detail."'

Ric's hands were clamped to the edge of the table. Dan-Dare's head was shaped like an antenna.

'"All I remember, Simon," Stod says to me, and the effort of recollection's almost killing him. Fortunately, what he was witnessing on the pitch was even more painful. "All I remember is Girder calling out for suggestions how to christen me."'

Their hopes seemed to hang in the fug-filled air of the bar, beckoning to the threesome.

'"And he says to me, the Girder, he says, "You are a cretin." "Think, Stod," I say to him. "Are you sure that's all he said?"'

Simon paused momentously.

'"Eh, it's Simian, Simon," says Stod, "if you don't mind. Not that being called a cretin is so terrible, like. Sticks and stones, and that. Also, I took a leaf out of the boss's book, looked up what it really means. It's no so bad . . ."'

Simon's voice faded into nothing.

When they looked into the air again, their hopes had fled and cigarette smoke was all they saw.

'A Mondeo?' Ric finally asked.

'Titanium-blue. Fuel injection. Enough air bags for him to construct himself a new blow-up doll. Power steering. Alloys. Form-fitting seats. Mini-disc. Air-conditioning.'

'Air-conditioning?' Dan-Dare objected. 'In the land of brass monkeys?'

'Says it'll impress the birds.'

They stared at the table where the keys would shortly be tossed. If only to stave off purchasing the next round, Ric broke the hush. 'Did he tell you about his run-in with the foreman?'

Probably they knew, but information had come to have the reassuring lull of lament.

'The devout old-timer, Hugh, comes up to him and tells him straight out what Simon wrote him in that anonymous letter. Says, "There's a rumour going round that you're blackmailing the boss." Stod thinks it's a joke, but Hugh insists it's not, and that he's warning him in case the employees turn nasty. "The boss is a sick man," Hugh says, "and if he doesn't get better soon, who knows how long he's going to last. There's some here feel their livelihoods are on the line, and they're connecting it to you, Stod." Pretty much as you wrote it, Simon. And Hugh goes on: "They're saying how else would a dimwit manage to rise above the ranks of chief bog-cleaner. A cretin, the boss said, when he fired you."'

Meanwhile, Simon had been thinking. 'What exactly is the disease Barr's suffering from?'

But nobody was listening. 'So what does our Simian reply to Archangel Hugh?' Ric went on. 'He's not ruffled one bit. He digs into the lucky-dip of his miserable bairnhood, from when his gran used to drag him to mass, and comes out with: "Thou shalt not covet thy neighbour's job."'

Ahead again, fourteen weeks this time, to where the late-May sunshine was still flooding in, despite the blinds he'd had fitted. Hugh refusing to be seated, his heavy sighs announcing: The Pantomime is Over.

'But surely, Hugh, a place could be found for him in PR, if it's not working out in research.'

Hugh was obdurate. Blood out of stone.

'Or tell me, what about his family? Do you know them at all?'

'Very suitable directors, I'd have thought, Mr Barr. The father with twenty years' experience as a full-time stotious drunkard, major investments in the betting industry. The sister, looking like the back end of an unwashed bus, would be ideally placed in sales. Only sad thing is the mother, who topped herself some years back. Though, on reflection, if she was ever dug up she'd be more than a match for her children.'

Hamish swivelled in his chair. What was his heart doing? 173? 185?

'Now, Hugh,' he objected, 'what's become of your Christian charity? I thought you went to St Mary's with his grandmother.'

'But now she's had a stroke.'

'You were the one who pleaded for him. I hardly need remind you that we're all doing pretty nicely for ourselves on the basis of my judgements . . .'

'Aye, but for how much longer if you let that dunder-head loose?'

He searched for baritone, but his strangulated throat gave him falsetto. 'I chose you, after all.'

'With all due respect, Mr Barr, if I thought you were comparing me to Stod – to Simon – I'd go home and gas myself, though it'd mean burning in the fires of hell.'

If he wished to help the family, in other words, he'd have to do so by himself.

193? Maybe a new high of 200? When Hugh had finally ceased tormenting him, and stormed out of his office, he decided he would stop again at the George Street Vintners on the way home.

But hardly had he tasted the first oblivion-yielding sip, over dinner, of what Morton the wine-merchant had promised him would be as good as eating lotus, when his wife's voice broke over him:

'Isn't it time for radioactive iodine?' Zoë asked. 'The endocrinologist, when I called him, told me it has an excellent success rate.'

'So now you're making secret calls to my doctor?' His eyes bulged so badly, he felt they would pop.

'Only because I'm so worried.' She had obviously been rehearsing. Her normally mobile features were hard-set, her hair had been sprayed into a helmet. 'You're not the man I married, you know. Your medication isn't working. You're going to kill yourself if you don't do something.'

'I'm doing something!' he cried. 'I'm atoning through the nose, if sin is what it's about.'

'Sin!' she snorted. 'But it's a secret, right?'

'I'm striking at the root.'

'We can't go on like this, you do know that?'

She'd be thinking of how they hadn't had sex for more than nine months. He managed the odd bit of porn on the video when she was out at tennis, but in the way geriatrics might watch gymnasts perform on isometric bars.

'So you'd wheel me off to Dounreay for recycling, or bury me like uranium?'

'You'd only have to be isolated for a week or so.'

He flung the Château Pommard over the rubber plant. 'And what about our children? You want them born with a Sellafield sign on their bibs?'

Her look was an amalgam of loathing and hope. 'You dare say that to me now? Now? When I'm about to turn forty-four and you've been refusing for the twelve years since I met you?'

To meet her stare would be to dissolve in acid. But even that might be welcome.

'Go package yourself!' she shouted. 'Take your suppurating gland and shove it up your arse!' She was walking out the door, tennis-racket in hand. 'Oh, and one final thing. I've booked for Morocco. I was sick of hearing about Iceland and the Fjords.'

How had he let her get ahead, when he was the one ahead of the entire field? He struck the martyr's pose. 'Forty degrees in the shade and maximum glare. That's just grand.'

'They've got ice-cubes.'

'You didn't think of Albania? Or the Congo?'

'I'm going to Morocco, far from the Scottish rain. I intend to enjoy myself for the first time in nearly a year. You're welcome to join me. If you don't, I'll draw my own conclusions – and, believe me, I'll act accordingly.'

The dream from which he awoke on the couch, ten minutes later, featured a plane. All his dreams, in the fits of sleep that visited him, had a vivid unreality, as if pasted to his aching eyeballs, a special sort of strangeness that made him think of the cartoons of his youth, when his mother would take him to the Jacey Cinema on Princes Street, insisting they sit in the front row to get their money's-worth.

On this occasion, a bomber, flying low over Ravelston Dykes, not unlike the ones used to pound Serbia, suddenly turned into a butterfly, as in the song about 'Woodstock'. Only, this was no red admiral or swallow-tail; a thick fat sponge-like creature, inestimably sinister, which was defying not only gravity but its own organic nature to be hurtling through the air at such velocity.

When it reached his house it hovered.

He could read the bombs, emblazoned T-4, which after a terrifying delay rained down upon him their lethal liquid droplets of hormone thyroxin.

None of the three could have said for sure whether it was by chance or by design that they met, one blustery Friday afternoon back in mid-April, in Princes Street Gardens, near the bandstand. The weekly seminar had become an occasional meeting, peetering out further when Ric, saying something about his father's illness, had ceased to show; until all three had become dimly aware that they were avoiding one another.

Now Ric was defying the seasons back in his coat again. The office girls were stretched out on the grass under a pale uncertain sun, while the weather's reluctant shift somehow confirmed the rout.

'I could have handled Majorca, Ibiza, Gran Canaria at a pinch.'

They barely made eye contact.

Simon's voice went unclothed, almost obscene. 'I bumped into Stod, Simian – Simon as I suppose we have to call him now – in the Grassmarket. He was viewing real estate, he said, he's meaning to move from Craigmillar. "Never down Clarks these days, Simon," I tell him. "I could fair damage a pint or five," he says, "but the lady-friend's more into wine bars." "Right," I say, cursing quietly since I'd decided to try and get him interested in my wee sister Laura.'

'Lady-friend?' Ric groaned. 'He said "lady-friend"?'

Dan-Dare was only just audible. 'He called me up a week or so back, wanted me to help him choose summer shirts, couldn't decide between

Ralph Lauren and Hugo Boss. She's some loaded bird from Scottish Widows.'

'Get to see her?'

'A photo. You don't want to know.'

'So much for Calvin,' Ric sighed. 'So much for Predestination.'

'Anti-frigging-nomian,' came Dan-Dare's echo.

The three were dispersing, each in his own direction, blown by personalised winds, ghost-like, each recalled to his own private purgatory.

His old friends were almost out of range when Simon remembered, turned, and called to them. 'Tuscany!' He raised his arms to heaven. 'The summer with his lady-friend in Tuscany, with a quick trip to the Vatican!'

Scotland: July and the Trades, an almost guaranteed certainty of rain. Fez, Morocco, and the sun was unlimited. The shutters were closed tight, but a sharp little beam still managed a dance as it radiated from the slats across the bed.

The voices from the street below spoke words whose purpose was comprehensible even if their language was not, and the sharp scent of commerce encouraged him to rise. Zoë was already up and out, and if he was patient she'd no doubt return dressed in some exotic new wrap which she'd remove to a dance of her own improvising, with much shaking of hips and batting of charcoaled eyelashes.

The whoosh of blood was faint, so he needed fingers on his wrist to count the heart-beat. Eighty wasn't back to normal, but at least he wasn't sprinting, and that was without medication. He'd slept for nearly five hours last night, if fitfully. Since arriving in Morocco he'd put on half a stone; and if his skin was clammy, then he hardly bothered since so was everyone else's. He smiled to himself as he touched the stain on the indigo-dyed sheet. He had made that happen, just the day before. His wife had paid him compliments and fed him candied fruit.

'The thyroxin level is still too high,' the specialist had told him the day before they left. 'How does it feel?'

Just as he hadn't found the words to describe the illness, so he couldn't describe what it was to be well again. 'In synch,' was all he could think to say. 'Like I'm back in time, or almost. As if I've paid my dues.'

'This remission, if that's what it is, may be short-lived, Mr Barr. Relapse is common with hyperthyroid, so don't be over-celebrating. It's only fair to warn you.'

'If it starts again, I'm for radioactive iodine.' He sounded almost flippant. 'Or whip it out once and for all.'

The specialist emphasised his tact and diplomacy in refraining from saying: 'I told you so from the start.'

The bed seemed to welcome him as he stretched out. Had it all been one big coincidence? Had he spent all that money, and made such a fool of himself at the firm, for the sake of a coincidence?

A fly's thick buzz brought him back to the sun's ray crossing the room, to the blue sky beyond, to his wife coming up the stairs from the market.

To the here, to the now.

Way back almost a whole month earlier, 21 June, and Hamish had been up and racing since first light.

217 . . . 225 . . . 236 . . . He forced himself up with downward-thrusting arms from his chairman's chair.

He knew he had to walk down that corridor linking his office to the door with THINK TANK freshly painted on it. He had to do what he'd long had to do. All the rest – the favours, gifts, promotions – was just avoiding the issue. Even if he'd bit the bullet and gone back to confession, it would have been hedging his bets. He was responsible: if not for Kosovo or the world's ills, maybe not even for his own sickness, then at least for the words that had issued from his mouth.

'Do you have a moment, Simon?' Not even the strangulated throat could account for the tremolo.

'Sure thing, boss. Come in, take a seat.' Stod stuck his finger as a marker in the guide-book he was studying, neglecting to notice that he was occupying the only chair in the room.

'Planning your holiday?' Hamish began, cursing his beat about the bush. 'First time in Italy?'

'Working on Siena now. Though it's only your holiday bonus that's made it possible, boss.'

'I need to talk to you, Simon.' His pupils were marooned amid convex off-white seas. His face was drawn and thin. The scent of fox he was emitting was pungent even to himself.

'I'm all ears, boss. Here, take my seat.'

But Hamish would not sit down. 'For some months now,' he forced, 'for nearly a year to be precise, I've been meaning to speak to you.' If his voice went any higher, only dogs would hear him. 'Ever since I fired you in fact.'

'Woh!' Stod warned. 'All water under the bridge, boss, all Arno under the Ponte Vecchio, if you catch my drift.'

'As you no doubt know, I've been suffering severely from an acute hyperthyroid condition. Don't sleep, can't work, racing ahead of everyone, a foreigner to my own self, and now my wife is threatening to leave me.'

Stod clasped his boss's shoulders in his two big hands. 'Listen to me, Girder – boss – now, listen to me. If there's anything, I mean *anything* I can do to make it easier. If you'd like me to step in, have a word with the wife, take over the reins here, run the show for a while?'

'There's a single thing you can do for me, Simon.'

'Anything means anything.'

'Please don't ask me to explain, because I can't. I haven't told a single living soul, since they'd think I'd finally cracked, and probably have me committed.'

'Anything!'

'What I'm asking you to do is forgive me.'

'What? For the sacking? But it was like giving me a clean slate, a boot up the bum, like a lesson, a kick-start, a tabula rasa!'

'Not for what I did.'

There now, it was almost out, the very word by which he'd condemned himself. He fell to his knees and squeezed his palms together.

'Forgive me, Simon, please, for calling you a cretin!'

Stod dragged his boss to his feet. 'But that's no big deal. Listen, boss, I followed your own advice. According to the dictionary, the origin of cretin is 'Christian'. Some link between being a total idiot and being godly.'

The two men were finally facing one other.

'So you see, boss, you didn't really insult me at all.'

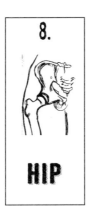

HIP

IT WAS ALL perfectly simple, at least it was to Laura's aunt Gloria, as she cleared away the Kleenex and restored the cap to the baby oil. So why the interest all of a sudden? First that Deirdre Darling from Age Matters, and now this Mr Stevenson, as he liked to be called, with a 'v', he insisted, not a 'ph' – not that she was ever likely to write it down, timetabling being The Lark's job. Just because she let on about how the pain in her worn-out hip was rooted three decades back – not the pain, exactly, that was all too present, day by day, minute by minute, but the reason why she'd never done anything to remedy it.

'You mean to say you've a sentimental attachment to your agony?' Mr Stevenson asked, just as he was losing control.

'If you want to put it that way.'

Which apparently he did, since it brought him off a treat.

'And so you suffer the torment of the damned,' said Deirdre, failing to conceal her outrage, 'and risk crippling yourself permanently, all because of some big mystery that happened thirty years back?' It almost made Deirdre spill her tea, though she had prepared it herself.

There would be nobody else using her room for the remainder of the day, the 'pantry' as Gloria called it, yet she liked to leave it spic and span. She had managed to satisfy three out of four hardy perennials that afternoon, not including Mr Stevenson, who was fast becoming a regular, improbable though this seemed, a handsome young man like him, with no obvious defect.

Wheeling herself forward on her tall office stool, she removed the plastic cover from the osteopath's table she'd been using ever since stooping to the divan became impracticable. One of the fringe benefits of all those sessions with the bone-cracker, when there was no more he could do to save her hip, he gave her the address for one of these tables specially designed to jack the client up to a respectable height – respectable, in this case, being what she considered 'a relative term'.

It was all perfectly simple, she thought, there was no great mystery to it. Unless of course The Lark was right. He did think up the most twisted things, stuck day in, day out in his booth by the door, smoking his French cigarettes, following on the surveillance screens what went on in all four rooms of his establishment.

'Ah, the mystery, Gloria,' he'd pronounced, when she'd stopped in for her chat, as she always did before starting. 'The mystery is that there is no mystery. You know men, they have to find an intrigue.'

'Women too,' she'd added, thinking of Deirdre. 'Apparently.'

She would have told them straight out, if only they'd believe her: that she had met Jamie Lofgren, the love of her life, thirty years before, and had lived on and off with him for five perfect months. That he'd been enchanted with her hips more than with any other part of her, and when they danced together he loved them even more than in bed. 'Your hips, Gloria, make everything right for me.' Though they hadn't made it right enough, given that he hanged himself without leaving so much as a note (his past had caught up with him, the downstairs neighbour said). Leaving nothing behind, in fact, other than debts she'd felt obliged to pay, and the one photo she had of them together, down the Plaza, doing the samba.

It was all so long ago. She could hardly remember more than the compliments he paid her. The sound of his voice was gone, not to mention the feel of his skin and the taste of him.

They would never understand, despite all their prying. Everyone had their own private thing. For her mother it'd been Julie Andrews in *The Sound of Music*. For her it was the way Jamie Lofgren idolised her hips.

'Keep 'em guessing,' was The Lark's advice, when she finally emerged from her pantry at five. His judgement was issued in an unplaceable accent – somewhere between Glasgow and Puerto Rico – which retained the gravitas of a lifetime spent people-watching. 'Take it from me, Gloria, some folks are hard to please.'

The email icon was flashing. Down the line, someone was waiting for the input from his office at BP Edinburgh. In Qatar the day was nearly over, and former drinking partners would be cursing him, wheeling out their insults about his bald spot and his empty life. But that was their tough luck, since they couldn't even load the programme without his help, let alone manipulate it. And if he had other fish to fry, under the name of Mr Stevenson, then didn't that only prove how wrong they were, with their petty jokes about his empty life?

What was clear, on consideration, was that it wasn't in character to be repeating the experience, least of all with a woman almost old enough to be his mother and with a game leg . . . to boot.

He chuckled at his own choice of words. Then he span round in his winged leather chair and stared blankly at the wall.

Gloria was a professional all right; she worked wonders with her hands, and once the oil was on them, what difference did it make if they did have a few wrinkles. He could always lie back and imagine Anna Kournikova, whom he hadn't caught enough of on TV. Or he could count the blessings of his nomadic life, and think himself back to the flesh-pots of Bangkok or Dubai.

Only, if he was honest with himself, and this was presumably the point of wasting his time here at BP's expense, pondering his destiny rather than managing the data for which he was paid a fortune – if he was straight with himself, he'd have to admit that Anna was as far from his mind in those moments with Gloria as Dubai was from Edinburgh. He was far too busy scanning the poor woman's face for winces. And ever since she'd spun the yarn about how her ruined hip was connected to her distant past, he'd been dreaming up some new question to ask her.

He wheeled round again, sat up straight at his desk, and put on a poor pretence of industriousness for the benefit of his secretary, who knocked nervously and placed a heap of faxes marked URGENT on his desk.

Not, he told himself, that he took the slightest pleasure in Gloria's discomfort. He had been a lot of places and tried a lot of things, such was his nature; but he'd never been one for gobbling live monkey brains or gambling on cockfights. Even as a child he'd not been the type to stick pins into frogs. He couldn't sit through *Crash*, and the gory scenes from *The World at War* left him cold, though the expats watched them endlessly. Call him unimaginative or empty, but for better or for worse an old-fashioned hand-job was his idea of fun.

Only, if he was honest with himself – again! And here he was, getting excited just at the thought of it – there was something special about dredging up Gloria's past, something that made him blast off in style.

Gloria, he thought, how typical. Couldn't she have thought of something more original!

What with the evening glow and the touch of warmth in the air, the fire didn't seem necessary, though her niece did look pale, as if her lovely long red hair were sapping her blood.

'You're usually good at guessing,' Laura said. 'So what do you think he does, when he's not pestering you with questions?'

Her aunt had given it thought. 'At first I thought a surgeon, given his interest in my malfunction. Then I thought a judge, since he's balding on top and I could see him in one of those wigs. He's definitely Edinburgh, though he's almost lost his accent. Stays in the Overseas House on Princes Street, if I'm not mistaken. Now I'm not so sure, but something abstract in any case, disconnected from the real world.'

'Sounds like computers,' Laura suggested.

'That's out of my ken, dear, but you could well be right.'

As she prepared the fish for her aunt's tea, Laura wondered if she shouldn't be more concerned. Not about the hip, there were enough folk worrying about that, and she did her bit, in any case, helping out with the messages whenever she had a chance. Rather, about the world of weirdos and no-hopers her aunt worked in – though of course she enjoyed her aunt's stories. Not that the rest of the family gave a damn, not even her prude of a brother, with their long faces whenever Auntie Gloria got mentioned.

'In another day and age,' her aunt said, over the plaice, 'I would have been a milkmaid. Same difference, almost, particularly as I only work with my hands these days.'

'It'd mean getting up earlier,' Laura put in, 'for the cows.'

'Yes, despite his name, The Lark has always been reasonable about my hours. Three to five, I told him, when we moved from Danube Street in the '80s. Means I get professional men who can choose their hours.'

The subtleties of her aunt's working code were not always easy to comprehend. But Laura had her own snobbery – some heads she despised, others she respected, even bald ones, like that of Mr Glen, the lawyer next door to Enzo's, who clearly had a fancy for her.

'Most of them are lambs, of course,' Gloria went on, 'rather than cows. My elderly gents especially, who have finally realised that there's nothing new under the sun.'

Her niece was picking at her fish.

'What's eating you, Laura, that you're not eating?'

Laura laid down her cutlery. 'You don't think he could be awkward, this so-called Mr Stevenson? I worry for you sometimes, Auntie Gloria.'

It was in vain that Gloria encouraged her niece to drop the 'Auntie'. 'He's a youngster, this one, rather toothsome. The problem with the young, of course, being their lack of imagination, as compared to the veterans. Awfully literal they tend to be. But what can you expect with their lack of real experience? Mrs Thatcher . . . John Major . . . Tony Blair . . .'

For her aunt, apparently, these names said it all. 'Maybe this Mr Stevenson's parents didn't love one another?' Laura tried. 'Maybe his stepfather molested him?' Psychology, she knew, had never been her strong point.

'I told him he was welcome to whatever he wished to know, but that he'd still not believe me.' Gloria retired to the couch. 'People are like that, it seems. Then I snagged his foreskin with my nail, just to remind him who's boss.'

Truth be told, it rather infuriated Deirdre, the way her client tidied up her flat before she paid her visits. Even the impossible bean-bags. Which meant that to feel useful and to find some mess she had to go delving into the backs of cupboards, reaching for bluebottle corpses and bacon rind set aside for blue tits months before. 'I brought you this jar of pills, Gloria,' she said. 'They're ibuprofen, since you tell me aspirin doesn't agree with you.'

'No need to shout, Deirdre dear. It's my hip, not my ears, that's defective.'

From the way her client inspected the jar, Deirdre knew it would never be opened. Stubborn, Gloria's middle name.

'It's always the same,' her client said, apropos of nothing, after gesturing to her to stop fussing and take a seat, 'with the married ladies.'

Their eyes crossed, but Deirdre couldn't tell if she was included in this club.

'They can't help thinking their husbands, just possibly, have been amongst my clients at the pantry. It eats away at them something terrible.'

Deirdre hoped the serenity of her smile would promote her to safety. In any case her husband was off abroad, on another round of research for his interminable book. So she had no worries on that score, for the present at least. 'Here,' Deirdre said, 'put your leg up on this.'

'Anything to oblige.'

Wasn't there something inevitably awkward, Deirdre finally asked herself, in being responsible for a woman only a few years her senior, who'd be as spry as she was, but for her hip? But since it was so, and since conversation was part of her brief, she went on: 'And have you been keeping busy, Gloria?'

'Oh, I've had my hands full!'

Deirdre was unsure if she was allowed to snigger. When her client had informed her of what she called her 'side-line', she'd felt it her duty to make discreet enquiries. To be informed, in no uncertain terms, by her client's relatives, that Gloria was perfectly well off; that if she lived in Dalry and worked in that awful place, it was her own choice.

'Still,' Gloria expanded, since conversation was flagging, 'at least it means I'm making more than the taxi fare home. It's beyond me now, the 44 bus.'

This was Deirdre's chance, though only now that it presented itself did she realise she'd been waiting for it. 'You know, don't you, Gloria, that I'd help you with the paperwork. I read yesterday that John Cleese has just had his done, and he's younger than either of us, despite his Ministry of Funny Walks. I've one old biddy down Leith, in her seventies, who's been given a whole new lease of life.'

'I've never been one for queues,' Gloria sighed. 'I've no wish to be creating problems for that nice Mr Dobson, expanding the NHS waiting-list.'

Deirdre tried to keep the irritation from showing. 'It's only going to get worse, you know. If there were at least a rational reason for your reluctance, rather than this nostalgic nonsense. It's not as if the rest of us don't have pains, you know.' Her voice was rising dangerously. 'Where would we be if we were all stuck in the tragedies of the past?'

Her client smiled as if to a petulant child. 'There's no tragedy about it, dear.' She passed her the jar of pills. 'Here,' she said, 'you might be needing these.'

Though she also helped with his accounts, it was mostly for the smell of the French cigarettes The Lark liked to smoke that Gloria spent a few minutes in his booth each day, before entering her pantry. Since she knew she'd never manage it, she liked to try and trick him into revealing his real name.

'What's wrong with The Lark?' he asked. 'Should remind you of spring, things rising and that.'

'I sometimes think,' she said, 'that it was my name, more than the awkward situation after Jamie died, that destined me for Fickle Fingers Massage Parlour.' She stressed each word in The Lark's establishment, to remind him how she deplored the name. 'What else, for a girl called Gloria?'

'You could have been a film star, Gloria, with looks like yours.'

She cleared her throat as she smiled. 'Is that the new girl?' she asked, pointing at one of the surveillance screens. 'She'll never beat the brewer's droop with houghmagandie like that!'

'Talk to her,' urged The Lark. 'Explain to her what haunches are for.'

When he passed her the diary, her wince looked to him worse than usual.

'Mr Stevenson?' Gloria signalled.

The Lark unlocked a drawer in his antique desk and pointed to a pile of twelve freshly minted fifty-pound notes. 'All from your new admirer,' he explained. 'He's paying way over the odds, doesn't seem to care. He's no problem, is he?' He aimed one hand at the screen that corresponded to her pantry, the other at the baseball bat collecting dust on the floor. 'Any monkey business and I'll be in there faster than a rat down a drain.'

She shook her head and struggled to her feet. Her face announced her inability to explain. 'You see any resemblance,' she asked instead, 'to the young Sinatra?'

The Lark gave it some thought. 'A Mob-man in the making?'

Her limp was particularly bad today, he observed, as the curtain closed behind her. He watched on screen as she hobbled into her pantry: getting worse by the day.

She had been rehearsing, but still he got to it first. 'And how are we today?' he asked.

It was her own line he'd pinched, from her strict-nurse days. Normally, the banter was second nature, but for once she was at a loss.

'I've been saving up for you,' he said, as he bent down to unlace his expensive brogues.

'Yes, Mr Stevenson. The Lark showed me, a very tidy sum.'

He squinted up at her. 'You know I didn't mean that.' He hardly kept the resentment from his voice.

Where, she wondered, did she usually rest her eyes when they were undressing? At least the Johnson's would give her something to be doing.

'Has it been giving you grief?' he asked, as he stretched out on the table.

Now that he was supine, she could finally relax. 'Not as much as this' – she grasped – 'must have been giving you.'

'It's a lot of misery to go through,' he moaned. 'For a mere ball and socket.'

'Ball,' she repeated, pinching his tightly sprung sack. 'And socket,' as she slid her hand down the shaft.

He was not so easily diverted. 'Tell me once again,' he commanded. 'About Jamie Lofgren and the samba.'

'You'll make me miss my stroke,' she said, trying to hide her smile.

'Tell me what he used to say to you.'

'I've told you it all already. Everything I can remember.'

'Tell me what he looked like.'

She switched her wrists to automatic pilot. 'It's all so long ago,' she said. 'In the one photo I have, he looks like everyone else did in the late '60s. I'll need to be inventing things if you want anything new.'

'Don't invent!' he ordered, between pants. 'Just tell it to me again. Tell me what he'd say to you about your hips.'

Discussing her aunt with her family was a sure non-starter, but with a total stranger Laura didn't see the harm. She couldn't have said how they got on to the subject, but it was presumably just an intro to questions about herself, starting with her hair, as always. Bar Sirius was hoaching, her friends were late, and he wasn't at all bad looking, if it weren't for the creepy smile.

'So – Laura did you say your name was?'

'Did I say?' She must have downed more Iguanas than she realised. He was setting them up as fast as she could knock them back. 'And you?'

He reached out his hand. 'Frank. Frank Utterson.'

'So what can I tell you, Frank? It was only ever a side-line, as she puts it.'

He seemed to find it intriguing, an aunt turning tricks.

'She's got a hip worn out, in total agony a lot of the time, so she limits her operation these days.' She frowned between gulps. 'Sorry, Gloria, to make you sound like a kitchen appliance.'

'Gloria?' he laughed. 'That's her real name?'

Was there a surge from the crowd round the bar? Was that why he bumped into her?

'So why don't you do something about this aunt of yours? They work wonders these days, with prostheses.'

'That's what the carer's always saying, from Age Matters. I don't know, maybe she's attached to her old hip. Maybe she's attached to the pain.' She thought she spied her pals, through the smoke. 'Not that psychology's ever been my forte.'

'So you're saying she chooses to suffer?'

It was time to change the subject. Or change man. 'What's your line, then, Frank?' she asked him.

'Computers,' he let out automatically. 'Data management and retrieval, more precisely, so you won't confuse me with the anoraks.'

She put her glass down, and looked him in the face, though her whole frame was shaking. 'Computers?'

'Must go to the loo,' he said, avoiding her stare. 'Back in a jiffy.'

She polished off her cocktail as she watched her pals approach, determined to get out of the bar before this Frank returned.

Deirdre had emailed her pest of a husband, she had taken the puppy for a walk, and still she had time on her hands.

In the Age Matters office it was easier, even if rather too much of her attention was being monopolised by Gloria's unreasonableness. Nobody, after all, she thought, and least of all a mother like herself, got to fifty without knowing her share of pain. But had she ever let her ingrown toenails fester, or her root canals or cysts? And yet didn't she have a past she was attached to, even if Heather, her only child, had dropped out of it? What gave anyone, and that anyone included her client, the right to inflict their misery on others? For even if Gloria didn't actively grumble, it was impossible now to visit her without absorbing some of the torment. Why, even her own clients at her grotesquely named place of work were presumably not immune to it!

It was a positive relief when the buzzer went, and in walked a stranger.

'Can I help you?' she asked, adjusting her face. 'On behalf of a relative? Please, take a seat.'

He finally removed his sunglasses. 'It's actually a dear cousin, or second cousin, about whom I've been hoping to see you.'

He looked around the shabby office, and smiled as if to say they all deserved better.

'She's been fortunate enough to benefit from the services of Age Matters. When I enquired, I was told you were in charge.'

Deirdre smiled: it made a change to have a handsome man in the office. 'And you are . . . ?'

'Mr Jekyll.' He chuckled. 'Yes, alas, like the story. Frank Jekyll.'

'And your cousin? It wouldn't be . . . ?' She was convinced: there were days that almost gave you faith. 'It wouldn't be a Gloria, by any chance, of Dalry?'

'The very same.'

Their eyes met across the desk, remaining engaged for longer than was strictly necessary. 'I have, like you I believe, been trying to convince her to alleviate her sufferings.'

'Don't I know it!' Deirdre whooped. 'I mean, in that I've been doing likewise ever since the day she was assigned to me. She gives me this ridiculous argument about the NHS waiting-lists. I've been racking my brains for a solution, I don't mind telling you.'

'While it's she who's really on the rack.'

The silence lasted until it risked becoming awkward. 'I have no qualms telling you that I've been getting no support, I don't mind telling you,' Deirdre complained, 'not even from her niece.'

'Ah, from Laura?'

'However, I don't suppose we can actually oblige her. For her own sake?'

His solidarity was a series of silent nods.

'The anomaly being that we can compel people to relieve their mental, but not their physical suffering.'

Concern was written all over his face, which had broken into a sweat. 'I have the money here,' he finally said, tapping the inside pocket of his immaculate jacket, while the words oozed out of him. 'I can think of no better way of spending it. Let her go private.'

Deirdre raised her eyebrows, wondering if he was *au fait* with her 'side-line'.

'Only, you'd need to avoid mentioning my name and, indeed, that you've ever met me. If she smells family charity, she'll refuse.'

'It'll be a pleasure, Mr Jekyll. I do believe it could be arranged. It'll be our conspiracy, if you like. Our benevolent conspiracy.'

She didn't stint on the flattery. Yet as she showed him from the office, five minutes later, his proposal seemed to have left him like a glove puppet with the hand removed.

She hastened to offer her own hand, both figurative and real.

Laura was a rare delight for her aunt on a Saturday night. 'Is everything fine, dear? You're looking thinner than ever.'

'I've come to see you specially, so let's not talk about myself. What I need is distraction.' She settled into an armchair. 'How about you?'

Her aunt had her feet up on the couch. 'Oh, I'm the same as ever.'

Laura prepared the G & Ts. Only after a good few were drunk, did she try: 'The man you mentioned?' Her question didn't emerge as casually as intended. 'Tell me again what he looks like.'

'You mean the one with all the questions?'

Laura nodded.

'He reminds me of a young Sinatra, though with a bald spot. Tall, impeccably dressed. Why do you ask?'

Laura got up and looked out the window to conceal her blush. 'Just curious.' The description, she told herself, could fit a hundred men in Edinburgh. 'And what about your carer, that Deirdre woman, is she still going on at you?'

'Oh, they're both obsessed,' Gloria sighed. 'I've told them everything I can recall. And now Deirdre's telling me that Age Matters has come up with the money so I can avoid the queue and have the operation done privately. I don't approve of private medicine, of course. But I'm thinking of accepting none the less.'

'No!' The shout left Laura before she could control it. 'I'm sorry, Auntie Gloria, I just don't like their interfering. Though sure, I'd be glad to see you out of pain.'

'My whole past is public now, you know. I even managed to recall how Jamie used to say I must have some Brazilian blood in me, the way I took to the samba. He'd been on the ships, so he knew that part of the world. But does that satisfy our Deirdre? Does that satisfy Mr Hyde?'

Laura's head jerked so violently that it almost cracked the window-pane. 'Mr Hyde? Mr *Hyde*?'

'I know, it's not very original, I told him I've known a dozen Hydes in my time, this being Auld Reekie. But that's what he's calling himself, he insists, now I've nothing more to recount.'

As she pressed a hand to her brow, Laura reminded herself that she had, after all, been looking for distraction.

'I suppose it's flattering in a way,' her aunt went on quietly. 'He's so interested in my past – my pain – that it's the only thing to bring him to the boil.'

'Did you say "past", Auntie Gloria, or "pain"?'

'When he finally gets there, two bottles of Johnson's finest later, you'd be hard put to say who's suffering worse, me or Mr Hyde.' She shook her head sceptically. 'Though I'm afraid he won't live up to his name.'

The icon was flashing. Qatar was still waiting – the poor sods. In a fanciful moment he even imagined the attendants at BP service stations up and down the country adding a penny to the price of petrol, because of his inaction.

Not that he had really been inactive. It hadn't been easy to track down Gloria's niece, who'd only been mentioned once, and that indirectly. Then there was Deirdre. There was also the matter of avoiding his cronies at the Overseas House, the irate phone calls from neglected girlfriends. The trip with the jemmy. Finally, the not inconsiderable effort put into lining up a psychiatrist, a Dr McAlpine, for later, as his conscience demanded.

His secretary interrupted with a knock at the door. 'You did say, sir, that if anyone asked for a Mr Jekyll, I should direct them to you?'

'Don't let us be disturbed,' he ordered, as his visitor took a seat. 'Hmm,' he purred, as he reached across the desk to graze her cheek with his lips, 'I was so hoping you'd come by.'

His co-conspirator scanned the office, for bugs or cameras, or maybe just admiring its expensive furniture. 'Can we speak freely, Mr Jekyll?'

He nodded as he adjusted some items on his desk and unconsciously started to doodle.

'I preferred a personal conference to the telephone. One can't be too careful.'

'How true, Mrs D, how true.'

There was a playful look in her eye. 'You computer buffs have a lot to answer for,' she started.

He was ready for all sorts of accusations, but not for this one.

'I'm being endlessly pestered on email by my husband. It quite cramps my style.' Her eyes glowed. 'When all my concentration is required, if our mission's to be successful.'

On the scrappaper in front of him, a stick man was emerging.

'Anyway,' she went on in hushed tones, 'Here's me just back from seeing our charge. I believe she's come round to it.' There was a look of childish glee on Deirdre's face. 'I couldn't fathom it at first. Then she showed me the broken lock on her door. Apparently, she's had a burglary. She says that nothing of value was stolen, just some personal item which she refused to specify. But I suppose it must have set her thinking how vulnerable she is. Not to mention the constant scourge of the pain.'

With the hand not holding the pencil, he dipped into his pocket and fiddled with his Nokia. A single key would bring The Lark on the line.

She was finding his eye hard to catch today, and his face wasn't showing as much delight as she had expected. Presumably, he was thinking about what it was going to cost him.

'And if,' he asked, 'by any chance, she were to balk at the last?'

He could at least repress his hopeful tone, Deirdre thought. Judging from his office, he wasn't short of a spare grand or two. 'I'm on the board of the clinic where we've booked her in. I didn't mention that? Well, Mr J, I've warned them that she may have second thoughts, but that deep down she's committed to going through with it.'

With the cocky angle of the chin, the sunglasses and smile, the stick man appeared to have usurped his maker's traits.

'You're not suggesting,' he said, 'that the replacement could be done without her consent?'

Deirdre hoped her blankness made it clear such foolishness could not reach her.

'What, against her will?'

She wondered if she had been wrong to put so much faith in her accomplice with the ridiculous name – almost as ridiculous, now it occurred to her, as her client's place of work.

'I certainly wouldn't put it like that. There'll be no question of coercion, just of making sure she receives the treatment she deserves.'

His pencil flickered until the stick man was almost erased by what appeared to be an 'X'.

Only when he inspected it closer, after his visitor had left, did he find that in fact it was a 'J'.

The thick wad of fifty-pound notes passed like a fat Havana under the nostrils of The Lark. 'Very generous, I'm sure,' he finally exhaled, 'Mr eh . . . is it Hyde today?'

'How should I know?' his customer said irritably. 'Stevenson, Utterson, Jekyll, Hyde, in the end it's all the same.'

With the money in his drawer, The Lark was empathic. 'There's a lot of wisdom in what you say.'

'I'm not trying to be wise,' his customer snipped. 'Just practical. This is in compensation, you understand, for the weeks that will be lost. You do understand it's a secret, that she'd never accept our charity, which is why it's going through the channel of Age Matters.'

A frown afflicted The Lark's forehead as he spotted some irregularity on one of his screens. 'It'll be a relief to me, I can tell you. Been trying for years to persuade her. I can't bear to see Gloria suffering like that. However stoical she is.' He pointed to her screen, where the room was eerily empty. The look on his face was that of an old-time ally.

'She's on her way?'

'That's right,' said The Lark. 'She'll be here in twenty minutes, do go into the pantry and make yourself at home. You can count on my discretion.'

'I trust so.'

He pushed back the curtain and steadied himself against the table. But even taking his time, making himself at home didn't prove easy, not with his suit sticking to the sweat, and the dizziness that threatened blackout from one moment to the next.

When, after a struggle, he was down to just his vest, he opened his briefcase and began removing the items he'd prepared, arranging them carefully on the mantelpiece.

First, a copy from the Registry of Deaths, on which the demise of James Lofgren, 'By hanging', on 4 June 1968, was recorded. Then, blown up from microfilm, an extract from *The Scotsman* obituaries, whose bald announcement he read over to himself: 'By suicide, Mr James Lofgren, of no fixed abode, former seaman, leaving no known kin.' And finally a man, dressed in a sharp '60s suit, his arm round a young and glamorous Gloria, caught in a moment of time, mid-samba.

He took out his Nokia and dialled Deirdre's pre-recorded number. 'So it's on for tomorrow?' he asked tersely. 'Right, I'll arrange the driver, he's an old acquaintance.' The look on his face, as he spoke, was an indecipherable mix of duty and despair. 'Don't worry, I'll be at your side from the moment she's under anaesthetic.'

Only when the final arrangements were made, did he at last stretch out on the table.

'This is for you,' The Lark announced, when Gloria had absorbed her fill of his French-cigarette smoke, and was grappling to her feet. 'She's a grand lass, your niece.'

In the relative privacy of the hall, she read the fax, which begged: 'Please call me, Auntie Gloria, I'm worried about you.'

She limped back to where The Lark was engrossed in his screens. 'If by any chance Laura calls me,' she told him, 'then say I'll ring when I'm through. It's a promise.'

The few yards between The Lark's den and her pantry had never seemed longer. But by taking them one step at a time, she traversed them.

'I see you've been preparing,' she launched, determined to speak first, 'Mr Hyde.'

He might have been on a mortician's table, for all the reaction she received. Except for the solitary bit of him that was ostentatiously alive.

'I'm afraid I have to tell you that I may be gone for a few weeks. The Lark'll let you know when I'm back in business.'

There was no show of surprise. There was no show at all.

She was well on her way to the toiletries table, when she froze, mid-hobble.

At last, he turned on the table in order to study her reaction, as she scrutinised the items arrayed on the mantelpiece. For a split-second her hand reached out instinctively towards the photograph. Then, like an officer on guard duty forced to watch a snake crawl up his trouser leg, she held her arm in check.

'You've been hard at work, I see.'

He was studying her so minutely that the skin tightened attractively across her face.

'You didn't think of calling yourself Rebus?' she suggested, as she moistened her palms with oil. 'Or Burke for that matter? Or Hare?'

His voice, when finally it emerged, sounded like it came from someone lying on top of him. 'And now the tomb's been desecrated?'

The smile with which she was set to answer him was spoiled, just before it arrived, by a grimace, as if she'd been stabbed.

'I don't believe you'll be needing these,' he muttered, pointing at her oily palms.

'What?' she managed. 'Like when you were a lad, in your wet dreams? Or on your bike without the stabilisers: Look, Mummy, no hands?'

Still, he did not smile.

'What'll you have me do, then?'

On this, he was decisive: 'Just stand here, where I can get to you.'

She staggered, unassisted, to the side of the table. 'Just stand here, you say. *Just* stand here?'

With his right arm out, he checked she was within reach. The brush of his fingers was enough to make her whole body convulse in pain.

'I only have to wave,' she sighed, when she'd recovered enough to speak, 'and The Lark'll be in here like a shot, baseball bat to the ready.'

Finally, he looked her in the eyes. 'But you wouldn't do that, now, would you?' he gasped. 'Not on this, our last encounter.'

9.

NAVEL

WHEN HELEN GOT cornered by Haring in the library cafeteria shortly before closing time, amid the moulded plastic, the Twix wrappers, and the images of impending eclipse, she prayed he wouldn't ask her for evidence of her research. She forgot, in her panic, that he had as little wish to read about the rituals of Covenanting as she had motivation to write on them.

'That's a bit of luck,' he cheered. 'I was just thinking you were the one for the job.'

It was so untrue that it was impossible to feel flattered.

'It's on behalf of our own dear Darling. He wants us to find some word which he believes holds the key to the mysteries of Mexican golf, thereby to the completion of the opus magnum.'

Poor Professor Darling: Head of Department, yet butt of all his colleagues' jokes. It pained her, the way they made fun of him and the book they were convinced he'd never complete. Her sympathy came not just because of her junior version of the self-same problem with completion. No, he was the only one in the Department who continued to treat her like before.

'It would only mean looking through some dictionaries. Seeing if there's anything that corresponds. Easy stuff, Helen, for a miracle-worker like yourself.'

She wondered how he dared, given she hadn't managed a stroke of work in nearly a year, ever since Japes (Professor Jasper) had dropped her as a lover, oblique stroke, Professor Jasper (Japes) had dropped her as a student.

'You could pack it into tomorrow,' Haring persisted, 'and still be free for the eclipse.'

Her mother, when she mentioned the Department, was merciless. 'If Darling's dead wood,' she said, 'then he should be floated down the river for logging.' She couldn't say a good word about Japes, obviously, that 'antique vulture' as she called him. So: 'Your Dr Haring sounds a likely lumberjack.'

'I see you hesitate,' Haring sighed, loading three heaped sugars into a beaker overflowing with thin grey liquid. 'But as your official supervisor —'

'My official supervisor?' At least she didn't let him away with that.

'As your supervisor, I should encourage you to consider your name on the acknowledgements page, not to mention my undying gratitude.'

He wasn't even a senior lecturer, yet already he was a creep. He didn't believe for a second that his Head of Department's book, never mind the acknowledgements page, would get written, and his own so-called gratitude would be expressed in the Aberdonian brogue with which it delighted him to baffle her.

'That's right,' he condescended, 'take time to think about it.'

As bad days went, and they did go, daily, this had been a stinker. Protracted indulgence in the worst of her weaknesses.

'So you've been at it again,' her mother would say, on her nightly phone call. 'I can tell it from your voice. You've been navel-gazing again, instead of getting out there and achieving.' Her mother would follow up, as she always did, with a reminder of how it had well-nigh destroyed her daughter between the ages of twelve and seventeen: day after day turned in upon herself, as if she were the be-all and end-all of creation.

'You on then, Helen?' Haring pushed. 'It's just a gesture that's required, so we can tell him we tried.'

Her mother had never understood that all her repeated warnings had achieved was to confirm her in her habit; while turning her navel – no mere figure of speech now, the literal one situated some unthinkable place on her person – into the site of virtually every anxiety and woe.

'Hmm?'

Maybe this challenge would be good for her: not just helping Poor Professor, stuck in the wilds of Mexico, but forcing the amorphous grey sludge which had once been her brain into a mould not of her own making, for a day. Maybe she'd even convince the Lumberjack – he had burnt his tongue on the coffee, at least – that she wasn't ripe for pulping.

'So, I'll do it.'

And the day began well.

Up early, she avoided turning on the telly, assisted by the idea that it would be full of star-gazers. She took a shower, even washed her hair.

True, she then stood in front of the mirror for the statutory fifteen minutes, torturing the flesh of her upper thighs and flanks. In the eleven months since the bust-up she'd put on nearly three stone, requiring her to find ever more injurious terms for the sight that greeted her every morning: for the orange skin (traditional); the cottage cheese (more accurate, and with pineapple chunks); the pebbles from Zogeria beach held in a cheesecloth sack (she rounded it off with a private reference, tailor-made to wound).

True, she did that. But she also tried what might turn into a whole new regime, skipping the bus, walking all the way from her Viewforth bed-sit to the University Library, via The Meadows, past enthusiasts staking out their turf for tomorrow's dimming of the sun.

And still she was one of the first among the stacks when the Library opened at nine. Up in Reference, she joined the few remaining researchers who'd found nowhere to go for their holidays, as was her case, or who had work overdue, as was her case – horribly.

If the first five minutes were almost fun, lugging dictionaries to her desk, stirring memories of before the debacle, when she'd still been able to concentrate, the next ten were troubling. Everyone else's research, including Poor Professor Darling's, seemed so much more compelling than her own.

Even when she'd arrived from the South, hadn't there been something laboured, artificial, about showing how the Covenanters, with their allegiance to The Guid Book, their desire to have a direct line to God, were mired in ritual and romance? And that was before her initial ideas had been twisted to fit in with Professor Jasper (as he was then). He had insisted that the Anthropology, not the History or Divinity Department, was the right home for such work, and he himself the right person to supervise her, even if he would soon be up for retirement.

So it was nearly half an hour before she was really geared up to start.

At which point, just as she was about to open the dictionaries and set to work she was distracted again, by an old classmate crossing George Square. He'd been on the MA, and now he'd already finished his PhD, something genuinely anthropological, on the hunting habits of an Ecuadorian tribe. Since then an offer of publication from OUP, she'd heard, and maybe even a job interview.

Why was it, Helen asked herself, sometime around mid-morning, that architects designed libraries to ensure maximum distraction, making it virtually impossible not to waste time by staring out the window?

It was as if the authorities had done a survey and awarded the commission to the solitary designer who vowed he'd never spent a day in a library in his life. In summer the students had to shade their eyes, while book titles faded in the sun. In winter the enormous windows made hypothermia a realistic risk, as the hail lashed against the glass, until they turned the heat up so high that drowsiness was certain.

Not that that would have been so bad, had they only designed the place so it was fit for a nap. But no, she'd searched every inch of the building, and not a single comfortable spot. When people were still talking to her, she'd done a private survey which confirmed that everybody – everybody, Jasper-Japes included – wanted the same thing from a library: a place to be quiet, private, a protective cell away from the eyes of the world.

What they got was a parody of an open-plan office but without the titillation.

Pushing aside the unopened dictionaries, Helen scrutinised the users as they wandered in: occasional members of the public, disoriented regulars who chose their desks with a precision a computer would envy, so as to be as diametrically distant from everyone else as possible. With six of them inside, the whole floor felt full. She could hear a fart at fifty yards, or watch a sentence being transferred verbatim from text to essay, despite the wiles of the cheat.

Lunch came hard on the heels of this digression, consisting of a Mars Bar and a packet of crisps in the basement cafeteria. She scoffed them on her feet, though her legs were trembling from the exertion of The Meadows. In case Haring should burst in, she pretended to be absorbed in the planets pinned to the grimy grey walls.

Elizabeth David and Marcella Hazan were her mother's sacred scribes. Her present diet was because of her mental state, she reassured herself, and the can of Irn-Bru a temporary blip. It was the Mars that summoned the Twix. And she had enough lucidity left to ask herself what she was really mourning when she rued the day that Marathon became Snickers.

Back upstairs, the afternoon dissolved, along with her guilt about Poor Professor Darling, who would be failing to finish his book again, this time because of her. The Mars, the Twix, and the Snickers dissolved too, under the acid additives of the Irn-Bru.

For a daring minute she thought of opening her own notes.

Three months, Haring had judged back in September (when he 'inherited her', as he put it). Three months to write it up. The research had been done, as far as he could see, and she seemed to have proved her point about the Covenanters' dependence on magic and mediums. (He'd dropped the Aberdonian brogue for once, so he may even have been sincere.) Which meant that she could be applying for jobs by the spring. Not in Edinburgh, obviously, he was swift to add, no openings here for the foreseeable future . . . Though elsewhere, surely, where she'd stand a very good chance, given – his voice lowered and his eye twitched – given the reference she could expect from . . . her favourite professor.

And she really was about to – surely – open her notes, get stuck in, when at precisely that moment a man with a moustache had to be watched as he crossed George Square, with a particularly urgent air about him.

Not an academic, she decided, but a lawyer on his way to sell a house. Or an MSP on his way to the Scottish Assembly. Or a brain surgeon en route to an urgent operation . . .

It was better, she persuaded herself, if marginally, than the day before, when she'd spent most of the afternoon watching an ant, which had somehow broken into the library to make off with the remains of her Twix.

Everybody – every ant! – with a sense of urgency, such clear-cut lives to live.

The vision of the moustachioed man didn't last long, objectively at least and there wasn't an ant in sight. But by four o'clock the spectre was visible of another evening at home, staring at the walls or listening to her mother drone into the answering machine, with her never-ending remedies for what she called 'The Depression' (capital T, capital D).

If only the walls were bare. If she'd had the courage to scrap the mementos: The Pet Shop Boys poster commemorating the one concert she convinced Japes to go to; Raeburn's painting of the skater that he gave her in the second month; the dog-eared map of the Isle of Spetses. Or if she'd even managed to chuck the box of Courabié biscuits bought on the island, with the logo whose faulty grammar Japes liked so much – 'For almost a century, high quality products and tradition are synonymous.' Or stopped repeating it to herself like a mantra. Or thrown the pebbles. Or at least unhitched the lengths of twine with which, after weeks of persuading, he had finally agreed to tie her up.

As if an extra few minutes would have done it, she was the last one out the building when it closed at five-thirty.

'I spent the day among the dictionaries,' she reported, from the phone box on Minto Street, omitting to mention that she'd never actually opened them. 'Couldn't find a single thing that corresponded to 'Duano', not in any of the languages or dialects of Central Mexico.'

Haring was out of breath. 'Not to worry,' he said. 'We've made the gesture. I'll email Darling tonight and tell him that the only equivalent we can find is some word in Nahuatl . . . signifying what . . . ?'

She knew he didn't expect her suggestion.

'Dead donkey! Signifying dead donkey! That'll do the trick.' Breathless though he was, he still managed to laugh at his own joke.

The Tucan Wine Bar was as hooked on the eclipse as everywhere else, a TV blasting out predictions about the weather, the sun's gases, protective spectacles. But at least the place was new, only having opened in the past ten months, which promoted it to a memory-free zone.

'A glass of white' would require opening her mouth, which meant her shame might spill out. So Helen pointed instead, until the barman got the idea.

She took her drink to a corner where she would be almost invisible, but to the folk at the bar. And they were more interested in the images on TV, humans now, not planets – if it qualified as human, Patrick Moore flailing round like a pantomime horse, his left arm attempting to point at the moon.

The wine's sharp metallic taste woke up her tongue, first alcohol in weeks. Normally, she limited herself to water with the meat pie she microwaved on weekdays; Coca-Cola with the M&S curry at weekends. Not that gulping down the wine was probably such a great idea, though if it went to her head, she thought, it might convince her she had one.

And now her glass was full again, as if by magic.

The rest were glued to the pantomime horse. So it had to be the dark-haired guy at the bar – hadn't she seen him in the library?

If this drink was on him, then presumably refusal was in order, even though she felt like accepting it, given that the first glass had barely begun to numb her.

Was rebuffing men like riding a bike? Even with two years out of the saddle, would it come back to her? Failing that, she reckoned, if he came over to pester her, this poor fool with money to burn, she could claim to be a foreigner. More of a foreigner than she really was, fluent only in Finnish or Urdu. Though an Urdu accent would probably be less off-putting to the locals, it occurred to her, than her Home Counties twang.

Wasn't it one of the things her mother had insisted on? That she was blind to the narrowness of the Scottish mind, Edinburgh in particular? Nothing like Cambridge, her mother always said, where along with Germaine at Newnham College, even if she hadn't known her personally, she had lived her greatest glories.

Had she been blind?

True, when she arrived she was full of the charms of the New Town, which was surely one-up on her mother's home-town, Bath. Buoyed up on her first-class degree from London, where she had come good after a slow start, even enthusiastic, in a vicarious way, for the foundation stones in the Museum of Scotland. Here was a place, she thought, as distinct from the cynical South where all that mattered was the price of property, here was a place where the spirit of the Covenanters hadn't died out entirely, where ideals still counted.

Did that mean blind?

Backs were now turned, awkward silences when she entered the room, furrowed brows and occasional sniggers. But maybe that was because she had betrayed the Ideal. If she was a small-time pariah, then maybe it was precisely because of national pride, or some code she'd infringed, on fidelity, duty, proportion?

Not that, for her, this was the worst thing. The worst thing didn't concern the others. No, the worst thing concerned Japes and Japes alone. The worst thing, for the moment at least, was that it was exactly a year since he'd invited her to Delphi.

Having decided to accept, she threw another drink down the hatch, with some effects at last.

The light was faint, admittedly, in her corner of the bar. Added to the fact that she always kept covered up. Yet the bloke at the bar had to be short-sighted or desperate to be wasting his hard-earned cash – the third glass was a 'chilled Sancerre', according to the waiter – on someone whose hair resembled rags and whose breasts were drooping, though she wasn't yet thirty.

He'd be better doing like the others, Helen thought, and sticking to TV. She seemed to be the only one unable to derive a thrill from the fact that for a couple of minutes the sun would be obscured.

'Would you like a change of flavour?' asked the note on the napkin that came with the glass. 'Or of colour?'

What she really wanted was to be left alone to her thoughts, however lugubrious they were proving.

She had to strain to focus on the bar. 'Red!' she mouthed, finally getting the idea across when she pointed at the crimson wall behind her.

He had claimed, Japes, that the choice of Delphi had nothing to do with his work. He'd already published his monograph on the sacred sites of Greece. And that in any case he'd forgotten all about work since falling in love with her – 'As irretrievably as only an old fool could,' he said, 'worthy of my nickname at last.'

Before she'd even accepted the invite, the emailed objections were clogging up her computer, on top of the Fed-Ex deliveries from Bath – 'Seems Mother,' Japes joked, 'is a full-time member of the vice squad.'

Despite which objections, spoken and written, Delphi was about to happen, until she dipped into a guide-book. The sanctuary had meant a great deal to the ancient world, Helen learned, with its magical Temple of Apollo at whose core was housed the omphalos, marking the centre of the earth, where the eagles had crossed, released from East and West by Zeus.

She'd had to run to the toilet, to avoid throwing up over the definition: for omphalos, read *navel-stone*!

A scene she might have to re-enact soon, she realised, if she kept on downing them at this rate. Which might not be so bad, maybe clear the system out, lose a pound or two. At least compared with the worst thing, the truly worst thing, now, fatal and unavoidable, which was that despite it all – Damn her! – her mother had been right.

Germaine notwithstanding, and for the wrong reasons no doubt, her own frustrations speaking, her hormones congealing amidst the Dalton china and the solid silver service, menopausal regrets for Newnham, an academic career she claimed she might have had, but for the side-track into stockbroking, but for Helen's father – whichever one he was.

In the early days, when she would run through it, she'd hoped each time would be the last. Whereas now it had become more of a daily routine. She replayed it the way other people go to the cinema, the way her hairdresser said her grandmother used to go to *The Sound of Music*, so frequently that they'd ended up letting her in for free.

For full cinematic effect, she had to shut her eyes and take a deep breath . . .

That this Jasper Vulture, with his one foot in the grave, might even be telling the truth, in that this might indeed be the first time he had fallen – yes, fallen – but that this didn't stop it being utterly classic, as if taken from some Merchant Ivory film. That he came from a totally different generation, painfully pre-Greer. That, having conquered Helen's young body, his pride would make him incapable of keeping it a secret. That in any case Edinburgh wouldn't be big enough for such indiscretions – even Bath was not. That she would open him up to pleasures and delights – she granted her daughter this, for she was her mother's child – which he would then, in a second infancy whose laws were as immutable as those of the first, feel obliged to try out with others of her ilk. That he would forget he'd once claimed to be expert on the rituals of Covenanting and shunt her on to some junior colleague who would treat her with fear and derision. That she was acting like a total frump, as if feminism had never happened, worse than that daughter out of *Absolutely Fabulous*. That once the word was out, her friends would keep their distance, and she'd find herself alone in a country that, for all it was part of the United Kingdom, was more foreign than France or Turkey. That she would receive rancorous calls, if not from the aggrieved old bag herself then from Japes's grown-up daughters, both of whom (her sources informed her) were figures in Edinburgh society. That in the end, of course, after his bout of madness, he would return, tail between his spindly legs, to his all-forgiving wife, for the meantime at least. While she, Helen, precisely because she'd been raised to be more than a stereotype, to take an active role in managing her own life, would look back on the whole unfortunate episode as if it hadn't happened to her at all, but to a 'brainless baba' (she cited this phrase without revealing her source), who had fallen for every outdated trick in the book. Whereupon she would begin indulging in her favourite activity involving that preferred part of her anatomy – the part by which she had formerly been nourished by her devoted mother; an activity she scarcely dared name, so nefarious was it in her daughter's case, and which would involve raking endlessly over the past, including these very warnings, spoken and written, which she was doubtless about to ignore.

Helen was withering by the second when, thankfully, came a packet of cheese and onion crisps, served up with a third glass of red, and the compliments, via the waiter, of 'the gentleman at the bar'.

She was knocking them back as if there were no tomorrow, which in some sense was right, since it would be exactly the same as today, eclipse notwithstanding.

'Thought you'd be more c & o than salt & vinegar,' announced the coaster. 'Have you bought your eclipse glasses yet?' Next to a signature: 'D-D'.

At least, she thought, if it had been the doomsday version of sunlessness. But in Edinburgh it would no doubt be only a bit missing, on the side, just like the rest of her life.

She'd barely taken a swig before the waiter was back. And, from the way he was hovering, this note expected a reply.

'Mind if I join you for a drink?'

Well, did she mind?

Another few glasses and she would be past minding anything at all. Sustaining a conversation would be an effort, as would fending him off. But with any luck, if he came closer, he'd be repulsed by the marshmallow he'd discover.

'Ten more minutes,' she scribbled on the coaster.

Of course, she thought, normally she'd have gone through it all during the afternoon in the library. But avoiding the dictionaries had eaten into her time. And once started, it was dangerous to stop mid-show.

It was a mystery, why, when she'd vetoed Delphi, Japes chose Spetses. For her part, she couldn't remember her mother ever having mentioned it – she was full of the Cyclades ('barring Mykonos,' she wailed, 'now it's become a gay ghetto'). And neither Zeus nor Apollo had ever made it the centre of anything.

She had helped him to pack, since by then he had a pile of his things at her flat, and had convinced him to discard some of the more fusty items, including the garters, the Brownie camera, the *Ancient Greek Lexicon* by Liddell and Scott. ('I don't suppose I'm allowed my pith helmet either,' he joked.) The plane had left from Prestwick at a romantically late hour, though he had felt obliged to apologise for it, cursing himself for skimping on a charter.

She'd hoped to see dolphins from the prow of the boat that carried them to the island, their eyes stinging from salt spray and lack of sleep. For a moment, as they disembarked, she expected the port policeman to hand her a telegram from her mother. But he only stopped to wish her and her father a pleasant stay on Spetses.

She didn't complain when Japes refused the horse-drawn carriage along the front, lugging their bags instead as far as the Yachting Club, where he'd felt obliged to haggle down the price from 14,000 to 12,000 drachmas a night. A lemon on the window-sill set off the turquoise of the sea, which she could almost reach out and touch. Before he kissed her, he wanted to hang up his short-sleeved shirts. A kitten chased its mother along the wall. Its erect little tail, she told him, sparing him the 'little', reminded her of his penis. He confessed to her what she'd known for months, about the Viagra, and she pretended to be amazed.

And later, once he'd got his strength back, she convinced him to hire a scooter – he claimed he'd been too old when they first hit the market. She sat pillion as he drove round the island, picking out spots for future swims; lighting on Zogeria Bay as their own private paradise, where he would be hunter-gatherer and she would be his prey – the roles were reversible, he hastened to add.

Those pebbles in paradise were so pink and smooth, she wanted to put them in his mouth.

And the only cloud over the whole ten days came when, in an awkward attempt to reciprocate, he forgot her problem and tried to insert one into that special place of hers, where in any case it would not fit.

She managed to restrain herself from striking him, but she swam out so far that he panicked and tried to summon the navy. Then she refused to speak to him for twenty-four hours. Until, at a loss for an escape route from Greek-Island Coventry, as desperate as if he'd crashed the scooter or passed her a fatal infection, he hired a two-masted schooner for the day, skipper and all, which he invited her to board, flowers in hand, by walking out of their hotel room straight into the sea.

There was a cheesecloth sack of these pebbles in her handbag when they arrived back at Prestwick.

In a solitary gesture which her mother might have been proud of, she swung it at his daughters who were waiting at Arrivals, with news of their mother's attempted suicide.

(Half-hearted attempt, her own mother judged.)

'Eh, a euro for your thoughts,' came a nervous-sounding voice.

Not that they were worth an old-fashioned penny, in Helen's own estimation: just lint picked up abroad. 'Holidays,' she forced out, amazing herself with the sound of her own voice.

'You mind if I join you?'

Too tired, tipsy, too pleased she can follow his accent, to say 'No.'

'What is it with holidays?' he asked, from the narrow bench facing her. 'I've this mate, Stod . . .'

They always had friends, she remembered, who were always more interesting than themselves. Not that he'd be totally unattractive, if he weren't so short and eager – and woozy to boot, presuming he'd been keeping pace with her.

'Stod's one of the Famous Four, that's what Simon's sister Laura calls our gang. Anyway, so Stod's off to Tuscany for his. Everyone's on about where they've booked their next holiday. He's not even staying for the eclipse. It must be the crap Scottish weather.'

'Probably,' she agreed.

'I've seen you in the Library. I go up there on my time off. Films, screenplays, and that.'

His voice was almost acceptable, so long as no articulate answer was expected. 'Too much wine.' She counted out the monosyllables. He had strong worker's hands, that made a welcome change.

Did he notice her staring? Was that why he reached out? 'Dan's the name,' he said. 'Though my friends call me Dan-Dare.'

Thirty-six hours Japes had lasted, post-Spetses, before his nerve gave out.

Her mother told her to demand it in writing that his breach of professional conduct would not be detrimental to her career.

Three weeks later she was reassigned to Lumberjack Haring, who knew as much about Covenanting as she knew about his own speciality: voodoo.

Two months later Professor Jasper was spotted at a conference in Bradford with an undergrad in tow, five years her junior.

'Come here often?' The words blurted out of her.

He shook his head and smiled. 'More of a pub man myself. But I was hoping to see Stod, who's off to Tuscany, or get introduced to his lady-friend Una, more like.'

It was as good a reason as her own, no doubt, even if it did sound odd.

'No luck though,' he plunged on boozily. 'So I spent my time more profitably.'

Was she really showing enquiry in her eyes?

'More profitably as I was, like . . . eh . . . like, you know . . .'

Helen should pick on someone her own age, her mother moaned. Or find some young fresher with testosterone to burn.

She soon tired of claiming that nobody was interested in Japes's hand-me-downs.

'Like, you know . . .' persisted Dan-Dare, 'in that I was admiring you.'

Helen knew her lip mustn't curl. She should be thankful he wasn't calling her 'Darlin'.

Her admirer's glass was shaking as it rose to his lips. 'It's a bit like the eclipse, you see?'

'Like the eclipse?' There was something she'd missed in his conceit. 'How's that?'

'Call me Dan-Dare, please.'

'Right, Dan – or Dare. So how's that?'

He chewed on his moustache. 'The eclipse,' he stammered, blushing redder than he already was. 'I was thinking how it was like . . .' His eyes rolled round for help. 'A bit like . . . like . . . if you don't mind me saying it . . .'

It could be rabies, Helen thought, with eyes like that. Until they finally came to rest.

'I was going to say: a bit like your belly-button.'

So there really was a final straw. This proved it.

It wasn't enough that her mother had the right to go on about it endlessly, that people tried to shove stones into it, but now the name of her neurosis was branded on her brow for perfect strangers to read.

'I don't think I can have heard you right. Say that again?'

No hesitation now. 'I said it reminds me of your belly-button. All circular and beautiful. Or as my mate Simon might say – he's the eloquent one of the Famous Four . . .' Dan-Dare was so busy rummaging for a word that he missed her look of amazement. 'It's like, shelestial,' he slurred. 'Like stellar. You should sell special glasses in case it drives us blind.'

Helen had heard of Sod's law, but this was something worse, almost eerie. Frozen to her seat, suddenly stone-cold sober, it was only in some far chamber of her mind that Dan, or Dare, was coming on strong, and that she ought to be resisting.

What in hell was he saying? Didn't she make a point of always buying extra-long T-shirts to be certain they stayed tucked in? She dared not look down, but her fingers crawled towards her midriff, not having far to go since it was coming down to meet her over the belt of her jeans.

Trying to cover up would be thumb-bashing. She had to play cool, for another few minutes, until out of here and home, where she could punish herself in private. If he'd stuck his tongue in her ear, it would have been child's play by comparison. Given which, why in God's name was she chirping, 'You mean to say, it's a beacon in the night sky?'

With his face more relaxed, he looked less like Robin Cook. He leaned across the table. 'Think *2001: A Space Odyssey*,' he crooned. 'The final scenes from *Men in Black*, when they gaze back from space at the beautiful wee disc of the earth.' He could almost begin to look pleased with himself. 'Not that I'm usually so bold, despite my name.'

How much longer was she required to keep up the act? She wanted to stretch out on her bed and let the sobs start. 'And does it drive creatures wild,' she asked, 'the way they're saying the eclipse does?'

'Animals climb the walls,' he drawled, gaining in confidence. 'Humans climb trees and start to howl, like in that Fellini film . . . Others make it their goddess and begin to pray to it . . . Though I'm the High Priest, the only one allowed to adore it in person.'

Surely, now, she should adjust her attire and leave. Very soon.

'I'm a Covenanter,' she slurred, trying to mollify her Home Counties' accent. 'One of those who signed the pact in Greyfriars Kirk, just a stone's throw from here, so they wouldn't have to be ruled by cardinals or kings.' It was a bit of a distortion, but she stamped on the pedant reminding her. 'Being adored is overrated.'

'Right, right, you're more Xena Warrior Princess,' he cheered. 'We're talking Merlin, Druids, Moses in the film of *The Ten Commandments*. Commandment number one: Thou shalt not cover thyself!'

'I've got to go soon,' Helen reminded herself more than announced.

'Stuff that!'

'Not that I want to deprive you earthlings of your Milky Way.' What was she saying? 'Or your Snickers.' It was an awful pun, she ought to be ashamed of herself.

He was busy scribbling on a coaster.

'Here,' he said. 'Here. I'd be really pleased if you rang this pagan up – if we survive the Big Day, that is. I meant what I said —'

'Even if your pal Simon would have put it better?'

It was exactly the nasty sort of thing her mother would have said. She wanted to take it back, apologise, ask him to forgive her.

But – 'You can't be keeping it to yourself,' he groaned, before she had the chance. 'It's a wonder of creation, it is, the corona on the path of totality!'

Maybe she should watch it after all, she decided, the moon taking a bite out the sun.

She was teetering when she got to her feet, but it was only when out in the night air that the drink really hit her.

She'd take a day off from wasting her time in the library.

Fuck the Lumberjack. Fuck Japes. Fuck the Covenanters.

She'd lie on her back in The Meadows. Yes, and if it really was going to be semi-dark, then why not in halter-neck and shorts.

HANDS/HEELS

THE CANCER WHICH they insist started in my spine – 'Your spine, Mr Somerville, your spine not your neck' – has spread so widely that doctors can no longer tell me from it. In order to finish everywhere, finishing me. The consultants refuse to be drawn on this, of course, though one young doctor, Darling according to her name tag, was kind enough not to deny it when I told her I had only days left to live.

But I didn't start writing so as to talk about my disease-eroded parts. Everything down to the funeral arrangements, taken care of, including the last will and testament, safe in the safe at Somerville & Glen, Legal Practice: half to Ric, my more or less estranged son; half to Gloria (whose address I tracked down). Everything taken care of – everything but the clamour of regrets visiting my bedside when the morphine wears off, the most insistent, making all the others jealous as it gropes at my pyjamas and shakes me.

But didn't I say I wasn't going to moan about what's left of me?

So Bermuda, 1966.

I'm twenty-four years old and my sister, Adelpha, is twenty-two. Our parents four years in the family grave, both victims of yellow fever. Working the docks by day – I'm built like my father, and can lift a 100 lb sack of flour in each arm, go on lifting for hours – I'm able to study in the evening, with the ambition of becoming a lawyer like my grandpa. I finish my day, bathe in Whale Bone Bay, before wrestling at night-school with the intricacies of tort, contract law, the verdicts handed down at the Old Bailey, four thousand miles away, by which folks on the island are still judged and punished.

I know what people say: that Adelpha looks so little like me, with her dark olive skin and crinkly hair, that our mother must have done the dirty. She jokes about it too, my sister, more so since we've been left alone to run the family cottage and the patch of land out back. Jokes about how I should watch her more closely or she'll turn out a wild one too; how I should kick the men who come sniffing her out, hanging round the veranda – though she'd soon enough complain if I really did. It's she who watches over me, more like, cooks her stews, which are simmering when I come home from class, my sheets clean. When she marries, she says, she'll make her husband take me in, at least until I'm at the bar. She could never leave her Archie, her only kith and kin.

I've gone over it often enough in my mind, but I'm still not sure when I first became aware of one man hanging round more than another, offering bunches of flowers, boxes of shortbread and crudely bound packages of a foul-smelling meat that called itself 'haggis'. First thing I remember for sure is a dinner. When I came in from class, my head reeling from judicial reviews, my muscles aching from sacks of rice, there was Adelpha dancing in the sitting-room to a record, rumba blaring on a gramophone he's brought. I watch them through the window. He dances well, and in his arms my sister looks gracious, despite her shabby frock, beautiful all over, with her exquisite long fingers – pianist's hands without the piano.

What should I call him, the intruder in tartan? By the name he went by then, Norrie Patterson? Or by one of the many names he adopted during his flight – Rat Richards, Dormant Wood, Tarrie McPhail, or, most cruelly, Hank Hands? Or should I use Jamie Lofgren, the assumed name under which he was sheltering, hopeful he'd thrown me off the scent, when I uncovered him in Edinburgh?

That first dinner, the Scotsman talked about his life as a sailor. It's all still fresh to me more than thirty years on. He was not much older than I was, and he had a smooth handsome face, a bit like the young

Sinatra, Brylcreemed hair. But the way he talked, over the rum, he might have been our grandfather, with a pipe, a beard, and brine on his clothes. I'd met sailors aplenty, but few of them could spin their yarns like this. He'd been everywhere, from Zanzibar to Colombo, from Perth to Reykjavik. He told us how he'd got drunk in Samoa and passed out under a statue, which he only realised on awakening the next day was of his compatriot, Robert Louis Stevenson.

Later, from his knapsack, he pulls a bottle of Scotch unlike any I've ever tasted. It doesn't burn the throat but makes me think of History, makes my head more lucid, not cloudier, before it takes its toll. I had never left our island, except out fishing. I had never been up in an aeroplane.

Norrie danced with my sister while I sank beneath the Scotch. I didn't dare check where she was sleeping when I finally awoke, in the small hours.

I can't seem to get my tenses consistent. But in whichever tense I write of those days and weeks, whether I use present or past, they are here now, in my hospital bed, as much as they ever were during my months of vagrancy and pursuit.

The other dockers told me I should be stricter on my sister. I thought they were just jealous, each of them wanted a share of Adelpha's olive favours. This was the 1960s, even in an outpost like Bermuda. I listened to the radio, I heard of rock and roll and free love, I saved up and bought records by the Beatles, which I played on Norrie's gramophone.

Later I would ask myself, frustrated in some one-dollar dive in Puerto Rico or Panama, if my rage was really just guilt. If I should've been firmer with Adelpha, more the macho brother out to save his sister's honour, and if my life devoted to revenge was just my way of avoiding self-reproach. But then I felt my hands tingle – my hands. Legal niceties, I told myself (I'd abandoned my law degree, but I still had the notions). Despite the shame I felt, there was enough rage left in me to keep me on his tail, by boat, rail, foot, by day and by night.

Two months or so after that first meal, he watches his ship cruise out of the Sound, Adelpha by his side. She's wearing a tartan mohair scarf, incongruous in the Bermudan heat. On the quay there's a whole crate of haggis – I'm almost used to its rancid taste by now. I see: flies, the white roofs of the cottages, Adelpha's new dress, the complacent smile on the marooned sailor's face.

What did he want from us? Did I ever figure that out? Adelpha was exquisite, but he must have met other beauties in other ports. We had no money but what I earned each week and our family home was going to ruin. Maybe he really was in love with her, though I tried, afterwards, to obliterate this thought. There were the songs he'd sing, of his boyhood, filling the whole house: 'Will ye no come back again, will you no . . .' He told me my ancestors must be Scottish, what with my freckles and interest in law. He insisted on teaching me to swing a golf club. He made himself useful round the house, fixing nets, bicycle wheels, storm blinds. Adelpha made progress in her dancing, and twice a week he would take her to Flanagan's, returning full of grumbles about how the natives of an exotic island should have a better sense of rhythm.

The alibi of his room in the boarding-house was dropped. He talked about marriage, claimed he'd found a way of making money on nautical insurance.

I almost got used to his songs, his hunt on the World Service for football results, his stories of poverty and flick-knives in the Gorbals of his native Glasgow.

October 1966, the typhoon warnings have passed; it's the season for marlin-fishing. I've told him that, since he's recalked it, he can use the skiff that was once my father's. I've also told him that on no account is Adelpha to accompany him, not with the weather still uncertain, hooks and flying tackle, the dodgy outboard motor he's convinced a neighbour to lend him.

So they wait until I've left for work. They take the back path to Mangrove Bay, where the boat is moored. They push out and drift, sunbathing. Maybe they have sex, awkwardly, on the bottom of the boat. He sets the outboard and heads west, where he's been told the fishing is good.

With Adelpha stretched out under our mother's tattered Christian Dior parasol, he hooks and baits two lines, lets them out. Maybe the lovebirds speak to one another, maybe they are silent, listening to the morning and the throb of the outboard. He is a sailor, he should be noticing the storm clouds mounting in the east. But he's too busy staring at her in the shade of the parasol. So when the wind rises and the sea grows choppy, and the marlin bites, and the line runs out, and Adelpha panics, all that occurs to him is to turn up the throttle and head for the shore.

But he does this too abruptly, and my sister, who's on her feet, is sent reeling by the wave which hits the boat. She stumbles, falls, tangles her leg in the line which whips round, he fails to cut the throttle and she's overboard, her hand in the propeller blades, her pianist's fingers, her palm, her long lovely bones. He sees the puff of blood, hears her scream, he knows she is a poor swimmer, maybe he imagines sharks' fins, in the distance, roving; he can see a trawler less than a mile off, flashing to enquire if he's in trouble.

Does he panic? Or does he think: Fuck this, I'm out of here ('outah he-ar' in his Glaswegian accent), sick of all these folk in their ridiculous shorts with their obsession about rainwater. Maybe he's tired of her endless orgasmic moans and her pain-in-the-arse brother with his stevedore muscles and his lawyer's pretensions, she's probably half-caste in any case, how would that go down in Glasgow? That's if she were ever to condescend to leave this godforsaken isle, the grown-up baby she feeds every day and whose bed she still makes, amusing herself with the stains . . .

I'm only guessing, of course – what do I know.

He shears the lines, ignores her cries as he speeds towards the coast. By the time the trawler reaches Adelpha, she has lost the remainder of her left hand, and a shark has taken a chunk out of her right thigh. The shock and blood loss have almost finished her off.

Yet she could have survived. I know she could have survived.

For four days I sat at her hospital bedside, her other hand in mine, talking to her, coaxing her, telling her how she would be fine, her leg would heal, inventing absurd consolations for her lost hand which make me cringe, today, now I'm the one in the hospital bed.

She only ever said the one thing, over and over again: 'He sailed away and left me.'

When she did die, after more than a hundred hours in hospital, it wasn't because of a severed hand or a damaged leg. She died because he'd sailed away and left her.

When I abandoned the hospital, my head reeling with fatigue and grief and rage, he already had a four-day start. At the docks they told me which boat he'd left on. They tried to keep the 'told you so' look from their faces.

I saw my sister into the family grave, would have carried the coffin myself if the vicar had let me. He counselled me forgiveness, reminded me how in only two years I'd complete my studies. From what he knew of Adelpha, he said, she would be proud if I became a distinguished Bermudan lawyer and started a family.

I left the island that evening, working my passage to Rio.

All I took with me was the little cash I'd saved and the photograph of the two of them. He, seated in front of the cottage, Adelpha on his lap, his arm round her shoulder, laughing.

By the time I found someone who recognised him, in Rio, Norrie Patterson had become Rat Richards. Greased by a handful of *real* and a bottle of cheap Scotch, the tongue of another Scotsman told me how he had shaved his head, grown a beard. The Rat was somewhere in the Panama Canal by now, but he knew I would come after him wherever he was.

The ship I joined required double shifts. But what did I care so long as I arrived in Auckland before him.

I was waiting on the dock when his ship berthed. It was strange to have travelled so far and still understand the language. The passengers came off first, then, hours later, the crew. But no Rat.

'The Rat? What rat?'

I showed the sailor the photo.

'He's the one we know as Dormant Wood, don't ask me why. The captain had him up dancing, playing the gigolo for the passengers. Until he jumped ship in Fiji, taking my passport with him. If you ever find him, kick him in the balls for me.' The crewman sized me up, maybe sensed my rage. 'On second thoughts, since it's not me that wants him childless, make that the shin.'

It wasn't my feet that were itching, it was my hands. As if I didn't get enough exercise for them, working the hawsers, I squeezed a tennis ball whenever I was idle: each month I'd have to replace it.

There were days, of course, whole weeks, when I thought I'd lost his trail, despaired of ever finding him. One bleak day in Vladivostok, I almost threw myself into a crack in the ice. I had started to hallucinate that Adelpha had never existed, nor our life in Bermuda, that I'd dreamed them up to justify the rancour that was my sole reason for living. On another occasion, in Porto, I met the very same Scottish sailor who'd betrayed The Rat in Rio. He informed me that Hank Hands knew I was still on his trail. I drew slim satisfaction from the knowledge that he lived like a fugitive.

The world grows smaller when you've been round it a couple of times in a ship. In moments of fever or delirium I would imagine he'd left the earth's surface and buried into the planet's core, from which still point he was laughing at me. But the rest of the time, in Yokohama or Miami, I knew I would find him in the end. Time was on my side. Sooner or later he would have to head for home.

The tenements he used to talk about had mostly been pulled down by the time I made it to Glasgow. I showed the photo to the undernourished children playing amid the rubble. It was spring 1968, I had been moving for nearly eighteen months, no two nights in the same bed, unless that bed or bunk was itself in motion.

I fed them sweeties.

'That's Tarrie!' they shouted. 'Whae's re darkie burd?'

Another few bribes extracted the story, in an accent I struggled to understand, of how Tarrie had returned home in the winter, had said he couldn't settle, had moved to the capital.

It was a beautiful day with buds on the trees when I arrived in Edinburgh. I'd seen poorer cities, but never one more austere, with that castle up on its hill, and those rows of buildings they called the 'New Town', though they didn't look new to me.

I took a room in a boarding-house in Learmonth. As I wandered the city, I found it so different, so ordered, that I realised, for the first time that I could live somewhere, here, go on living, after my business was done – Bermuda was over for me, every minute I'd be thinking of Adelpha. There were lawyers everywhere, maybe I could qualify, at last, join the Establishment we used to hear so much about in the colony. I admit I even forgot, for whole hours at a time while wandering the gardens and parks, what remained to be done, before my new life could begin.

'What took you so long?' he says to me – 'Jamie Lofgren' he's now calling himself.

I thought I'd want to ask him: Why? But now he's in front of me, trembling, I no longer care. 'I thought I'd got you in Antofagasta, then again in Mogadishu.'

'And in Bari,' he says, 'in Singapore, in Port Canning – I saw you in all of them.'

'You could have stabbed me.'

'I guess I could have.'

He stands up and reaches into a drawer. Now, I think, he will shoot me. I should care, but I can't. But no, he pulls out a length of rope in which is tied a hangman's noose. He looks at my hands – one of them would suffice.

'You should save those for whatever you'll be doing next,' he says.

He puts the noose over his head himself, then hands me the rope.

'Don't you want to leave a note?' I ask. It's all happening so quickly, after so many months of anticipation, too quickly for me to take it in.

He thinks about it for a second. 'I wouldn't know what to say. I'd like it all to perish along with me.'

I can't get him to protract it. He doesn't even resist as I pull the noose tight, or when I hitch it onto the butcher's hook protruding from a beam, just the involuntary kicking of the legs as the impulse to live fights its last.

I clean my fingerprints from the door handle before I leave. I'm thinking about beginnings, endings . . .

That woman doctor I like, Dr Darling, came and sat at my bedside. 'You've been writing,' she said. 'Would you like to read me some?'

Suddenly the futility.

'Lies,' I told her. 'All lies, or nearly, and a very rushed denouement.'

She was too discreet to pry. For as long as she sat there, I didn't feel so bad. But when she left, with two hours until the next injection, the triteness of my invention – that's too dignified a word; of my lies, my lies – left me feeling emptier than ever.

What is certainly true is that Jamie changed me forever, in his death began my new life. His stories had been wheeling round my head for months, but only now he was gone could I make them my own. He'd opened up worlds, languages, lives. Though all I made of his legacy was to become an embittered and now cancerous lawyer, this fact shouldn't lead me to underestimate what he gave to me. With him out of the way, there was no looking back.

Until now, that is; when I have to look back further.

November 1967, Lochend Road, Edinburgh.

The first time I met Jamie, he was overtaking me on the stairs of the tenement. I'd heard him moving in two days before, though all he'd arrived with was a bed. What struck me was the box he was carrying, which was giving off an odour I'd never smelt before. He turned to me and I'm sure he grimaced. Unlike Bermudan Archie, whom I later saw on photographs, I am not – I mean was not, then, even before the cancer reduced me – 6 ft 4 in. of solid stevedore muscle. I was 5 ft 3 in., dumpy, ginger-headed, gnawed away from within by regrets, oozing eczema and pus which I'd no sooner buff, than, toadlike, I oozed them back again.

'You the downstairs neighbour?' he asked, adjusting his face to a smile.

'What's in the box?'

He found that funny, for some reason – the cocky bastard. 'That's Chinese cooking,' he said, as if it was the most natural thing in Lochend.

'What?' I said. 'All the way from China?' I'd squirt poison if he didn't stop laughing.

'All the way from the Chinese restaurant down Great Junction Street.'

I'd noticed it, just hadn't imagined anyone would actually risk their life eating that stuff.

'Aye, right,' I muttered, before retreating indoors, to Rita's recriminations about the midden of the flat.

The winter of 1967 was a vicious one, for me at least, home at dawn after seven hours in a night-watchman's hut, all the work I could find. Any relief I felt at release from the Portakabin, with its fag-ends and porno mags, turned to ice from the gale blowing down Lochend Road, straight from the Arctic, vinegar-sodden newspaper pokes whipping against my legs.

Rita would be getting up as I fell into bed. We were only twenty-six but we felt like sixty, already married nearly a decade. I'd long since given up vexing my nails against her nylon nightie. She resented me, of course, but wouldn't have known how to put it into words. I'd lie soaking up her heat, thinking it was all she was good for, a glorified human water-bottle, as I failed to get to sleep, listening, half-heartedly at first, then with real interest, more interest than I could summon for anything but the football results and the finer aspects of the Craft (the symbol of the Ashlar was much on my mind in those days) – I'd listen to the groans of my neighbour and whichever bird he'd picked up the night before. He told me he was into dancing, seemed like a jessies' game to me, but this was making me think again, the way he'd come back with a different bird each night, real yelpers too, some of them, and the occasional screamer, who would inspire me to have a go, unsuccessfully, at myself.

The afternoons would hardly have started before night fell, barely leaving me time to get up, fix my beans on toast, curse Rita for not getting in more exciting food. Of course, I'd have eaten beans on toast in any case, but why couldn't we have something interesting for a change, if neighbours were eating panda and bamboo, or whatever it was. I'd bash my head against the mystery of the Ashlar for a while, then I'd go upstairs. I'd heard the latest bird leaving, so I knew the coast was clear.

He'd be seated at the window, tumbler of rum at his side.

'Come away in, Ewey,' he'd say, though he knew I liked to be called by my full name, Ewan. 'What can I fix you?'

He didn't need to work, had saved a good wee bit, he explained to me, from his days on the ships, and was determined to spend it in style. He always looked dapper, with his flowery shirts and his tan, especially compared to me, of course, who was particularly noisome in that era.

'I was just going over in my mind,' Jamie would start, like he really had nothing else to do. Then he'd tell me about Samoa and the palm trees, about swimming over Granada coral reefs, about a lock of hair some sweetheart from the Falklands had given him – since lost, he claimed, though I didn't see how he could have lost such a treasure (I imagined it a sleek pelt, nothing like Rita's moleskin perm). He told me about a contest in Veracruz where you held onto a metal handle along with an opponent, and paid a torturer to crank up a generator until the electric current became so unbearable that one of you would crack.

He could fair spin a yarn, I'll say that for him, maybe that's why he went to sea in the first place. He told me about some French poet who ran arms, about Shogun before it became a TV series. He seemed to know something about everything, though he couldn't have been more than a year or two older than me. When he realised I was in the Craft, he told me about a Neapolitan prince called Raimondo di Sangro, from the 1700s, who was the first Grand Master of Italy. In his chapel, he said, along with a statue of a dead Christ covered in a veil, were corpses of his servants he'd murdered with some special fluid that froze their veins, so he could pull off their skin and inspect their arteries.

I was sitting in his front room in Lochend Road, on the crates and tea-chests he used for furniture. But in the meantime I was everywhere.

The bastard, I hated him already, and all he had experienced.

But I kept going back for more.

I'm not imagining the fact that the doctors, as they pass on their rounds, have to remind themselves that I'm really still alive, in mind if not body.

It did improve, my mind, after Jamie died. The seeds he planted sprouted, and the shoots I repotted, warmed and tended, so by the time Wee Ric was born (a horrible mistake from a rare drunken night, or that's what Rita claimed at least, and I must admit that the boy grew to resemble me, poor sod) I had an Open University degree, and a place in a new law practice on Howe Street. Nobody liked me much, that didn't change, but I was a devil for the details.

My mind improved but my body didn't, and even my own son

would turn away from me in distaste – when he grew big enough to do so without risking an instant skelp. Bad turned to worse, and now I look like some sort of stone Buddha, with every organ bloated and my hair out; and my son who says he's too busy to visit me in hospital, though he's been unemployed for over a year.

It'll be any day now. My organs are so full of chemicals and radiation that nobody would want them. I don't suppose Rita will come to the funeral.

But this wasn't supposed to be about me or my parts. At least not about their current collapse.

I began noticing I wasn't the only one spending time upstairs. I'd be down Leith docks, pretending I was looking for alternative work but really noting where all the ships had come from. I'd become an expert in nautical flags – 'shipspotting' I suppose you'd call it, and probably I wore an anorak (I'd have called it a jerkin in those days). I'd come home expecting my tea. But no, instead of cooking, Rita had gone straight upstairs, hadn't even bothered to drop off the messages.

She'd be sitting there smoking, telling Jamie about the thrills of the office. He never seemed to tire of listening to her, though he'd keep one eye on the street outside.

'Downstairs,' I'd say to the wife, in the way I did those days.

'I was just telling Jamie here —' she'd start, in a cloud of Player's smoke.

'Save it! You go and get the tea on.'

Not that I was jealous, exactly, but I didn't like her getting ideas. He'd be making her restless, the way he'd done with me, making it impossible to concentrate on the pools, not to mention the Ashlar. I suppose I was embarrassed, too, that he should see what a brainless slag I was married to – the cunt upstairs had class where women were concerned, so how could he find Rita anything but un-metre un-made? He who was expecting Gloria from one minute to the next . . .

He told me he'd met her at the Scala, and though it wasn't his usual style, this time it might stick.

'Too right,' I chimed, barely concealing my drool. Gloria looked a million dollars, like something out of Hollywood: Grace Kelly meets Sophia Loren, ice and fire.

Five minutes later, she'd barely be out of her fur coat and they'd be dancing together in the front room. He'd ask me to keep an eye out, tell him if I saw anyone particular coming down the road.

Half an hour later, I'd no longer be able to ignore the banging of Rita's broom handle on the floor, spoiling the samba, and her screams about how my tea would be burnt to a frazzle.

It was worse, too, listening to them at it, when I knew the partner. Sounded like the ceiling was about to cave in. Though even that wasn't as bad as the noise their feet made when they danced, which drove me mad because it was just the opposite: so light, as though they weren't human.

'How come you don't make more noise when you're dancing?' I asked him one afternoon. It was into spring by then and the windows were open in his flat.

'You only have to bang, you know, if we're disturbing you. Like Rita does.'

No need to remind me, I thought – arsehole. 'It's not that,' I said, feeling the eczema sprout on my elbows. 'It'd actually be easier if it sounded more like footsteps.'

He put his rum down and stood on tiptoes like some kind of Rudolf Nureyev. 'Look,' he said, 'the secret is in keeping the heels from touching the ground.'

We'll see about that, I thought – adding his explanation to the long list of things I'd make him pay for, if I ever got the chance.

I was starting to fear he was invulnerable when I went up one evening, Rita was out at the Bingo, and found him rigid by the window.

'Oh, fuck,' he was muttering, white as the proverbial sheet.

I joined him at the window. He was staring at a tall thickset man who was coming down Lochend Road, a hood over his head against the rain. Abruptly, the man looked up at the light, and the tension broke. 'Shit,' he moaned, drinking straight from the bottle, still trembling. 'I thought it was him.'

I pretended not to be interested. But I knew I'd found the gap in his defences. He was afraid, scared witless, and no amount of tiptoe pirouettes would make me forget it. Of somebody, clearly, somebody tall and burly, presumably from his past.

After I left him, I went down the Spar and purchased, along with a couple of bottles of Irn-Bru, to celebrate, a nicely bound notepad. I'd almost forgotten how to hold a pen for anything but the pools, but into that pad I noted everything I could remember of what he had told me.

It's a habit I've never quite lost . . .

And here I was, just writing about writing, when Doctor Darling comes up and interrupts. She asks me if I've had many visitors. I tell her I amn't a very likeable person, that even the Brothers from the Lodge have practically given up on me. She does me the kindness of pretending not to take me seriously . . .

It took me another month or so to get the rest out of Jamie, but now he was rattled I knew I would reach his terrified core if I just kept burrowing.

I can hardly be bothered using up what remains of my energies writing it down. In my own warped way I've written it already. Yes, he arrives in Bermuda under a different name. Yes, he falls in love with a beauty called Adelpha, who has a massive great big brother called Archie. Yes, he intends to settle. Yes, he goes out fishing with her, she gets dragged into the water, the shark-infested water, has her hand sheared by the propeller, and yes, he panics, always terrified of blood he says, and flees, no sooner back on dry land than he comes to his senses, but knows it is too late, that if her brother ever finds him, he's dead meat.

'I shouldn't be telling you all this, Ewey,' he'd moan, over his drink. 'But I'm that exhausted, with the running, the knowing what he'd do to me.'

For the sequel, the chase, I admit I did use some of the limited resources of my imagination, supplemented by what I've been able to find out about Bermuda, and even – I flatter myself – a touch of Joseph Conrad. What is certain is that Jamie fled the island on the first boat, ignorant of whether Adelpha was dead or alive. I never once heard him express guilt or regret, just fear, which had multiplied, he explained, when he called up the neighbour whose outboard he'd borrowed that day and found that Adelpha had indeed died and that her brother had left the island in pursuit.

For more than a year he kept moving, changing his name, his

appearance, setting false trails. And yes, he did see Archie in Bari, in Singapore, in Port Canning. After which he thought he'd given him the slip, returned to Glasgow; whence, because he felt too conspicuous in his hometown, to Edinburgh.

In the days and weeks that followed his protracted confession, I started appreciating this Revenging Angel, Archie. I too would stare out the window, but longingly. And when that didn't work, I thought of taking matters into my own greasy hands.

If I couldn't summon the Angel, then I would play the Fiend.

It was a Thursday in May 1968. There were riots on the streets of Paris, and we'd been discussing them at the Lodge, with me being more vocal than ever, gaining in confidence by the day. Rita was nowhere to be found; there was nothing on the stove. I could hear the heel-less dancing, but it wasn't Gloria I found in Jamie's arms, it was the wife, *my* wife, learning what he called the salsa – he didn't even let go of her when I entered, but went on explaining, to that lump whose sense of rhythm was even worse than mine, that you tap on the one and step on the two.

'Get away, hen,' I order her. 'I've got to speak with Jamie here.'

I turn to him with an appalled look.

'I've seen him,' I say, once Rita's skulked off.

'Seen who?' He switches the music off.

'Down the Capstan and Anchor, a gigantic geezer with arms like fuckin' tree trunks, funny accent, asking about someone called Hank Hands. He was putting out a perfect description of you.'

Jamie sinks to the floor, his head on his chest.

'Fortunately,' I go on, 'there was nobody there knows you, except me, who said nothing obviously, except to ask him where he was from.'

'Bermuda? He said Bermuda?'

I nod, fatally (forgetting he'd be unlikely to blow his cover). 'But look,' I say, 'he's not onto you yet. He's only been in the city a couple of days. You can still get away.' I'm having trouble hiding my glee: the idea of ordinary footsteps, heels and all, on the ceiling again!

'I can't,' he says. 'No more. Not with Gloria. Not my whole life running.'

Struggling to suppress my laughter, I leave him to come to his senses.

It was so much fun watching Jamie shitting himself that I'd probably have left it at that. He even lost his sure sense of beat, and on the rare occasions he put on music, I could hear he was struggling to keep time. He and Gloria withdrew from the Lothian Latin championships. He went out less and less, and to get into his flat required a complex code of rings and knocks.

I might have left it at that. By that time I was signed up for a law class due to start in autumn. I'd taken to studying in my night-watchman's hut. The world of legal disputation was opening up to me.

But: 'What's this?' I said to Rita. 'What the fuck's the meaning of this?'

She raised her hands as if it was obvious. The windows were open, I remember, it was high summer, and I wondered what the chances were of my throwing the plate from the dining-table straight into space.

'Where's the potatoes?' I asked, in my most reasonable voice. 'I can see the fish, I can see the beans, but where, dearest, are the potatoes?'

She pointed.

'That's what you call potatoes?' Reasonable no longer. 'I said, where's the fucking tatties?'

'It's rice,' she said.

'I'm no stupid, I can see that. You're not answering my question.'

Rita was hovering, ready to make a dash for it if plates started flying. 'I thought, for a change —'

'—To offer me a dinner with no potatoes? You call that a change? It's a fucking travesty.' I was pleased with my choice of words.

'It was Jamie's idea. He says he often has dinner with other things. Sometimes noodles, like Italian, or rice, like Chinese. Says he likes the change.'

No, I thought, I won't throw the plate out the window. I'll even eat his rice-shit.

For this, decidedly, would be his very Last Supper.

'Oh Jesus, Jamie,' I start, once I've digested, gone out for a stroll, got through his security at the door.

He seems calmer now, resigned.

'That's me just back from the Capstan and Anchor,' I say. 'He was there again, your Archie. Only this time there's somebody there knows you, by sight at least. Archie's telling us all how he's wanting to tell you about some estate you've inherited in Bermuda. So this idiot who knows you tells him how you live in Lochend Road. He doesn't know the number, but it's just a matter of time.'

Jamie doesn't say a word, like he's been waiting for it.

'Look,' I say, 'you can still make a break for it. Out the back and over the wall.'

The noose he takes out reminds me how he's been a sailor, very shipshape. He attaches it to the butcher's hook he's screwed into a lintel above his door, and tests it for length.

Is he bluffing?

He hardly seems to notice my presence, as if he's gone already.

Now, I tell myself, announce the truth. Tell him how you've just been having him on, putting a little excitement into his life, showing him the effect he's had on you, with all his tales of adventure. Now! Do it! For Gloria's sake, if not for his, she doesn't deserve to ruin her face with tears and wrinkles, just because you look like some prematurely spawned toad!

From downstairs I hear the crate being kicked away, but am disappointed I don't hear the thud. Until it occurs to me, chuckling, that this is one final time that his heels won't be touching the ground.

We went on living for another few years in Lochend Road, until I got my law degree and could afford to move out. Archibald never showed up, needless to say, though I often wished he would. I was going to the Lodge less and less, though I continued to be interested in the origins of the Order. Rita left me when Ric was ten. I didn't object. Two years ago, around the time that Ric dropped out of university, I spotted Gloria again, at Fickle Fingers Massage Parlour, limping a bit but still looking great. I think I managed to escape without her recognising me.

Dr Darling tells me it is time to put my pen down and take my medication. The denouement still seems rushed. All I can see is the way Jamie looked when he went to fetch the rope. I hope I look half as dignified.

11.

HAIR

BEN CRUACHAN, AT 3,689 feet, would knock a decision, surely, into his practically bald pate.

And so, long before it was light – not that it properly got dark, on a night like this in August – Fraser Glen was up, dressed in his Rohans, and into the car. Resolved, too, though he'd climbed it twice before by the easy route, to take it from the south side, for maximum catharsis, where it rose extra steep from Loch Awe.

The loch was mercury when he arrived two hours later and finally opened the car door. Even the widgeon by the bank, barely visible in the half-light, seemed hesitant to spoil the surface. Windless, suspended, a sparrowhawk in the elm behind the lay-by shook off the dew and flashed a sceptical eye towards the early intruder. If other beings inhabited this earth, they didn't want it known, such was the silence, which only an occasional trout dared to break, jumping for breakfast.

If she could see him here, he thought, where he was fully alive, rather than in town as Mr Bland (it wasn't the worst of Archie's nicknames for him). As always when finally he broke loose of the city's stranglehold, Fraser wondered why he'd been neglecting his hills – not since Archie's condition turned ominous, not since Ben Lomond in the snow, when he still had enough on his scalp to make the visits plausible. Back then, despite the worries about how he'd manage without his senior partner's instinct and investments, it had been easy: 'The usual, yes, short back and Connick.' Compared to now, with Archie six foot under, and the impending fiasco last Friday of him tentatively saying, 'I don't suppose, Laura, there's much you can do with the few remaining strands.'

A grouse, disturbed by the car door, broke cover and complained for fifty yards across the hillside.

From this, surely, he could draw strength: from his own country, from the sense he inhaled like the air, that it didn't matter he didn't go to night-clubs, own a DVD, hadn't seen *The Matrix*, didn't have shares in any dot-coms – at least not to Laura. Yes, he'd come to a decision: whether to declare himself, now he was freed from Archie's curse, and the alibi of the fortnightly visit was a farce; or to move the office from next door to Enzo's Salon, to anywhere he couldn't simply stare out the window and see her, coming down the street, going out for lunch, into the backyard with the bin-bags full of empty tubes and curls.

He stamped the driving from his legs, drew on his walking boots, startling the hush with so much intemperate human. He peered up at the distant crags. He'd been negligent of the Bens and Stobs these past two years. But maybe he still had credit from his Munro-bagging days. Would the hills help him now, he wondered, in his hairless hour of need?

When the sun finally nosed above the horizon, inhaling from the air the residue of chill, countless dew-drops were propelled into prismatic overactivity. A rabbit left its burrow to check on the upward lumber of this heavy pair of hooves. Spiders' webs were drying to silver, left and right. All of which he'd have shown her, including the warm green scallop of ferns, where some creature had recently been sleeping.

The first two hundred feet, he felt his full thirty-eight years sing to him with twinging thigh and wheezing lung. But gradually he found a rhythm. By four hundred feet the last of the morning mists had cleared, and the gun-greys and graphites had emerged back into colour and dimension.

Twelve years ago, he surely wouldn't have hesitated. Of course, he'd have been in his twenties, like her, but that wasn't all. He'd been a person in his own right, more or less, and he'd even had a girlfriend or two (depending on how you defined the term) at university. But then he'd started working, and added to the stress of the job came the pressure from his boss. By the time he realised what Mr Somerville was doing to him — still 'Ewan' in those days; he'd not yet renamed himself 'Archie' — the years of undermining had taken their toll. Not that his boss was any more scathing and sinister to him than to anyone else (his own son included). Yet the effect was disastrous none the less, till what was left was not just weakened and gullible, plain and undesirable, but also out of every girl-charming habit.

Fraser stopped, sat down at random, then noticed it wasn't random, given the seasonal colour — her colour, almost — of the dew-soaked bracken beside him, in which he promptly buried his face.

By the time he'd noticed his disintegration, it was the same story as his hair — already too late. Day by day, jibe by Archie jibe, strand by strand. Until he was unable to imagine that anyone could have the slightest interest — even his clients were only ones for whom Archie thought 'niceness' the sole priority.

Once he was confident. Now he was not. Knowing it only made it worse.

Back on his feet, and steadily rising, he was already stripped to T-shirt and shorts, and it wasn't even ten yet. The air was thick with pollen as he pushed through broom towards what he guessed, from the tinkle, was a burn. The midges were hiding under their fronds, aware it was Icarus if they exposed their wings to this heat.

He admired the slough of an adder when he bent over, cupped a cool palmful of peat-brown water to his lips. Things could be even worse, he realised, he could be besotted and styleless, he could be Asinine-in-Person (as Archie called him on bad days), in a country with no mountains, only flat land and towns.

Countless days he'd spent in the glens, always hoping, but never once seeing a wildcat. Foxes, of course, weasels, monarchs of the glen with moss hanging off their antlers, even a brown bear, presumably escaped from some safari park — but never the blessing of a wildcat.

The second handful from the burn he poured over his head; he'd need to remember to put on his cap.

If he were to stay stock-still, make himself a canopy of rowan, and if he were graced by the visit of a wildcat, its pink coral tongue lapping at the burn, then he might even forget about Laura for the duration: her smile, her pale complexion, her hair, her love of antiquity, her loathing of her brother. More to the point, he'd forget all the futile and utterly unhelpful things he'd ever said to her, seated in the swivel chair beneath her scissors and combs, or bumping into her at the library or Bar Sirius – 'bumping into' being the convenient term for the meetings he staged (as many as were consistent with coincidence).

Their first encounter set the precedent, when he'd finally built up the nerve, almost two years ago, after weeks of admiring her from the office.

'What'll it be, sir?'

'Eh, no need to call me "sir", Miss.'

'Laura's the name.'

'Miss Laura.'

'Just Laura's fine.'

'That's nice!'

And then the awkward silence.

'A trim?'

'I'm Mr Glen, you see, from Somerville and Glen next door.'

Awkward silence part two, sustained by an idiotic smile greeting them both in the mirror.

'It's my first time, I've got to admit, though Enzo's been saying I must, when he pops in for the odd bit of legal advice.'

'Right. So . . . ?'

'And I believe, from what he tells me, that you're fairly new here yourself.'

He immediately hoped she hadn't heard that particular inanity, given that she'd gone to fetch the book of styles to help him choose.

'And what would you advise?'

She pointed to a head that called itself a 'Harry Connick Jnr'.

'Absolutely. That's what I'd have gone for: short back and sides.'

The whole scenario was bad, admittedly. Though anything he'd said two years back, when he still had hair enough for a Harry, was small fry compared to now.

It was as if his innards had met at a convention and held a vote on what would incommode their owner most: the follicles won the day, and got a standing ovation for their offer of strike, walk-out, then mass suicide. However they conceived of their collapse, the resulting baldness made him blush to his defunct roots before he'd even set foot inside Enzo's.

No kindle of wildcat kittens could exempt him from this.

'Ah! Mr Glen!'

He could almost have laughed if it hadn't been so tragic.

'I'm glad you've decided to keep coming.' Laura eased him into the smock. 'So what'll it be?'

'A squirt of Pledge and a polish?' he almost said, but resisted, though it might have been better to get the absurdity into the open. Instead, he tried a fatuous attempt to change the subject, he could hardly remember what to, though it had happened only last Friday – some nonsense about enjoying *The Odyssey*. Now there was a hero who didn't need to worry about hair loss!

'The usual, then?' she interrupted.

'Oh, I think so.' He'd intended a conspiratorial chuckle, but what came out sounded more like a strangled yelp, so Laura thought she'd caught his ear with her scissors.

Half an hour later, following the course of the burn, when he looked down his car was just like a Dinkey toy in the distance, and the ancient ruin of Kilchurn Castle at the head of the loch looked almost inhabitable. To the west he thought he could see as far as the Paps of Jura.

Too early still for his pack-lunch, now was the time he would normally have relished the first stiff inhalation, the nicotine kick in the country-cleared lungs. Not that the thought of why he'd given up wasn't exhilarating: the power of sacrifice when there was so little else to offer her. The loss of two stone, the vague outline of biceps and abs, all of which had brought sarcastic comments not just from Archie but also from the octogenarian owner of the Laigh Coffee House, where he invariably took lunch.

Tearing off his T-shirt, Fraser wrung it for sweat and consigned it to his rucksack.

There remained the option of growing a moustache, or a buzz with the trimmer on ear-hairs, or a tidy-up of whiskers. He'd confirmed it was all doable the last time Enzo had been in about his taxes. Not that he really thought he could bring himself.

He gazed up and tried to guess how far he still had to climb. It was hard to say which part of him was aching most. A bit of physical pain wasn't bad, though, take the mind off the other worries, such as how the practice would survive with his tormentor gone, all that ruthlessness and cunning. Or the worry, now, about whether, if he ever made it to the summit, he'd have the energy left for decision.

'Excuse me!' he spluttered.

'Excuse us,' the man got out, disentangling himself from the woman's embrace, shielding her as she slipped on a blouse. 'Don't we know each other?'

He'd have avoided them if he could, but he'd vaulted over the dilapidated dry-stane dyke smack into the midst of their bivouac, virtually trampling on the pair of intertwined sunbathers.

'Mr Glen, isn't it?' said the male, composing himself more rapidly than his partner. 'Of Somerville and Glen?'

'Somerville RIP,' said the female, who was decent now, and seemed keen to atone for the nudity.

'I'm afraid so.' His grim undertaker's nod was somewhat ludicrous, Fraser guessed, in the context. 'And you . . . ,' he finally twigged, 'you're Mr Morton, if I'm not mistaken, George Street Vintners?'

The handshakes seemed incongruous too, perched up here in the land of thrift and ptarmigan.

'Small world.'

'And this is my fiancée,' said Morton. 'Heather.'

'Appropriately named!' Which was meant to sound jolly, but came out like a riddle. 'In the circumstances,' he added, gesturing to where it stretched out as far as the eye could see. 'If you get what I mean.'

'I was one of Archie's doctors,' she explained. 'At the Infirmary.'

He felt the need to explain: 'His real name was Ewan, you know, though for some strange reason he took the nickname Archie a while back.'

She didn't know what to say to that. On her blouse she wore a curious Aztec brooch. She was a lot younger than Morton, and an oddly knowing look on her face made Fraser wonder if Archie – it would be like him – had told her about the amorous aspirations of Mr Bland.

He pointed to the empty. 'Vosne-Romanée '85. I see you've been enjoying yourselves round the campfire.'

'We don't often get the chance,' she said defensively. 'Even in usual weather, let alone this.'

'If you'd like . . . ?' Morton made a half-hearted gesture of invitation to join them on the tarpaulin.

Fraser shook his head too strongly. 'Heading up?' he asked.

'That was yesterday.'

'Today's for sunbathing.'

'Almost killed us,' Morton moaned, 'or killed me, more precisely.'

There were many things he'd like to ask Archie's doctor. Maybe, on his deathbed, he'd explained why he was so bitter about the world, maybe he'd confessed to her how he'd purposefully set out to destroy his colleague's sense of confidence and self?

'I'll be heading on, then.'

'Mind and not get burned,' she advised.

If Fraser heard her, he made no sign. 'I'm determined to make it to the summit. Some big decisions when I reach it.' Here now, it was public, so there was no going back on it.

'Let it all become clear to you!' cheered the wine-merchant. 'Once you're standing on the cairn.'

The only problem with picking up a rhythm on the sheep-track which cut across the hillside beneath the heugh was that it left his mind free to wander. Whatever coolness there should have been at this height – above 2,000 feet by now – was defeated by the stillness as much as by the midday sun above. When he was a lad, long before Laura was born, there'd been whole weeks like this, it wasn't just nostalgia, never out of his shorts. Whereas now no winter, but no real summer either, as if the weather were leaving it to the humans – to him! – to inject the intensity.

After the Ice Blue Body Shop shampoo, the bottles of Rogaine and the capsules of Propecia, he'd gone as far as a Harley Street trichologist, making up some feeble excuse that Archie refused to believe for taking the day off work. Then he'd thought of a psychiatrist, since wasn't there something sick – masochistic? – about losing his hair at the very time when he needed it most? It was as if his hair, too, was echoing Archie, telling him: 'Get away with you! Ya wimp! Get a life! Ye can forget counting the days till the next appointment, 'cos if we have our way, there's not gonna be one!' He tried to object to himself – he wouldn't have dared argue with Archie – that maybe his hair was saying just the opposite, that he should exit, subito, from the office, five yards up Howe Street, into Enzo's Salon, straight up to her and declare his passion, now and forever. Before he went definitively Brynner.

Post-Harley Street, pre-psychiatrist, he'd neither got a life nor declared, he'd only watched in panic as the dome turned tonsure, the hairline receded, until even the bunchy bits behind his ears had started shedding, and the occiput went bare. Archie, by now in hospital and hairless himself, had thanked him acidly for keeping him company.

Since Laura didn't mention it, with her 'Harry Connick usual?', he'd had to mention it for her: sometime in May, borrowing from Archie's own idea (after prior removal of the acid).

'Very thoughtful of you, Mr Glen,' she said. 'Keeping Mr Somerville company like that.'

'Not that he's very great company,' he sighed, 'to be honest. Very withering and sour, if the truth be told.'

'You should introduce him to my brother Simon.'

He wished he didn't look so ridiculous, with that bib round his neck to catch the occasional runaway hair. 'You still live with your family, Laura?' It was a struggle to make it sound like a question, given how much he knew.

'Not for much longer, surely.'

'You've not got . . . ?' For more than a month he had forbidden himself to tail her, so he couldn't be one hundred per cent sure. 'You've no beau you could move in with?'

'I've got a brother I'm escaping. I've an interest in the past, in antiquities, whatever. And I've got what you see.' She opened her hands, and invited him to inspect her in the mirror.

'Which is?'

He should have answered his own question, dammit! Should have forced it out. Which is everything! Which is Beauty, Life, my Love!

'Which is . . . no so very bad. Right?'

Scents of tall grass, sodden peat, crushed blaeberry. The dampness of the moss seeped into him, stretched out. As his skin prickled in the heat, the poison-Archie that had been infecting him for so long was being cured by the antidote of the hills.

If she'd been with him, he could have told her the names of the peaks in the panorama, trying his tongue on their sonorous Gaelic. What did their age difference matter – look at Morton with the doctor, generations apart. This size, this scope, this barrenness, this Scotland, the unforeseen splendour of a sun-drunken day. And the colour of her hair too. None of your ginger, which sounded common, or auburn, which was English. None of your carrot, which would do for Archie (when he still had his), but in this case too brash. He had looked in the thesaurus, found nothing. Which left Scottish: her colouring, its emblem.

'Scottish!' Fraser hollered at the top of his voice.

'Sco . . . o . . . tiiiish,' came back the echo.

One final foot-slog and he'd surely be at the top. The Mars bar he was counting on had turned to mush. His sandwiches had that heinous wrapped-up smell. Only the apple was edible. But what did he care. Now that poison-Archie was neutralised, his whole shirpit system would be kicking in for the first time in years.

'You cannot be serious,' his boss had said to him when he'd caught him by the window again, the day before he entered the Infirmary for the fatal last time. 'What possible interest do you think she could have?' He'd apparently decided, as he was dying, that jibes were not enough. 'In Jenners Man.'

'Jenners sell Kenzo! Jenners even sell Comme des Garçons!' The shame of doing research into what might be fashionable didn't seem so shameful now he was under direct assault; and even his suspicion that Comme des Garçons wasn't really for garçons couldn't hold him back.

'So Bland's been swotting up on his brands. You must be kidding. Weekends in the Borders? Evenings at the bowls? Lunch at the Laigh? The acme of excitement a half pint of lager, an Indian carry-out – kurma, mind, none of your vindaloos – and an early night in bed with *The Heart of Midlothian*?'

Not all of which was true, he'd wanted to object – but didn't.

'Forget it, Fraser, please,' Archie said, turning to leave. 'She'll be out with the brainless likes of my son Ric, getting pissed on Hooches and bombed out on Ecstasy. You should hire yourself some stiff little spinster, when I'm gone, someone in tweeds that you can hope to bribe off.'

From where he was panting, baking, on the final sgurr, the peaks of Glencoe came into distant view.

It wasn't just geography that was urging him. History too, with its clearances, massacres, even what the car radio had told him on the way up, how wolves would not survive in the Highlands since their habitat was destroyed. It all came to melancholy nothing in the end, so why not make the most of it on the path to oblivion.

He could try sincere but light: 'I'd just like to tell you, Laura, how much these sessions under the clippers have come to mean to me. If you'd be up for it, I'd like to ask you out, on a date.'

His lungs were set to implode on the incline, his knees were screaming, and his sconce was getting singed under the three-o'clock sun.

Or jokey and familiar: 'Wouldn't we make an interesting couple, me with my billiard ball, and you with your copious locks?'

At least the pain of exertion meant there was nothing left for the extra effort of embarrassment.

Or classic and avuncular: 'You must be aware of how I've admired you from afar, been enthralled by the tales of your abominable brother. So now it's time to think of a rosier future: for you, and if you can find a place in your heart, for both of us.'

Even the heather was thinning now as the peak came into view, beaten flat by the habitual wind and rain. A single angry raven patrolled the air above.

Or as Archie might have suggested, all warp and cunning: 'I've got this flat whose owners would be delighted to have someone in it whom I can recommend, free of charge.' Or why not: 'I've two tickets for a Greek Island cruise, stops in archaeological high-spots.' Or even: 'I've a client, a Professor Darling, who'd be glad to help you with university entrance.'

At least he had the excuse of oxygen deficiency: sick ideas all, even the most innocuous. The only point was to do it, announce it, win her. He'd go in at ten-thirty tomorrow morning, just as she was beginning her tea-break . . . invite her to lunch for starters, not to the Laigh but somewhere younger, more anonymous, like Café Rouge or Est Est Est . . . and there he would put it to her, like any reasonable suitor.

One last effort and he'd be there, at the mountain-top. Here was the cairn in the middle of the narrow promontory of the peak. When finally he got there, he had to spread his arms out to balance on its topmost stone.

'Woh!' Fraser shouted, against the vertigo, against the explosion inside his overheated head. 'Now, Laura, please, be mine!'

When he looked at himself in the rear-view mirror, sometime after midnight, after almost collapsing from dehydration on the descent, finally making it to the car on his hands and knees, he saw what he took to be a demon, baked in the fires of hell.

With all the windows down, and his shirt still off, and the speed up over 50, the night air almost cooled him. The occasional hallucination might be due to not having slept in nearly forty hours, as well as to the broiled state of his brain.

He knew, as he sped into Edinburgh along the Corstorphine Road – so near to where she was sleeping! – that he should go home, take an ice-cold shower, cover himself in Calamine lotion, change his clothes, see to the blisters that were turning his scalp into mountains of Mars.

Howe Street was empty, but, living dangerously, he parked on the double-yellow line in front of the office. If he went home, he realised, he'd never summon the nerve to get out again.

The wait for the dawn of Monday morning was not too long. In the first light, he confirmed the damage in the bathroom mirror: the sunburn was bad enough on the chest, but came to a climax on his cranium, where the freshly hairless skin had been as untried as a new-born babe's. The crisp white shirt he took from the closet felt like Brillo. The legal tome in his hand as he stood by the window – *Delict* – grew heavier by the second as the perspiration soaked into it from his shoulders and arms. By the end of today he would know, if not sooner, if she might, ever, be induced to love him. Ninety-nine per cent chance by evening he'd not only be in the Infirmary so recently vacated by Archie, with second-degree burns, but also peering into the utter emptiness of the remainder of his life.

He closed the blinds, as he always did shortly before nine. Stood, swaying, at his post.

And there was no mistaking her, even through heat-stewed eyelids, as she came over the brow of George Street, down past Heriot Row Gardens, a heavier bag than usual causing her to list, a start-of-week face as she came into close-up.

He had another hour and a half to survive.

No dozing! Not that that was likely, tied here to the stake, the flames rising round him.

10.30 a.m.

Out of the office, onto the street, the white shirt already worse for wear, heat blisters discharging their abundant blood and pus. Glance across the Forth at the storm clouds rising over Fife – so much for the heatwave, just enough of it to bring his blood to the boil.

Four determined strides on his mountain-wrecked legs and he was at the entrance to Enzo's. He didn't dare look inside in case he caught her eye and saw his fate inscribed. He opened the glass door brusquely, and only when he was safely inside did he venture to look around.

There was a single client, apparently, an elderly rinse by the window being cooed to by Enzo's second-in-command. Where was she? Where was Laura? All he could make out in the rapidly gathering gloom was Enzo himself at the back, with some poor girl he was shearing.

He closed his eyes. When he opened them again, it would not be true. It had to be sun-stroke, delirium – anything but that!

'No!' The refusal left him of its own accord. Forwards he staggered. 'No! Please! Don't do it!'

'Too late.' Laura turned to him and smiled.

An unwilling collaborator, Enzo drooped in mourning.

'But you can't!'

A single strand was all that remained of what had been her tresses, their innumerable fibres of unnameable hue reduced to ersatz otter.

'But why? Why?'

Nobody seemed to find it surprising that Mr Glen, the lawyer from next door, should be standing there shouting in the oddest of clothes, his skin turned to brick.

'I told her,' Enzo grieved. 'Mr Glen, I told her.'

'He told me.'

'She won't even let me keep the lengths for a wig.' Enzo pointed at the floor – 'Look!' – where he seemed to be paddling in a pool of his own blood.

'The bin with them!' Her face, brutally exposed, more jubilant and juvenile than he'd ever seen before.

'For weeks I try to dissuade her.'

Laura was shaking a perilously light head. 'It would have taken a revolution, Mr Glen,' she said, 'like a *deus ex machina*. You can't be blaming Enzo, he's just the executioner.'

Nobody thought to ask Fraser why he was there; nor did he himself, as he fixed, helplessly, the trajectory of the final tress falling floorward.

'But . . . But I . . .'

'That's that!' she whooped, reaching out to touch some foot, made of marble, that she'd parked beneath the mirror in which she was confirming the catastrophe.

What had he wanted to say? She looked a dire five years younger, like a furless cat, a newly shorn sheep. Whatever it was he'd been intending, it surely wasn't —

'I came too late.'

'Too late for what?'

Though probably he didn't hear her question, retreating down the salon with an appalled look on his vulcanised visage, bumping into the rinse by the door, running into the rain which had just begun to pelt.

From where he lay, squirming, on the office floor, he could hear it lash against the windows. Summer, he figured, was over. He cursed himself for such a superficial thought, worrying about the weather, when a lot more was over than some stupid season.

What – Jesus! – had he been thinking of, up among the crags? His wily Greek cruises scarcely any more absurd than his offer of love and affection. However poisonous, Archie was right: she was barely out of her teens, with friends, hobbies, a life about to open, palpably no interest in an ossified redskin lawyer; not for lunch, dinner, not for a date, not for a moment, henceforth not even for a haircut, since no hair would ever grow again on the incandescent surface of this particular sad planet.

Never would she climb Cruachan with her hand in his. Never would they bivouac together. Never touch, never share, never mingle or wonder what the other was thinking. He had had his chance, and he'd blown it. The utter impossibility of starting again was all too apparent now.

The fits of fever were a relief, when they hit him, easing away the afternoon in shivers and sweats, visitations of the ghost of Archie, 'I told you so' etched on his face. The phone beeped, no doubt. Appointments came, rang, rattled, went.

Laura, he realised, sometime near seven, would have left by now. Enzo would be doing the till, clearing up. There was nothing to wait for but the eternity of evening, the slow fall of night, and then, first thing, the bin men announcing the obnoxious arrival of another day – they might even spot him through the window, melted plasma on the lino.

Only – bin men?

BIN MEN?!

The spring to his feet was sudden: another four blisters burst.

'Not on my life! Bland may be right, but even Bland can break!'

Delirious now, and heedless, he dashed to the window to check: there was Enzo, struggling up Howe Street through the rain. The salon must be closed. All the neighbours knew him, and even if they saw him and reported him to the police, what did he care, so long as he got to it first.

Lurching down the corridor towards the back of the building, he pushed past Archie's Bermudan memorabilia, unbolted the heavy rear door, swung it open.

The rain was cover too, hurling it down, turning instantly to steam on his inflamed head and shoulders.

At the bottom of the stone steps that led down to the yard, Fraser grabbed the railings, forgot for a second that despite the Rohan shorts, he wasn't wearing the boots that matched, hoisted his leg up, and just avoided impaling his foot on the spike.

So what, he thought, a bit of tetanus would probably be good for him in his present fevered state.

All he had to defeat now was the wooden stockade that Enzo had built round the back to protect his salon from burglary. The padlock on the door was invincible. Even sacrificing a few fingers to the razor-wire on top, he wouldn't be able to hoist himself over. But if not over, why not under, there was a nine-inch gap, more than enough for a worm like himself.

Headlong on the sodden gravel, he inched his way forward until his head, then his shoulders, were protruding. 'Ha, ha!' he laughed hysterically. 'Designed against intruders? But human, not lizard!'

Inching forward on his chest, to the side, ignoring the burning, where the top five layers of skin were turning to paste, thankful for lubrication . . . until, there, with half his torso under, Fraser could see them: the four black plastic bin-bags, goal of all his wriggle.

Another two inches, and he could touch the first of them with his lizard's claw. One more writhe, another last squirm – and he was stuck.

'Shit!' he muttered, into the puddle which was threatening to drown him in its two-inch depths.

Reaching from the last of his vertebrae, down through the shoulder – let it dislocate if that'd yield an extra inch – through elbow, finger, nail, till he could pinch it.

That was all he needed: he yanked the bag towards him, twisted his head to the side, sank his teeth into its delectable polythene. Pulled apart a small tear.

Out rolled empty cans of hairspray, bottles of conditioner, curlers, cotton-buds, some ugly drab curls. Oh, but here . . . 'Fuck you, poison-Archie, I got lucky first time!' Here, rolled up in their sarcophagus of towelling, a whole fleece of it, of them, of her – of Scotland!

By reaching out, he could grab them, holding the tresses in his mouth until he had every last one of them. And he could stay here, savouring, until he shrank a bit with the night cold, at which point retreat.

Unless—

'Mr Glen?!' came the astonished voice. 'I thought it might be a badger.'

He tried to wriggle back: nothing doing.

Forward: ditto.

While her hair unfurled in the torrential rain, anointing him.

'I was just finishing myself off with the trimmer, in private,' Laura explained, as if it weren't so very surprising after all, to find him immobile and prone in the yard, covered in her hair. 'And trying to summon the nerve to get out of here, in my new shorn state.'

He tried to raise his face for her to kick; but the strength was gone from his neck. He tried to speak; but his mouth filled with puddle.

'So why didn't you ask me?'

She was descending the steps towards him, smiling.

'See, as my fairy auntie Gloria might say, if you're really that keen, you can have the pubes and all.'

12.

BREAST

THE OPPONENTS' SPOKESMAN was shaking his head in the snell summer breeze. 'You've got to be joking. You are joking I presume?'

'Like in five-a-side, no?'

'But this is eleven-a-side.' The Clermiston captain did a quick recount. 'Even if there is only nine of us.'

The Sparta Athletic coach declined to be embarrassed. As instigator, founder, chief-organiser of the controversial club, as the one who dealt with the police when the homophobes got nervous, he felt he'd seen it all. 'No shots above the midriff.'

'Do we get to see him at least, the freak, if we agree to this nonsense?'

Coach glanced over to goal, where Bobby, who'd been playing for the team for nearly two years now, ever since Ian got incarcerated for art-fraud, was well disguised under a padded body-warmer, and was avoiding the training shots being fired at him. Catching Coach's inquisitive stare, the goalkeeper smiled that winning smile of his that seemed to say, 'Not that I give a shit', then shook his head none the less.

'No can do. He's a bit shy as yet.'

'Fuck that then,' returned the Clermiston captain. 'No deal. I'll never get the boys to buy it. How do we even know it's for real?'

Impatient as ever to get started, Rory, the chief Sparta striker, dribbled up to the centre spot. 'What's the delay?'

'No delay,' Coach explained, long-sufferingly. 'I thought their captain might show some understanding, given last season we agreed to no sliding tackles, seeing hows he'd smashed his shin the night before. But we'll still thrash them, despite our local difficulty.'

With which, Coach withdrew to the touch-line, to watch his prediction come to naught. By the half-time whistle they were lucky to have conceded only four, while, despite the efforts of Rory, who was giving his all in attack, they'd notched up only one.

Over oranges, huddling from the rain in the nearest bus-shelter, Coach was operatic. 'Look, Bobby, if you cannae catch the ball on your chest —'

'— Nor can I be cloitering in the mud while the Clermiston queer-bashers trample on it.'

'Then maybe you should come up to mid-field.' He turned to his favourite defender. 'Vijay, you could drop back to goal.'

'Against my religion, boss. Ramadan, don't you know.'

'Tadger?'

'Wi' ma circulation? I'd perish of hypothermia if I hud to hauld that still.'

Coach turned imploringly to Proteus, senior member of the team.

'You know, Coach, I'd help you out if I could,' Proteus explained. 'But I'm making inroads with their left-half. He's telling me how he's wanting Oscar Wilde for his eighteenth birthday.'

'So it's down to you, Bobby.'

'Eh, Agatha, Coach, if you don't mind. My inspiration.'

Coach was used to it, apparently. 'When the ball comes at you, try turning the other cheek, so to speak.'

'The other orb,' Proteus corrected.

Most of the team had drifted off in the direction of Broughton Street and their various late-night amusements by the time Janice joined her old school pal in the Tap, near the Art College, where she was doing her degree. Ever since she'd split up from Hutton – 'Hut' – more than a year before, she'd found it hard to make the effort. But tonight she'd put her hair up and her make-up on, while the shortness of her skirt asserted it was summer. Still, it took her a couple of tequilas before she had the nerve.

'So what's it feel like?' she finally asked, smiling and shifting.

'You should know.' Bobby didn't seem the least put out.

'You're not trying to tell me it's similar to what we feel.'

'We?'

'The girls, women.' Her downward glance was discreet, but in that loose-fitting jacket, it was impossible to tell. 'You'll be giving birth next, I suppose?' She didn't mean it cattily. 'Or hiring yourself as a wet nurse?'

But Bobby was unperturbed. 'I might do. Though I'm more interested in the fun along the way. You see, I've not lost all hope in you, Janice. That Hutton creep, with his awful songs, was just a deviation. Ever since school, I've known you've an eye for the girls.'

It was hard to tell if her shiver was just the cold, or maybe the last swig of tequila going down. 'But what did you need to tell the whole damn team about it for?'

'I let in six today; it's bleeding hard when you can't use your chest.'

'A bunch of philistines like that?'

He gave it thought, apparently, because her next shot of liquor came served with his pre-prepared speech, less tongue-in-cheek than usual: 'First, Janice, they'd have noticed me skiving the communal bath. Second, they're not all philistines, they're every type, that's what I like about Sparta Athletic.'

'Every type of queer, that is.' Everything came with a barb tonight.

'Not so fast. There's Rory, back from his honeymoon.'

'What? Rory-Consummation?'

'There's some of them from Broughton, some from Boroughmuir. But Ian, Flora's ex, who was in goal before me —'

'What? Tit-Ian? A real goalkeeper's tradition with the tits.'

'Very funny.' Bobby refused to laugh. 'But as I was saying, Ian went to The Academy. And there's Proteus – so called – who claims he used to snog with Tony Blair at Fettes. It's a classless society.'

'And now one hermaphrodite?'

The crush was intensifying round their table as last orders were called.

'The doctor says it's perfectly benign. I can have it removed any time, a simple enough operation.'

'You could even donate it, like that Sheffield racist did, only specifying it's to go to goalkeepers who're gay.'

If she was trying to get him riled, she was not succeeding. He was as cool as he was handsome; as handsome as cool. 'I could do,' he smiled, then leaned so far across the table, their noses were almost touching. He sounded like out of some '50s B-movie: 'Why won't you understand, Janice, that I haven't given up on converting you, for the Sapphic sisters.'

'Fuck you.'

'If you'd like to, of course, but I should warn you that for the moment I'm only endowed with the breast, not the other female parts.'

Janice had barely climbed into the taxi, still cursing herself for having missed the last bus home, when she spotted Esther, her best friend from college, who lived two flats down.

'That's magic, Jan,' came the lager-fuelled thanks. 'I was wondering how I'd make it home.'

Esther was looking very artsy, her hair in sticky-uppy tufts – very Björk, Janice judged.

'What's the matter, Jan?' her friend asked. 'Still no songs from the Hut? Did you see his name, my gran pointed it out to me, in the Book Festival programme?'

'He's just pretending he's depressed. What Hut really is is raj, that's what he is.' She could hardly tell Esther that she was raj too: at herself for having wasted another Saturday night with Bobby. Her friend would only reply, as she always did, that how could it not be a write-off, given there was no chance. So: 'I've been thinking about tits,' she started, hoping it didn't sound too abrupt, closing the plastic window that shut off the driver of the taxi.

Esther wasn't fazed. 'Like in painting them?'

'Like in how weird it is to have them.'

Esther's head was shaking. 'You should get them sucked once in a while, that'd take your mind off them.'

'You may be right.'

'Sure I'm right, so long as it's the right bloke on the other end. You heard about your queer friend Bobby?'

'You know about it too?'

'Everyone knows about it. I'm pals with Flora, mind? She still keeps an interest in the team.'

'So you'll know what it looks like, Miss Know-it-all.'

The taxi pulled up in front of their tenement.

'It takes all types,' Esther said. 'The long droopy ones and the taut little pears. The raspberry nipple and the wide brown biscuit.'

Janice refused to accept a contribution to the cab. 'That's boys' talk, Esther, you got it off them.'

'Who's the know-it-all now?' she called from the door, as she fumbled for her keys.

By four o'clock the next day Esther's hangover was starting to wear off, so she could risk the call. 'I spoke to Janice,' she explained.

'So?' Flora sounded even more bored than the usual Sunday: maybe doing her toenails. 'If Bobby's got a lymphoma, then why doesn't he have it removed?'

Esther looked at her hair in the mirror: artsy had turned pigsty overnight. 'A lipoma, Flo. If it was a lymphoma he'd be half-dead by now.'

'Anyway, according to Ian, who keeps himself informed, it's just some fatty tissue, nothing like a real breast, more like a cyst.'

'That's where you're mistaken.' Esther hadn't meant to fib, but now it came out she didn't really regret it. 'In fact it's rather beautiful, according to Janice.'

'What? His liposuction or whatever? Away wi' you!'

'According to Janice. You remember Carole Bouquet in that Spanish film we went to see, where the old guy who's obsessed with her finally gets her top off?'

'Nuh.' Flora sounded more bored than amazed.

'You mind Uma Thurman in *Dangerous Liaisons*, when Malkovich lifts off her nightdress?'

'Bullshit!' If Flora really was varnishing her nails, then she'd just tipped over the bottle.

'He keeps it well concealed, I grant you.'

'What side's it on, then? If Janice is the expert?'

The more it continued, the more Esther was enjoying the conversation. 'I asked Janice the very same question. So what she says to me, she says, "That's for me to know . . . and for you to find out." Then her voice drops an octave, and she finishes off, saying, "Darling."'

Flora almost gasped.

'That's right, Darling.'

The crowd of one, not including Coach, was bigger than usual for a Sparta mid-week fixture; what's more, out at Currie.

'We were counting on rain,' Coach explained. 'Most of the Balerno Tigers don't have boots with studs. They'd have been sliding every which way.' He directed her gaze upwards to the cloudless sky.

'Still nil-all?' Flora asked. She was trying to look enthusiastic, even carrying a miniature rainbow flag in support.

'But we're only started five minutes.' As in confirmation, the Tigers' striker dribbled past the last of the Sparta defence, and shot.

'Woh!' shouted Coach.

'Better!' came the echo from the team.

'Did you see that?' he said to Flora 'What a save!'

'It was only doing two miles an hour.'

After which, despite the interference of Rory's exertions, even the attack was going places, so Coach could hardly contain himself as Tadger tore up the wing, crossed to Proteus, who dared for once to use his head, and put the ball firmly in the back of the Tigers' net (where the net would have been, had the groundsman received an adequate bribe).

It was a good five minutes before Coach was able to rejoin Flora on the Sparta goal-line. 'You see that? It's up the other end we need to be, for the action, like.'

'I want to chat to Bobby. Ian's been asking how he's doing.'

'No distracting him now.' Coach interposed himself. 'Hey, Agatha,' he called, 'how d'you manage it?'

'I borrowed my brother's cricket box and my wee sister's bra. Works not too bad.'

Flora could barely feign interest in the antics on the field. 'Did you say "Agatha"?' she whispered in Coach's direction.

'Saint Agatha, properly.'

She felt an idiot having to ask, but since she'd come all the way. 'Agatha as in Christie?'

'Agatha as in ask your Ian.'

'He's not my Ian. I'm off with Joe, remember? Ian's inside.'

'Just as well. A hopeless goalie if ever there was one. Never caught a ball in his life, and on the rare occasion he got to it, he'd Van Damme it out of existence.'

'And Agatha?'

'He's no Gordon Banks, I grant you.'

'But his name?'

'As I was saying, ask your Ian. Apparently he first feels the new boob in front of some painting in the National Gallery, of Saint Agatha, who's had hers cut off so they're sitting in a dish in front of her. So he says anyway.'

'You're joking.'

'I don't know what it is about Sparta's goalies. First your Ian, now Agatha. Culture creep, I call it, right insidious. Next we'll have Vijay thinking he's Salman Rushdie, we've already got a Proteus, and then Rory'll be posing as the Immaculate Conception.'

Even without the unripe peaches, Flora would have been welcome in the bunker at half-time, having been present at Sparta's inaugural match years back, and having managed to impersonate some interest, even after Ian's incarceration.

'News of Double-Barrel?' Vijay asked. 'Still working on his erotic masterpiece?'

Flora, closing in, merely shrugged. By stumbling a bit, she even managed to brush against it; though it, of course, turned out to be the rigid plastic of the cricket box. Horrible idea: where it had been, was now.

'I hear it's Agatha,' she joked, squeezing onto the bench beside Bobby, peeling him a peach. 'I'd have expected something Brazilian.'

'So you heard, then, about my five days in Paris – or the Bois de Boulogne I should say. Those trannies are something.'

What infuriated her most was thinking she was ahead, only to be shocked by what came next. 'You serious?'

'But I couldn't face all that silicone and surgery. No, this is fine as it is, the natural way.'

Somewhat charily, she handed him the peach. 'You're not in any danger then?'

'No more than any C-cup.' He spat the stone in Coach's direction.

'Speaking of which, do you think your Ian . . . ? I mean, I could always pay him a visit at Saughton, if you thought . . . ?'

'He's no my Ian!' she snapped. 'Why can't people get that through their heads. Anyway, I specifically remember him saying he's not interested in herm-Aphro-dities.'

He smiled, but didn't correct her mistake. 'Shame.'

She needed to keep his interest up. 'I heard from Esther about Janice.'

'Esther? Does Agatha know Esther?'

'She certainly seems to know you. Tells me that Janice has got a bit of a crush.'

'With or without the new addition? That is the question.'

'You're twisted, you are.'

'As your knickers, my dear,' came the instant response.

As he re-emerged for the second half on the touch-line, Coach was wearing his kilt. 'Has its advantages, after, for the club,' he explained to Flora. 'Ease of access.'

She was wondering why she bothered, especially when she had to watch Bobby – he was still plain Bobby to her – let a lob drift over his shoulder, the second through his legs, bringing the score to two-all, with the inevitability rising, like the evening haar, of the final result.

'You don't think,' she said, for want of a better line, 'that the Tigers might ask for a test to determine the opposition's gender?'

Coach, humourless as ever, said, 'There's nothing in the regulations about X or Y chromosomes. Sparta's always had an open-door policy, no exclusions.'

'And Bobby could start a nursery school in the goalmouth.'

It was a mean thing to say, and it only made her feel worse. The topic of children was taboo with Joe, and each monthly period was an open accusation. Flora was determined to leave while the score was still at a draw, so as not to be abandoning a sinking ship. But then came the harangue from the touch-line.

'Saint Agatha,' the orator began, 'from Sicily, patron saint of Catania, third-century AD.'

'Shit!' murmured Coach. 'Some Tiger prank to wreck our concentration.'

'According to online Britannica: Agatha is cited in the martyrology of Saint Jerome and the Martyrologium Hieron-anon-anon . . .'

The orator, cursing, went back into rehearsal.

'Who's the Cicero?' Proteus asked.

'It's pathetic,' Coach chafed, 'if they think that's gonna put us off.'

Proteus's glance at goal, from where the object of the homily was straining to hear, did not confirm Coach's confidence.

'Hieron . . . ym . . .ian . . . um! Daughter of a distinguished family and remarkable for her beauty of person.'

'Woah! Wehh! Tell us more!' Most of the cheer was coming, alas, from the Sparta side, while their eponymous goalkeeper, no longer quite in goal, raised his hands in acknowledgement of the praise.

'Pursued by the Senator Quintianus with avowals of love.' The Tiger orator paused. 'That's *cruised* for the benefit of you uncultured oafs.'

'Right! Too true!'

'Resolutely spurned by the pious Christian virgin —'

'Yay! Hail virgin!' The bounds of credibility were so far stretched that even Coach joined in.

'Quintianus then subjected Agatha to various cruel tortures, especially inhuman being his order to cut off her breasts.'

'Boo! Rubbish! Fuck that!'

Flora pointed to where the Tigers' own goalie, the one player on the field unmoved by the oration, was dribbling unobtrusively down the wing, avoiding Coach's leg, which jabbed out too late.

'Goal!' the Tiger cheered childishly, when he'd lain down and headed it over Sparta's unmanned goalline. 'The decider!'

Even his own team-mates seemed less than overjoyed, when they turned to discover their victory.

It was presumably not by chance that Esther met Flora the following evening, the Thursday, in the Seattle Coffee Company at the top of Waterstone's on Princes Street.

Esther took the chance of going to Reference, to look up 'lipoma', and then somehow got lost in the hideous details of *Foxe's Book of Martyrs*. Flora, vaguely looking for Joe's birthday present – not that she was sure he deserved one – checked in a book for the portrait of

Saint Agatha in the National, before drifting towards Erotica. It was only once she'd chosen *The Bountiful Breast*, and got it gift-wrapped, that she realised it would do better for Janice than for Joe.

'Here,' she said to Esther when they met, 'this is for Janice, a wee gift.'

Esther was looking tired, her skin spotty. 'Sneak a peak?' she asked, fiddling with the wrapping.

'It's nothing,' Flora said, shaking her head. 'Just a wee nothing.'

Their chocolate-chip cookies were reduced to crumbs, their double lattes dregs, before either of them felt up to talking.

'So who in fact has actually seen it?' Esther asked. 'How about at the match, his team-mates?'

'You think they're interested? Be allergic to anything reminding them of their mum.'

'But would it? Remind them of their mum, I mean? A niggardly wee wart like that?' Esther spotted her friend's sidelong glance. 'As I imagine it to be, I mean. Despite what Janice says about Uma Thurman.'

'You may well be right,' Flora agreed. 'D'you mind the first episode of *Queer as Folk*? The muscly great hunk who gets invited back to Vince's? Then, when he takes off his shirt, he's got this big armadillo shell strapped over his pot belly?'

'Too right!'

Enjoying herself now, Esther forgot about her spots, and ordered a couple more cookies, as well as top-ups on their lattes.

'Beats me where they dig them up,' she whispered, across her drawing board, to which was pinned a sheet of A3 paper showing half an outline in uncommitted charcoal.

'A scunner,' Janice agreed in undertones. 'That ridiculous pose Leonardo has him lying in, and it wouldn't surprise me if he hasn't wiped his bum this morning.'

Esther suppressed a giggle.

'Everything all right there, ladies?' said Mr Leonard, the life-drawing teacher, coming round for a look.

Janice tried to cover up, but he was having none of it. 'Come now, Janice, none of your schoolgirl prudery here, this is college.' He pushed aside her forearm, then had to struggle not to twitch. 'Hmmm. Very . . . interesting. And let's see yours, Esther?'

She angled her drawing-board towards him.

'Come on,' he said, 'that's hardly even an outline. And you know we don't start there. From the inside out!'

It was obvious to both of them that Mr Leonard was buying time.

'Can I ask you, Janice?' he said, with the tremor under control. 'These . . . eh . . . what should we call them?'

'Breasts?' she suggested. 'Beauteous globes? Eh . . . gorgeous nipples from which all of life derives?'

Esther, unable to control her giggles, made a dash for the door.

'As you say,' said Mr Leonard. 'There's doubtless some reason why the model, though as far as I can see a male, has one of them.'

'That's right, Mr Leonard,' Janice chirped, somehow keeping a straight face. 'It's because the other one's in the dish in front of him.'

'Right. And that would be because . . . ?'

'I guess he's got mixed feelings about them?'

Mr Leonard's eyebrows were fixed in a frown. 'Quite,' he said emphatically. 'Though you are remembering this is life-drawing, not a free-for-all.'

Janice was stonily serious. 'True. But I was only doing like you said, working from the inside out, and that's how it came out.'

The class was breaking up and Janice was gone by the time Esther controlled herself. She realised she'd have to give Flora's present to her later; though in the meantime, maybe, without even tearing the wrapping, she could have a wee look at it herself. Surely Jan wouldn't mind?

It wasn't the first time she'd been invited back to Bobby's, but the first time to Agatha's, and the first time by herself. It was a lot tidier than she remembered, neater than her own place, and virtually nothing, bar the enormous tube of KY by the bed, gave away his tastes.

'I was just doodling circles,' Janice was explaining to him, 'trying not to stare at the scabby wee skelf of a model. And that was what came out, to poor Leonardo's horror, him who thinks himself so liberal.'

'You gonna show me?' Bobby was pouring the sixth tequila of the evening. 'Not too much for me, though, with the big match tomorrow.'

Somewhat coyly, never taking her eyes off his face, Janice unscrolled the drawing on his dining-room table, which he'd covered with Scottish Executive blotters filched from work.

'No bad!' he applauded.

She rolled it up too hastily, shoved it in its tube. 'Who's it tomorrow?' she asked, striving to show interest.

'A mighty relegation battle against Thor's Hordes from Corstorphine.' His shrug – Thor's Hordes! – admitted it was all too silly for words.

She was stretched out on his couch, and the tequila bottle looked like it might not survive the night. 'I hear you've bought yourself protection.'

'I finally made it to the sports shop. Who knows what the terylene attendant thought I was doing with a women's-boxing breast-guard. Not least because I insisted on trying it for size.'

She took another swig. 'I wish I had half your nerve.'

'Not that I'm wearing it now,' he sighed, coming over beside her, kneeling on the spotless rug at her feet. 'If you'd like to check?'

'Quit teasing.' She tried to sit up. 'I think I've drunk too much.'

'Who's teasing?' His voice was a purr. 'You're not still thinking about that bam-heid songster, Hut? Even if he is about to star in the Festival.'

She scratched her forehead and hid her eyes. 'Stuff Hut,' she said. 'Stuff his songs. It's us – so to speak. It couldn't really go anywhere, could it, Bobby – I mean Agatha?'

'As you yourself have pointed out, it could go round . . . in circles.' He was tracing the outline of her breasts with his finger. 'It could even lead to better things . . . better girls . . . I hesitate to say, better breasts.'

'Always the initiator. Why so keen to convert me?'

'I don't like to see you waste yourself.'

Shaking her head, past caring, she lay back on the sofa, closed her eyes.

'Here,' he breathed, unbuttoning his shirt. 'It's maybe better you don't look in any case, it's not such a pretty sight.' He leaned over towards her. 'And think of what I'm sacrificing too, as you mould your lips to this, my dear . . . in a sweet round O.'

The rain, next day, was back to usual form, though as Thor's Hordes all wore boots, as well as the ridiculous horned helmets in which they arrived, it didn't really help.

'Get that ridiculous headgear off!' cried Coach from the touch-line. 'Apart from anything, it's dangerous.'

'What about your kilt?' their captain screamed back. 'You think that's not a liability?'

'It's not a kilt,' Proteus retorted, denying the evidence of the Ancient Gunn tartan. 'If those are Viking helmets, then that' – he pointed to Coach's kilt – 'is what's called a *peplos*. As worn by the myrmidons of Sparta.'

'That'll be right,' their captain puffed, as he shuffled back towards his goal, just in time to trip an unleashed Rory, who would otherwise doubtless have opened the score.

'Tough luck,' Thor's centre-back consoled the bruised Sparta striker. 'Almost scored,' he said, with a special emphasis on *scored*. 'Almost . . . consummated?'

In disgust, Rory hobbled towards defence. 'Cheeky bastardi,' he complained in his best Italian, as Coach applied the numbing spray. 'What'd they say to you, Agatha?' he asked, turning to his goalkeeper, who was looking more than usually distracted.

Intensive care wasn't about to distract Coach, however. 'Let Vijay take the free-kick!' he hollered.

'They told me I wouldn't know the meaning of martyrdom until I'd seen them put away a half-dozen goals.'

'Cheeky bastardi.'

'Away you run now, Rory,' his keeper ordered. 'Scuttle up their end for a bit. I'm busy here thinking.'

Vijay's shot was a bender all right, but bending the wrong direction, so it landed at the feet of Thor's left-winger ('Kon-Tiki', according to his strip).

Coach, ever intuitive to the tide of play, was retreating down the touch-line towards the Sparta goal.

Kon-Tiki passed it to his captain, who brushed past Sparta's sweeper, passed it out to the other winger ('Oden'), who only just fluffed an ambitious one-two involving a back-heel, but not so badly that he wasn't able to lay the ball up again for Kon, on the edge of the Sparta penalty box —

And that was when it happened, such that nobody, but nobody, could believe their eyes.

'Oh no!' moaned Coach.

'That's that then,' sighed Tadger.

Epitaphs were everywhere, as the enormous boot of Kon, in cartoon slow motion, pulled back for the kick.

'Agatha!' shouted Coach, just in time to wrench him from his brooding.

The boot of Kon fired forward, releasing a furious stab of the instep, sending the ball screaming towards the top-right-hand corner . . .

'At which point . . .'

'Yeh?'

'At which point . . .'

'Get on with it!'

'At which point' – according to Coach, at least, who took up the story in the pub sixty minutes later, for those of his team who'd turned away in despair – 'At which point, as if all this Agatha stuff were merely to cover his true name, Gordon Banks —'

'Dino Zoff.'

'Alan Rough, the famous perm.'

'At which point he leaps like a cat.'

'Like a salmon on spate.'

The object of their eulogies had so many drinks in front of him, he didn't know where to start. All of Sparta was in celebration over reprieve from relegation, while he alone seemed unconvinced, preoccupied.

'So he hangs in the air for a full five seconds, as the ball swerves away from him. But then he just goes on soaring, soaring, until he's up there in the sky, and the ball's more like a ball-bearing, clamped into his magnet hands.'

'The great god Shiva,' Vijay gasped, 'ascending for Yoni.'

Proteus looked sceptical. 'Isn't Yoni female?'

But nobody was listening.

'Pure inspiration,' came Rory's cheer.

'Like Agatha saw an angel,' was Coach's final judgement.

'So who was shagging you last night?' Tadger asked his keeper, who was staring into his cups, with a face more like he'd seen a ghost than an angel. 'What happened? How come you've never done it before?'

'Hell!' snapped their saviour. 'Would I tell you if I knew?'

'And that was that,' Coach summed up. 'If you'd seen the Hordes, the way I did, it was clear they realised it was over. Not a chance. With a goalie making saves like that, they might as well pack up their horns and quit.'

13.

VEINS

WASN'T IT HIS father's doing, for going and dying in the first place? Stuff him.

Then, of course, the ridiculously large sum of money his dad had left him, without which this trip wouldn't have been imaginable – not that Ric could really resent this, he'd been in Naples nearly a week and was almost convinced he was enjoying it. More money than he could ever have dreamed, more shares, equities, mutuals, bonds, property, even after they'd been divvied up with that unlikely glamour queen from his father's past.

Whoever she was, this Gloria, good luck to her. If she'd been rubbing up against Ewan Somerville – 'Archie' as he'd nicknamed himself in recent years, for some unfathomable reason – then she deserved a medal as well as half the inheritance.

The mirror by the ice-cream parlour on the piazza San Domenico was returning Ric's sceptical gaze, while his amarena ice-cream melted. The sky was the oddest shade of southern sea-blue, which meant the afternoon was reaching its close. Yet still he couldn't summon the nerve to walk round the corner into Prince Raimondo's chapel.

Was the resemblance really so close, he wondered, between himself and his dad, beyond the colouring, the stature, the beadiness of eye?

His father's doing, he thought, this fretting here, as if so-called

Archie had been trying to tell him something from the way he left his books about Prince Raimondo, where they couldn't be missed, stacked floor to ceiling in the Williams Street flat. There'd been ample time for him to arrange his things, since the cancer had been slow to take hold. But no, he'd left it to his son to sort through all the books, along with the dusty Masonic regalia and the endless stuff about Bermuda – as if Archie would ever have gone on holiday in the first place, let alone to Bermuda.

Ric knew he should have gone in to see his dad during the final weeks, in May. So what if his dad didn't deserve it, always the mean-spirited, crabbit, cantankerous presence, until the family fell apart, at which point he became a crabbit, cantankerous absence. Should have visited him in the Infirmary, if only to economise on guilt, especially with the surprise of the will. And then, maybe he'd have learned about the obsession with Raimondo.

Only, the sight of him: it really was too much. With his carrot curls all gone and everything bloated up in him like some inflated terracotta frog.

It wasn't as if he'd been busy, during the spring, when Archie was fading. Not looking for a job, particularly, or even hanging about with his usual pals, Simon and Dan-Dare, not since Stod, last of the Famous Four, had hit the jackpot. With Stod taken up on some girlfriend, planning a holiday in Tuscany of all places, they'd each been going their own ways, forlornly. His dad left messages on the machine, long rambling monologues about anything and everything (anything but the essential: 'Get over here quick, son, 'cos the frog's about to croak').

But still he hadn't budged, not until some doctor rang him, 'Darling', Ric remembered, because for a wonderful moment he thought some woman was chatting him up. She told him his father was in his final hours, though by the time he got there all he could do was squeeze his hand, hoping he realised who it was, belatedly, at his bedside.

What's more, if he'd gone to see him, then maybe he'd have found out about Gloria, and it wouldn't have been so excruciating sitting next to her in the office of his dad's junior partner, Mr Glen. Her ridiculous yarn, about how she hardly knew his father at all, had been going out with the upstairs neighbour in Lochend, under whose flat his parents had lived, back in the '60s. How her boyfriend had killed himself, at which point Ewan – 'Not much older than yourself' – had been kind to her.

Kind? His father? It was all he could do not to laugh.

The Williams Street flat stank of human; the bed was unmade. Ric had laid out the few 'personal effects' handed to him by the doctor: the Timex watch, the toothbrush, the slippers, the Parker pen. There was the notebook too, of which Ric had skimmed a couple of pages, before he realised it was some nonsense scribbled during his dad's final days, some ludicrous fantasy about being a Bermudan giant named Archie.

The kitchen was a disaster area, scores of empty baked-bean cans gathering mould. The whole place too miserable for words, home of a man who was practically a millionaire when he died.

The evening of the funeral, he resolved to leave the whole lot to Capability Scotland, then sell the flat and be done with it. He only had to do something with the stack of books beside the bed. Taking a look at which, there it was, the statue he was now about to see in the flesh – in the marble – the *Veiled Christ* of the sculptor Sanmartino. It was the jewel among the commissions of Prince Raimondo di Sangro, the Freemason who, to judge from all the books on him, was his father's one true hero.

It wasn't for want of trying that he'd ended up in Naples alone. He'd wanted this to be a holiday, the sort he'd never in fact had, his first time abroad. The last thing Ric had wished was that it should become any sort of mission or quest. Far from it; he'd imagined the sort of time Stod was planning with his woman from the Widows, something romantic, with lots of seafood, sex and swimming (he'd been so keen, he'd overlooked the fact he didn't know how to swim).

One or two of the girls from Clarks Bar had been tempted, especially when he'd told them they could have a single room. When they declined, he'd even tried Laura, Simon's younger sister, biting back the shock he got when he walked into Enzo's Salon and saw her with her hair shorn.

'Pompeii?' he tried. 'All those statues and ruins?'

She only looked embarrassed, reluctant to leave the head she was working on, though, viewed from near the door, it looked practically bald and curiously red.

Ric had bought and studied the *Rough Guide*, and when he finally arrived in Naples, after a forty-two-hour train ride, he kept reminding himself he didn't need to scrimp and save, counting every lira until he lost himself among the zeros.

The Napoli T'Amo albergo on the packed Via Toledo seemed friendly. He'd have plenty of time for the rest of Italy, the usual tourist spots, Florence, Rome, Venice – not that he was in any rush to see Raimondo's chapel, no, it was one of many ports of call.

Indeed he refused to visit it immediately, spent the first few days wandering round the city, drinking coffee so dense it kept him awake at night, making bets with himself on the chance of pedestrians reaching the far pavement alive. He went alone to Pompeii, dragging himself from villa to villa, telling himself that he'd be better off studying the erotic murals in the *lupanar* than spending hours in front of the corpses of the poor sods who'd died struggling under the ash. He visited Lake Avernus, near to which, as he read in his guide, Aeneas had found the cave that opened into the underworld; though when he got there it looked more like a polluted pond than the mouth to Hades. In the evenings, after spinning out as much time as was decent over his pizza, he sat in the hotel lobby, reading from his father's books on Raimondo.

At least, Ric thought, as the last of his ice-cream dripped onto his shoes – at least it meant he was prepared. From the photos, he knew by heart each detail of the interior of the chapel, with its amazing range of bizarre statues. He particularly liked the one of Raimondo's ancestor climbing out of his tomb, the one of the man caught in a marble net, not to mention *Modesty*, whose full female figure was covered by a veil that only highlighted her nakedness, nipple-erection and all. There was the maze-like floor with its Masonic symbolism, which presumably his father could read. As well, of course, as the masterpiece of Christ taken down from the cross and covered in a veil.

Yet for all he'd read about Raimondo, for all his father's innumerable notes in the margins, Ric couldn't get it straight.

Raimondo was a philosopher, a man of the Enlightenment, rationalist, inventor, liberal, the first Grand Master Mason of the whole of Italy. But then Raimondo was a magician, an alchemist, an elitist attached to the Ancient and Accepted Scottish Right, excommunicated by the Pope for occult dealings. Light and obscurity? Revealing and concealment? Over the three months since his father's funeral, he'd hit his head against the Prince's contradictions. Until the only way, he'd decided, was to go and see for himself, in the chapel that was the Prince's chief legacy to the world.

Though if he didn't get a move on, he realised, pick himself up and shift, he'd have left it too late yet another day.

The nine-thousand-lire entry fee seemed steep, until Ric reminded himself it was only three pounds, just three out of the hundreds of thousands now collecting interest in his bank. He paid an extra five thousand lire for the guided tour in English, then stepped hesitantly inside.

The statues went round the wall as expected, though *Modesty* was even more provocative than the pictures of her, like the winner of some eighteenth-century wet-T-shirt competition, with tight little rosebuds round her crotch. Here was Raimondo's ancestor, still clambering out of his tomb. And the figure caught in the net. However, when Ric finally turned his eyes to the centre of the chapel, he realised that nothing he'd seen in his father's books had prepared him for the *Cristo Velato*.

Here were the nails, the crown of thorns. And here was Christ himself, raised on a couch so every last rib was visible, head to the right, the entire body unbelievably present, palpable, dead, covered.

'And see,' the guide put in, 'the holes in the hands and feet.'

Every feature was noble, sad, real; all the nobler, sadder, realer, for being covered in this veil.

'At the time the people of Naples were not believing,' the guide went on. 'They said Raimondo had invented a process to turn a veil into marble.'

And it was true, Ric realised dizzily: there was no veil, just a single marble surface, opaque, with nothing inside or underneath. It was beautiful, extraordinary, like a hoax – just surface. Suddenly queasy, he felt like escaping, rushing into the evening air.

'And down the stairs, of course . . .' twittered the guide, moving on, making the sort of spooky noises that wouldn't have frightened a toddler.

'What in hell's name are these?' Ric moaned, failing to unfix his gaze.

The guide was overjoyed. 'Raimondo, as you see, was a true man of science. Upstairs is surface, but here in the crypt is all depths. Our Prince would not be satisfied with the wax models popular then.'

'But these?' Ric was pointing, childishly. Before him were two gilt baroque frames, inside which were the remains of what had once been a man and a woman, reduced now to nothing but skull, bones, and the infinite complexities of vein and artery. It was as if their blood had been turned to stone – literally.

'The story tells how Raimondo injects what he calls his "silver liquids" into two of his servants, who are still alive of course at the time, otherwise the heart would not have pumped the blood to the extremities.'

The evidence was undeniable, down to every last capillary.

'So then the liquid freezes. Raimondo can pull back the skin, remove the organs.'

'Bbbut,' Ric stammered, 'but they're dead! His servants are dead! Guinea-pigs! What's enlightened about that? No wonder the Masons don't mention this. He's a murderer!'

Delighted with the effect, the guide shadowed his customer up the steps out of the crypt. At the top, he thrust out his hand for a tip, which Ric, still lost in the filigree tracery of the servants' time-darkened veins, failed to register. One of the servants even had an arm raised, as if he was waving – Raimondo's sick sense of humour?

'Thus to the Masons of his Lodge,' the guide concluded, 'Raimondo demonstrates the principle from *De Motu Cordis*, by your Englishman William Harvey: "Blood is life itself".'

Ric brushed aside the outstretched hand. 'Fuck off!' he blurted, as he rushed for the door. 'And I'm not English in any case, wanker.' He knew it sounded feeble, but it was all that occurred to him. 'I'm Scottish!' he cried, as the chapel door swung closed.

The sun was setting behind the San Domenico church, and he couldn't have said how long he'd been sitting mindlessly in the piazza, staring at the passers-by, when a voice brought him back to the present.

'Hey, Mr Redhead,' it said, in a Brooklyn–Italian accent. 'You'll turn into a statue yourself.'

The voice belonged to a tall man in his forties whom Ric suspected he'd seen before. He was rather bedraggled, with something about him that made Ric think of a hooded crow on a fence post, on the look out for carrion.

'Now you know why the mothers of Naples say, "Arriva Raimondo!" to terrify their kids. You could do with a drink, right?' The stranger presented his card: JOHNNY ZUCCHINI, it said, in embossed red letters, THEATRICAL AGENT.

'How did you know I was in the chapel?' Ric asked, ashamed of the nervousness in his voice. Back in Edinburgh, even unemployed, he felt streetwise; here he felt like a granny, full of guide-book warnings about rip-off merchants and the Camorra.

'How could I not notice you?' crooned the agent. 'A passionate man like you, with that great head of hair.'

Ten minutes later, with the beer fizzing inside him, Ric realised that Zucchini had been right. 'So I did need that drink.'

'And let me tell you something else you need. Some action. To make you feel you're part of something. What you were looking for in the chapel, maybe here in Naples, no?'

Was he serious? 'What I need is to be home in my bed. I'm culture-shocked. What are you in any case, a theatrical agent or a priest?'

'I'm both,' Zucchini answered. 'And Allya is my God.'

Ric ignored the pun, if that's what it was.

'I've been on the look-out for a red-head. I want the four hundred to include all of mankind, like the United Colors of Benetton. And you know' – the agent fixed his potential client in the eyes – 'in Italy red hair is connected with spices, the devil, many sexy things.'

Ric knew he shouldn't feel flattered. 'You mean you've been spying on me because of my hair?'

Zucchini made a sign which Ric remembered from his father, something Masonic. 'I'm interested in anyone who's interested in Raimondo. Given that Allya is the modern-day equivalent, making the mysteries of life visible. Turning inside outside.'

Ric saw the hoodie jump off his post.

'And your very own chance to enter *The Guinness Book of Records.*'

There were plenty of obvious questions, but Ric refused to ask them.

'In only ten days' time, as I'm sure you know, don't be shy, it's been in all the press, Allya sets out to satisfy four hundred men in twenty-four hours. The Guinness judges will confirm it. All types, big men, ugly, black, yellow, handsome redheads like yourself.'

Ric leant back as if Zucchini had just farted. 'You mean satisfy . . . ?'

The agent nodded. 'You've heard of Annabel Chong, in *The World's Biggest Gang Bang*?'

'That's disgusting,' Ric said. 'It's fucking filthy.'

'There you're wrong. It's good clean fucking, my fire-headed friend. Sponsored by Manix.'

Ric knew he shouldn't ask. 'Who's Manix?'

'The trojans. Japanese preservatives.'

Ric saw a wooden horse rolling into the city; slant-eyed additives with names like E143.

'You know?' Zucchini pulled out a handful of foil-wrapped condoms, just as Ric summoned sufficient outrage to get to his feet. 'Here,' said Zucchini, stuffing the prophylactics, along with the calling card, into the pocket of Ric's brand-new Trussardi jacket.

'You're crazy, Mr Zucchini,' Ric cursed, beating his retreat.

'We could put little devil horns on you,' he called. 'It'd be molto sexy!'

For three days straight it rained, the sort of thick wet drape upon the city that almost relieved Ric of his homesickness. He sat in the lobby of Napoli T'Amo, hoping somebody would speak to him, which was better than lying in his room, where he'd only stare endlessly at the postcards of Raimondo's so-called anatomical machines, or, worse, replay the meeting with Zucchini. He walked tirelessly through crowded dripping streets, dodging children on scooters. He ate and ate, but no matter how much pizza he consumed he was unable to spend more than a fiver. He picked up a copy of *Pleasure Palace*, the book he'd seen that presenter-guy make a fool of himself over at the Book Festival, but if it was an 'erotic masterpiece', as was claimed, then it was lost on him since he couldn't get through chapter one. He tried to call Simon, in Scotland. He wondered where the red-light district was hiding. He wondered if, when he got home, he would go back to university, now he could afford it. He went into a barber's shop, then changed his mind, and left after the shampoo. He stared out of the lobby at the pedestrians, who all seemed rushed, busy, purposeful.

It was such a relief when the sun reappeared that he got up early, determined to overcome his fear of boats, and sail to Capri.

The sea in the Bay was calm, the air was cleansed by the rain, the city looked splendidly historic as he left it. Out on deck, his guide-book told him about the wonders of the Grotta Azzura, Tiberius's Villa, and when he read about how the Quisisana Hotel was one of the top ten in the world, frequented by film stars and supermodels, he decided to spend the night there and finally put to use the platinum card his nauseating Clydesdale manager had urged upon him when the inheritance was deposited.

And for once the guide-book was right, it really was superb. He sat on the terrace of the restaurant Da Gemma, a plate of linguine alla marinara and the incomparable view in front of him. Unlike the pissheads of his youth (who'd tried to run him down in the Ford versions of the word), he wouldn't repeat the mistake of stressing the *i* of Capri. He found it hard to remember why he'd been such a wimp the past few days.

He told himself to forget it, in any case, as he digested his lunch on a walk round the east side of the isle, strolling through thick scents of lemon groves, past the Faraglione rocks which stuck up like sharks' teeth from the sea, around which beautiful suntanned bodies were bathing. At Tiberius's Leap, here, said the guide-book – Ric went as close to the precipice as he dared – the Emperor used to toss his lovers, often mere children, once he'd tired of them.

His body was pleasantly weary from exertion when, towards evening, he checked in to the Quisisana.

'No, no luggage,' he said, brandishing his platinum.

It seemed like the enormous bedroom had a noise-extractor, everything so sponge-like, felted, thick. The dinner was quickly beyond the range of Ric's culinary adjectives, and only once did he think of his father's baked beans. He even understood a few words of the conversation shared by the couple across from him – film stars, surely, he reckoned.

Over grappa, Ric wished he'd been more insistent with Simon's sister, even if she looked weird with her hair short, even if people might have thought they were related, because of their colouring. What a waste, her hair. But what a waste, too, to have a room like this, and to spend the night alone in it.

He was about to step into the warm buzz of the cicada-filled air, when he heard the sound of keyboards tapping in a room off the hall, where businessmen were checking their stocks and shares.

Reminding himself he had the right, he sat down at an empty terminal, did a quick search for Raimondo. What came up, nothing new, made him realise how much he'd learned already. He chuckled as he checked the temperature in Edinburgh. He was barely even aware of typing A-L-L-Y-A. But he sat upright quick enough, and checked nobody was watching, when her website flashed up, with Allya in person, in colour, in her birthday suit and high-heels, long blonde hair falling over her breasts, her thumb in her mouth.

On the following page, he read the announcement, in English:

> Allya says: 'Give me four hundred men, and I'll do it! This is your chance, you amateurs, to show the world the meaning of love. And I mean SHOW! Seeing is believing. So don't let me down!'

The discreetly lit piazzetta was buzzing with the beautiful, the rich, the presumably famous. Ric drank another three grappas and wished he were asleep. In the phone box someone had forgotten a bouquet of lime-blossom.

'Hey, Mr Flamehead!' cheered Zucchini, after a couple of rings. 'I knew I could count on you. What number would you like?'

In the four days that remained, Ric managed to make it as far as Vesuvius, until he realised that his poor head for heights would allow him no further than the base. The owner of Napoli T'Amo, taking pity perhaps, offered to show him some nightspots, but Ric was content just to sit in the lobby. The chef in his regular pizzeria, when he found out he was Scottish, rattled off the entire Premier League, before asking him if there was anything he should add to his calzone – didn't they eat sheep's stomach back home? The obnoxious guide at the chapel asked if Ric would be interested, given he was visiting every day, in a season ticket.

'I'm leaving tomorrow,' Ric replied, 'for Mantua.'

The guide shook his head. 'The Mantegna frescoes are fine,' he said, with a look of injured dignity. 'But all that Giulio Romano . . .'

Ric pulled a poor impression of a knowledgeable face.

The guide turned his back. 'For people,' he added gloomily, 'with no imagination.'

Ric studied the sign in front of the Palazzo Te the following evening when he got off the train in Mantua, around dusk. It announced in several languages that the palace was closed for the weekend due to 'Essential Restructuration Works'. He was about to turn away, a surge of relief shunting aside his initial disappointment, when he heard a voice he recognised shout:

'Over there! The side-door!'

Ric turned in time to see Johnny Zucchini draw up in a limousine and be hustled into the palace.

The side-door opened under the hand of a ferocious-looking bouncer. As he stumbled inside, Ric wondered what sort of bribe had been paid to close down this national monument for two whole days – unless the mayor of Mantua was one of the four hundred? For all Ric knew, maybe the authorities were proud to have their city the site of this record-breaking event – an event where, according to Zucchini on the phone, 'something essential would be revealed'.

'On film,' Zucchini now added, sidling up. 'Or DVD, more exactly, and for eternity.'

Ric followed his leader through an enormous Renaissance chamber decorated with paintings of horses, until he reached a further hall, this one already half-full with men. These walls covered with paintings of tigers, elephants, camels, babies sucking on goat-teats. Up in the corner a huge bearded god with a fish-tail and a whopping great erection about to make out with some bare-breasted woman.

'Jove seduces Olympia,' said a dignified-looking gent standing next to him, who had overheard Zucchini speaking English.

'Oh, I see,' responded Ric, quite the eager schoolboy. 'I've been studying some art myself.'

'Giovanni Pezzini,' the man said, stretching out his hand.

'Ric Somerville. But, eh . . .' He searched for a pseudonym. 'But you can call me Archie. I'm Scottish.'

'I teach Art History here in my home town,' the gent explained, 'when I am not at the Courtauld Institute in London. So you will forgive my local pride.'

If Zucchini was a hoodie, Ric thought, then this Pezzini was an owl, with his head sunk down in his shoulders, his big round eyes, the oddly innocent look.

'This is Giulio Romano's room devoted to Amore and Psiche,' the Art Historian explained, unperturbed by the rush of Zucchini, who thrust a form at Ric. 'Naturally, it was intended for the Big Event, but now I learn that dinner will be served here and in the Hall of the Horses next door. Which means that with Allya it'll be in the Sala dei Giganti, the Giants' Room.' He seemed to find it amusing. 'Here is light and love-play. There the gods are angry.'

Ric wondered how the owlish academic could be so relaxed. 'What number are you, Mr Pezzini, if you don't mind me asking?'

The Art Historian shook his head sadly. 'I'm an old man, as you see. Here as custodian, to check nobody messes with the frescoes. And you?'

Ric looked around for an exit. 'Number sixteen,' he gulped, 'apparently.'

One hundred and fifty bodies, Ric reckoned, in Amore and Psiche, a further two hundred and fifty with the Horses; noise-level high, testosterone count through the exalted roof. The pasta was cold and glutinous, the suckling pigs undercooked. The local Art Historian, whom Ric was determined not to let out of his sight, apologised profusely for 'this execrable sampling of Mantuan fare'. The crowds of men were unimpressed by Zucchini's speeches about 'Quantity into Quality' and 'The Enigma Revealed'.

Yet if not for this, Ric thought to himself, as he pushed the watery panna cotta round his plate, if it wasn't for something mysterious, then why were they here in the first place? It couldn't have much to do with pleasure, surely, since how long did each man get?

60 x 24 was 1,440, and divided by 400, equalled roughly . . . three and a half minutes each? Pleasure? Surely not. Even his mate Dan-

Dare, who found Pamela Anderson a turn-on, would be defeated.

It was an interesting idea, what the rest of the Famous Four would say if they could see him now, but it was interrupted by the bouncer who strode up with an order.

'He asks,' Pezzini translated, 'for the form which you must sign.'

Ric took everything from his pockets before he found it. 'Be glad to sign,' he said, 'if I can just know what it says.'

'It says,' explained Pezzini, 'that you accept without condition that the Great Event be filmed, then commercialised.'

'So in a month's time my own dad —' Ric stopped short. 'In a month's time my pal Dan-Dare could be watching me on the job, from the comfort of his own home?'

'You've heard of Messalina, Signor Archie, the Emperor Claudius' wife?'

For once he really had. 'Heard her mentioned once, by my friend Simon's sister, who's into all that classics stuff.'

'She did twenty-two men in twenty-four hours, according to Pliny the Elder. There is a long tradition. Our most famous porn star of today, Cicciolina, was recently a Member of Parliament.'

'And him?' he asked, pointing at a priest sitting opposite. 'You think he's for real?'

'He told me he's resigning from the church. Or maybe it's Zucchini's idea of fun to have him dress up.' The Art Historian pointed to the postcards of Raimondo's servants which Ric had removed from his pockets. 'I had forgotten these poveri,' he said. 'Even they – I believe you have the expression? – even they are making an exhibition of themselves.'

The show which followed the food was an improvement, to judge from the applause of the diners. To a strident song in English, in which the singer claimed she 'Don't Want No Short-Dicked Man', a dozen chorus-girls strutted between the plates, undressing as they went. Zucchini roared encouragement through loudspeakers, with 'fluffers' being the only word Ric could make out (a universal term, apparently, whatever it signified).

With a heart that sank and rose at once, leaving him feeling stranded somewhere in between, Ric finally admitted to himself that he'd never sat through a single porno movie. Despite Dan-Dare's enthusiasm, embarrassment forever got the better of him. Given his poor track record with girls, even before his father's illness, this was more nakedness than he had ever seen before.

Feeling more alone than ever, he turned needily to his neighbour. 'I've never been big on pornography,' he confessed.

'No?' His neighbour was concentrating on the last of the chorus-girls, who was massaging herself with a melon. She halved it, spilling the seeds on the table. 'Ecco!' Pezzini pointed. 'There's the problem with pornography. Always the – what do you call it? The paradox of the *scena di godimento*?'

Ric raised his shoulders helplessly.

The Art Historian pointed to a fresco of an ancient bearded deity who was ejaculating rivers.

'Ah! Dan-Dare calls it the "come-shot".'

'To demonstrate the pleasure,' the custodian pronounced, looking more owlish than ever, 'the pleasure is defeated.'

Any chance Ric might have had to think about this was itself defeated by the roar from Zucchini in full flow, and by a pair of Japanese women who came up, dressed in skimpy kimonos, pushing an enormous barrel on wheels.

'Manix *plego*!' they shouted. 'Manix *plego*!'

Following orders, Ric lucky-dipped, coming up with a parti-coloured handful, from 'Tickler' to 'King-Size'. Embarrassment, he realised, was an understatement. Shame would be more to the point.

The doors opened, and in walked two earnest-looking men who, Ric reckoned, seemed even more awkward than himself. The crowd cheered and waved. Sixty years ago, Ric thought, they'd have been doing it for Il Duce. His dad had drummed it into him as a boy: Fascists versus Freemasons.

'Here come the Guinness judges.'

More used to confirming how many fools can cram into a phone box, Ric imagined, or how many raw eggs can be imbibed upside-down.

'But I told you 16!'

Ric knew it sounded petulant, and that in all honesty he didn't care a toss if he was number 16, 17, or 25, for that matter, so long as he wasn't in the hundreds, when his nerves would surely be spent with waiting, and when Allya too – she hadn't shown her face yet, or any other part of herself – would be well past her prime.

'But Mr Zucchini, you promised! Here's me all the way from Naples. From Scotland!' If nothing else, complaining delayed the moment when he had to follow suit and strip off.

The long walk past gigantic sculpted eagles, through open-air courtyards, just the first thirty of them, plus Pezzini the curator – all this had been stressful enough. But now came the undressing, compared to which school showers were child's play.

Zucchini went into confab with the rebellious priest. Whether bona fide or impersonator, he was refusing to raise his cassock if he had to be number seventeen.

'Seventeen,' explained the ever-philosophical Pezzini, 'is an unlucky number for Italians. Like your thirteen.'

Ric almost intervened: what did he care, the whole thing so ridiculous. Grotesque, as Simon would say, the whole thing grotesque. And here he was part of it, willing, hopeful, as if he were contributing to the well-being of the world.

'Surreal!' he muttered, to get it off his chest.

The owl nodded knowingly. 'Berlusconi meets the Renaissance.'

Watching his fellow-aspirers strip, some furtively, others ironically, Ric felt his courage ebb. His nerve, and not only his nerve, slackened perceptibly. It was a quarter to midnight. 'Only an hour to go.'

'Or less,' corrected the curator. 'With ten minutes per wave of five.'

'Wave of five?'

Pezzini pointed at his behind, his flies, his mouth, and to finish he waggled both hands. 'Five men at a time.'

So he hadn't been far wrong, feeling part of a troop about to go over the top. 'Get the poppies ready,' Ric sighed, walking nervously to the corner, from where he got a glimpse into the Giants' Room, whose centre was dominated by an enormous bed.

And grotesquer!

'What in hell's name is this?' He turned to the Art Historian as if he were personally responsible.

The owl-face only smiled. 'You should have studied Mantua before Naples. I told you, here the gods are angry. Vasari says that nobody can go in there without feeling that everything – the mountains, buildings, pillars, stones – will crash down upon them.'

Whatever Vasari was, it was right: every last inch of the walls was covered in what looked like enormous cartoons of giants – collapsing, ruining, doomed.

'You know Gombrich, Signor Archie?'

Ric nodded unconvincingly, before being jostled by the advance of the first five, naked, as they filed into line.

'Gombrich writes that this famous room is "catastrophe of form".'

Ric could hardly concentrate for staring at the openers, being expertly brought to an appropriate state of readiness by five of the chorus-girls.

'There must exist an Italian word,' mused the owl.

'What?' Ric asked. 'For "Gombrich"?'

'For "fluffer". I don't know it, in any case. As for Gombrich, he says that for Giulio Romano, author of these giants, the goal of the room is not the drama of defeated Titans, but rather "to show representation itself".'

He had showered before leaving Naples, but now that he was down to his boxers, Ric felt grubby, sweaty. The ginger hair on his body looked gaudier than ever.

'Daring Dong!' called Zucchini, a cry which Ric understood when carried quickly forward was a penis-pump – his father had something similar, after the prostate operation – the sort that sucked rather than blew.

'Number four in trouble,' commented the curator. 'In pole position, we have the rector of Mantua University, also reputed head of the local Cosa Nostra. Number two, Party Secretary of the Northern League. Three, some Austrian VIP. Four, the one in trouble, the Cardinal of Milan—'

Ric looked up from where he had been fazing out again, over the postcards of Raimondo's victims.

'Only joking!'

Ric relaxed his left hand, with which he'd been unconsciously squeezing his right forearm, like a tourniquet, so the veins now stood out, blue and alarming.

'Bravo, Signor Archie. But I think you mistake the part of your anatomy.'

Ric was about to explain, when he was relieved of the need by the tallest of the fluffers, who reduced him unceremoniously to the state of nudity she was herself displaying, then attempted to divert the blood from Ric's forearm to where it would shortly be required, if Allya's record-breaking attempt were to prove successful.

Yet wasn't it obvious that it was well-nigh impossible to concentrate his desire, lust, ambition, whatever it was, when its ostensible object was practically invisible?

Here he was, twenty-five past twelve, with the number '17' printed in felt-tip on his right shoulder-blade, in line at the entrance to the Room of the Giants, trying desperately to catch a glimpse of Allya. But on the bed was what looked like an enormous octopus, with male arms and legs for tentacles.

'Jesus!' Ric moaned to himself. 'It's nauseating.'

The noise was not unlike a stable at night-time, all snorting and snuffling, over which came the orders of Zucchini, the curses of the fluffers, the shouts of the chief grip, the lighting engineers, and of course the director (Frank Copula according to the director's chair). The late-summer fug, the halogens, the crush of the bodies, professional and amateur; the nerves, the hesitation, the fear, the fumble – each had its own acrid stench.

Not for the first time, Ric wondered what on earth he'd let himself in for. Why was he doing it? Why was Allya doing it – surely not just for profit? Why were four hundred men about to risk humiliation?

He'd hardly started figuring, when the priest, still in his cassock, passed Ric a poster. It announced Frank Copula's INTERNATIONALLY ACCLAIMED MOVIE (director's credits: *A Poke-In-Lips Now*, *The Sodfinger*) in which Ric might soon have a part, but whose title – *Allya Beats All Comers* – only succeeded in sinking his spirits further.

'Che cazzo fai?' The tall fluffer drew Ric violently from his musings on cinema stardom.

'She says,' interpreted Pezzini, who had elbowed through the crowd, still explaining the frescoes with incongruous civic pride, 'How can I say it, she is disappointed that you're not maintaining the posture to which she has erected you.'

Ric wasn't listening. 'You mean that after all this, I don't even have a choice of position?' He was pointing at numbers 10 and 12, who were stumbling back to the Guinness judges, who glanced in turn at their respective Manix, confirming results, before dropping the wrinkled sheathes in a bucket.

'As in a nuclear power plant,' noted Pezzini, pointing at the judges' long rubber gloves and face-masks.

'Not only do I have to be unlucky seventeen,' Ric whined, 'but I'm going to be stuffed just any old where?'

The priest, with his cassock finally up, was making eany-meany-miny-mo gestures that suggested he was working on the same question.

'You intend,' asked the curator, 'to go fast or go slow?'

Ric tried to oblige the fluffer with his hands as he pondered. 'If I go fast, then it's good for the cause. But amn't I also doing this for me? Shouldn't I go slow to make the most of it, take home some memories?'

The curator's finger drooped expressively. 'If you continue like this, Signor Archie, you'll be lucky to go at all.'

'Quindice!' came the order from Zucchini, more hooded crow than ever.

Number 16, ever more real than pretend, was crossing himself.

For a moment, by craning, Ric glimpsed an Allya arm and empty hand, until it disappeared, full of 15.

'Seidice!'

The priest stepped bravely forward; Ric didn't dare look at which position he was assigned. 'You'll wait for me?' he appealed to his friend. It was all happening too quickly.

'"In bocca al lupo", we say here. "Break a leg", you say. Here —' He looked at Ric and frowned. 'Hmm . . . we say: into the mouth of the wolf!'

Ric tried not to think of the implications.

'On, Manix!' the curator exhorted him. 'Up, flesh!'

'And your hairs!' cried Zucchini. 'Make them stand up as well!'

That, five minutes later, he had managed it, was surely beyond doubt. He saw the Guinness judges check, then manually turn the scoreboard. Yet how he had succeeded, through the confused jolt and crush, required an action replay. He sat, still undressed, in the antechamber, getting his breath back and trying to piece it together.

'I did it,' he sighed. 'Don't ask me how, but the judges checked the Manix. I saw the scoreboard move.'

The curator beamed with avuncular pride.

On such a perilous high, Ric's need to talk was imperative. 'I didn't think I'd manage it. You saw me. It was touch and go – so to speak. Number thirteen finally finishes, gets up, and I'm on.'

'On?'

'Right, for a second I wasn't sure myself, between the cameramen, the bodies, and I still can't actually see any of Allya. But one of the fluffers gets me on track, I'm lying half on my side I think, and the whole octopus shifts practically on top of me. I guess I'm in Allya's—'

'—Basta!'

The words were tumbling out of Ric faster than he could control. 'First I think I'm going to be crushed, and it's not made any easier by the fact that all I can see are these bits of men's heaving bodies, number twelve's arse, number sixteen's greasy scalp, and beyond them the Giants, the Titans, being slaughtered and submerged under rocks, and Zucchini who keeps shouting at me to make my hair more visible.'

Ric's rib-cage was mounting in waves as his story escaped. The curator laid a protective hand on his shoulder. '*Calma, calma,*' he muttered.

At the touch of the hand, Ric took a deep breath, gazed around in panic, and despite his every resolution, burst into tears.

'Oh, you idiot,' he moaned, cursing himself for bubbling now, of all times, after he'd managed to keep his eyes dry for the past six months. 'Oh, the shame of it . . . Fucking disgusting . . . And that poor exploited woman . . .'

The sobs, when they started, seemed like they would never stop, despite the attentions of his protector, then two of the fluffers who were moved to hold him maternally, despite his drooling, to their decidedly unmaternal breasts.

'It's his fault!' Ric finally gasped, between the body-wracking sobs. 'It's all . . . his . . . fucking . . . fault.' He was pointing to the postcards on top of his clothes.

'Of Raimondo?'

'My father's. For getting me involved in the first place. Then . . .' Ric gulped, 'these miserable creatures, nothing but veins. For making me a sex pervert, for giving me red hair. It's all his fault, for that and everything else!'

The fit of tears was long, but the night, they knew, would be longer.

'And where's the fault?' asked the Art Historian, finally, when Ric had ceased to sob. The fluffers stepped back, clucking.

Ric thought, enormously, for a second.

'Signor Archie, you were just about to be crushed,' the curator prompted.

'I'm sorry about all that greeting.'

'Greeting?'

'The tears.'

'Please don't apologise.'

Ric shook himself, stood up, looking fresh again and feeling alive, lighter than he had for a long time. 'Right,' he continued, 'when finally I get a glimpse of the ceiling, of the big guy in the middle—'

'That's Jove.'

'Who's casting his lightning on the Giants. And all the wonders round him: the lions, winged horses, the goddesses with their tits out. Let me up there! I'm thinking. Let me up there away from here!'

The curator, pleased with his protégé, was translating for the fluffers in a whisper.

'I've been going at it for a couple of minutes, though it's practically impossible to move, and poor Allya's presumably pinned between the five of us, so I'm wondering if I'm ever going to make it – only, then I suddenly think of Raimondo's servants . . . of their veins . . . of my family . . . of something we say in English . . . and for some reason it brings me to the brink.' Ric gasped to catch his breath. 'So when Allya gives me a squeeze, down there you know, with her—'

'Sì!'

'That's me, I'm finally freed from all this heaving human flesh, up there with the gods, and I'm shooting my bolt as well!'

His audience nodded sagely.

The voice of Zucchini could be heard in the background, calling on twenty-six.

Even three months later, long after he'd said goodbye to Pezzini, left Mantua; after Florence and Rome; long after the Great Event had been reduced to a quiver of disgust, a videotaped aberration called *Allya Beats All Comers*; even three months later, it would still be haunting Ric – just what it was that set him off, that turned him into a statistic for *The Guinness Book of Records*.

Already he was back at university, settling in to his brand-new flat in Heriot Row, fussing over the guest-list for his house-warming – Dan-Dare, Stod and his woman, Simon, Fraser Glen the lawyer, Simon's sister Laura (who'd got rich all of a sudden, a gift from some unmentionable aunt) – when it struck him, once again, as amazing.

'There's Raimondo with his servants,' Ric had said to himself decisively, 'and my dad with his Gloria.'

He had swallowed, taken a deep breath.

'And here's me now with Allya.'

He'd smiled to himself, full of future.

'So blood really does run thicker than water?'

CORPUS KEY

Adelpha

Sister of Archie; orphan; lover of 'Jamie Lofgren'.

Alex Haring *aka 'Lumberjack'*

Lecturer and temporary Chairman, Department of Anthropology, University of Edinburgh; supervisor of Helen; specialist in voodoo.

Allya

Porn star; client of Johnny Zucchini; aspirant to *The Guinness Book of Records.*

Archie

Bermudan docker; student in Law; brother of Adelpha.

Bobby *aka 'Agatha'*

Scottish Executive clerk; friend of Janice; Sparta Athletic goalkeeper.

Clarence *aka 'G'*

Nobleman; brother and victim of King Richard III; occasional dreamer and visionary.

Brother Clovis

French priest; pilgrim to Iona.

'Coach'

Founder and trainer, Sparta Athletic Football Club.

Dan *aka 'Dan–Dare'*

Member of the 'Famous Four'; film-buff.

Deidre Darling *aka 'D', 'Dee', 'Mrs D'*

Volunteer worker, Age Matters; wife of Professor Peter Darling; carer of Gloria.

Enzo

Owner and manager, Enzo's Hairdressing Salon, Howe Street; neighbour and client of Somerville and Glen.

Esther

Student at Edinburgh College of Art; friend of Flora and Janice.

Ewan Somerville *aka 'Ewey', 'Archie'*

Former night-watchman; senior partner, Somerville and Glen, Legal Practice, Howe Street; former husband of Rita; father of Ric; former downstairs neighbour of 'Jamie Lofgren', Lochend Road; sometime Freemason; patient of Dr Heather Darling, The Royal Infirmary.

Flora *aka 'Flo'*

Office worker; former lover of Ian; fiancée of Joe; friend of Esther and Janice; occasional supporter of Sparta Athletic.

Fraser Glen *aka 'Jenners Man', 'Mr Bland'*

Junior partner, Somerville and Glen, Legal Practice; former Munro-bagger; client and admirer of Laura.

Gloria

Part-time masseuse, Fickle Fingers Massage Parlour; aunt of Laura; former lover (1967–8) of 'Jamie Lofgren'.

Hamish Barr *aka 'Girder'*

Owner and Managing Director, Barr Packaging Inc.; inventor of the 'New-Condensed Crate'; husband of Zoë; employer of Hugh and Stod; lapsed Catholic.

Dr Heather Darling

Surgeon, The Royal Infirmary; daughter of Peter and Deirdre Darling; lover of Roger Morton; doctor to Brother Clovis and Ewan Somerville.

Helen

Doctoral student, University of Edinburgh; former supervisee and lover of Professor Jasper; current supervisee of Alex Haring.

Helen's Mother

Stockbroker; former student of Newnham College, Cambridge; resident of Bath.

Hugh

Foreman, Barr Packaging Inc.; devout Roman Catholic; fellow parishioner with Stod's grandmother.

Hutton *aka 'Hut'*

Former singer-songwriter; former boyfriend of Janice; psychoanalytic patient of Dr McAlpine; presenter, Edinburgh International Book Festival.

Ian *aka 'Tit–Ian'*

Former art dealer, Phillips Auction House; art-forger; inmate of Saughton Prison; former boyfriend of Flora; former goalkeeper of Sparta Athletic.

'Jamie Lofgren' *aka 'Norrie Paterson', 'Rat Richards', 'Dormant Wood', 'Tarrie McPhail', 'Hank Hands'*

Former seaman; former lover of Adelpha; former lover of Gloria (1967–8); former upstairs neighbour of Ewan and Rita Somerville, Lochend Road; dance champion; suicide.

Janice *aka 'Jan'*

Student at Edinburgh College of Art; former girlfriend of Hutton; friend of Flora, Esther, Bobby.

BODY LANGUAGE

Professor Jasper *aka 'Japes'*

Professor of Anthropology, University of Edinburgh; specialist in ancient civilisations; former supervisor and lover of Helen.

Joe

Assistant, Phillips Auction House; fiancé of Flora.

Johnny Zucchini

Theatrical Agent; manager of Allya.

'The Lark'

Owner and manager, Fickle Fingers Massage Parlour.

Laura *aka 'Laure'*

Hairdresser, Enzo's Salon, Howe Street; sister of Simon; niece of Gloria; classics and antiquities enthusiast.

Mr Leonard *aka 'Leonardo'*

Instructor in life-drawing, Edinburgh College of Art.

Dr McAlpine

Psychoanalyst to Hutton.

Okay Richards

Arts Presenter, Scottish TV; client, Enzo's Salon.

'Ol' Brockit' *aka* '*G*'

Saughton Prison warden; widower; father of Rory.

Professor Peter Darling *aka* '*P*', '*Van Helsing*'

Professor and Chairman, Department of Anthropology, University of Edinburgh; husband of Deirdre; father of Heather; author of (unfinished) *20th-Century American Colonialism.*

Mr Pezzini

Art Historian, Courtauld Institute, London; art curator, Mantua.

Pierre—Loup Liberman

French novelist, author of *Pleasure Palace*; guest speaker at the Edinburgh International Book Festival.

'Proteus'

Senior member of Sparta Athletic.

Raimondo di Sangro di Sansevero

Eighteenth-century Neapolitan prince; inventor, rationalist, magician, murderer; first Grand Master Mason of Italy; devisor of Sansevero chapel statuary.

BODY LANGUAGE

Ric Somerville *aka 'Archie'*

Unemployed; former student of Biology, Heriot Watt University; son of Ewan and Rita; member of the 'Famous Four'.

Rita Somerville

Office-worker; wife of Ewan, mother of Ric.

Roger Morton *aka 'The Monster'*

Owner and manager, Morton Vintners, George Street; brother of Deirdre Darling; lover of Heather Darling.

Rory *aka 'Rory–Consummation'*

Bank customer advisor; fiancé and husband of Una; Sparta Athletic striker.

Simon

Student of Divinity, University of Edinburgh; brother of Laura; founder member of the 'Famous Four'; advocate of Antinomianism.

'Mr Stevenson' *aka 'Mr Jekyll', 'Mr Hyde', 'Frank Utterson'*

Computer Systems Analyst, BP; client of Gloria.

'Stod' *aka 'Simian', 'Simon'*

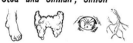

Employee and rising star, Barr Packaging Inc.; member of the 'Famous Four'; boyfriend of Una.

'Tadger'

Winger for Sparta Athletic.

Una

Fund manager, Scottish Widows; fiancée and wife of Rory; girlfriend of Stod; yoga enthusiast.

Vijay

Defender, Sparta Athletic.

Zoë Barr

Wife of Hamish; tennis-player.